Praise for natio
SUSA

SU

"Grant's skill at rounding out all her characters
always makes her story sing!"
—*RT Book Reviews*

THE WARLORD'S DAUGHTER

"Her latest Tale of the Borderlands...
is passion and adventure as only Grant can provide."
—*RT Book Reviews*

MOONSTRUCK

"A gripping, sexy new series! I could not put it down!"
—*New York Times* bestselling author Gena Showalter

"This is a can't-put-down read that draws you in from the
first page and doesn't let go until the tension-filled
final chapters. *Moonstruck* is terrific. I highly recommend it."
—Linnea Sinclair, RITA® Award-winning author of
The Down Home Zombie Blues

HOW TO LOSE AN EXTRATERRESTRIAL IN 10 DAYS

"For readers who want strong heroines and sexy alien hunks,
[Susan Grant] is definitely still the go-to author."
—*The Romance Reader*

MY FAVORITE EARTHLING

"Susan Grant writes heroes to die for!"
—*USA TODAY* bestselling author Susan Kearney

"I loved this book! I can't rave about this novel enough.
From an arranged marriage to royal espionage to saving Earth,
this is not a book to be missed!"
—Sylvia Day, bestselling author of *Pleasures of the Night*

THE LAST WARRIOR

SUSAN GRANT

HQN™

Recycling programs
for this product may
not exist in your area.

ISBN-13: 978-0-373-77542-2

THE LAST WARRIOR

Copyright © 2011 by Susan Grant

www.HQNBooks.com

Printed in U.S.A.

ACKNOWLEDGMENTS

I couldn't create my stories without the help
of all the wonderful and generous people in my life.
Big thanks to Caro, aka Midnight Line Editor, Corey Collins
for the horse help, Donna-Marie for early reads
and the use of her lovely mountain home,
my editor Tracy Martin, my agent Ethan Ellenberg,
George Meyer for all the brainstorming and loving support,
and, as always, my two wonderful kids, Connor and Courtney.

For Caroline Phipps,
with gratitude, for helping guide me back to the joy of writing.

THE LAST
WARRIOR

PROLOGUE

SHEER TERROR PROPELLED Elsabeth through a gauntlet of reaching, sympathetic hands as the people of the Kurel ghetto spilled out of their houses, into the alleys and streets. "The king sent soldiers," someone called out to her. "Talking sense into them, your mother and father are."

No. A moan of fear rose up in her throat. No one could talk sense into Tassagon soldiers, thickheaded ax-wielding thugs. Not even her parents, the shining stars of Kurel Town.

Her famous-physician father turned no one away from his clinic, not even Tassagons desperate enough for cures to risk setting foot inside the ghetto walls. Her beautiful mother, "the healer's angel," ably assisted him. Elsabeth feared they'd be confident enough, and crazy enough, to try talking peace to a people who did not know the meaning of the word.

"Are soldiers inside the gates?" Elsabeth cried to those she passed. Sweat and frightened tears streamed down her cheeks as she gulped air, breath after breath, step after step.

"Yes," came the answers, with hands upturned, helpless.

Soldiers, here. It had never happened before. Superstitious beliefs kept Tassagons from venturing inside Kurel Town, an overcrowded but orderly warren of row houses and shops. Most were certain they'd fall victim to the wizardry and charlatanry that allegedly occurred inside the walls, and left them alone. Both peoples had shared the capital peacefully, until King Xim had ascended to the throne. A few short months after being crowned, his deep distrust of her people was culminating in this: soldiers inside the ghetto.

At the gates, a crowd had gathered. Between the bodies, she caught glimpses of bright blue-and-white military uniforms, but no sign of her mother's shining blond curls or the tall, lean frame of her father, his long auburn hair always neatly tied at the back of his neck.

She knew now what she'd find. She knew.

"Beth, no. Don't go closer." Some tried to hold her back, but she broke free. No stopping her from her destination. A gut-deep dark knowledge of what she'd find had taken over many streets ago, driving her through the crowd to a scene she could not absorb, let alone believe.

Her boots scraped to a halt over the gravel in the

road. For a moment the world went silent. Then a steady sound like a metronome arose as she took in the sight of her mother lying on her back in a pool of blood, her limbs flung crazily.

Like a discarded rag doll, stuck in paint. In those seconds, Elsabeth was oddly detached as she turned her disbelieving eyes to her father, who lay on his stomach, two arrows in his back, his outstretched arms forever frozen in the act of leaping to shield his wife from the arrow that had lodged in her throat.

The metronome was her heartbeat, and it surged in volume and speed until it was drowned out by a howl of unimaginable grief.

Hers.

"They're dead," the others were telling her, hands stroking, holding, trying to soothe what was utterly inconsolable. "Dead…"

The loss was incomprehensible—not only to her but to all in the ghetto. Her mother and father's blazing personalities had eclipsed all who encountered them, including their own daughter. She'd grown up in their shadows, content with her place there, assisting by logging supplies and organizing shelves, working for hours. Tucked away in the hushed peace of the medical storage room, she'd wondered how two people whom everyone noticed could have had a child as invisible as she, whose only adventures were confined to the storybooks she read.

And now they were gone, taken suddenly and brutally, leaving her reeling in a world she'd never imagined facing on her own.

Beside the burning bonfires of their funeral pyres, she rocked on her knees, weeping. King Xim had done this, a madman sitting on a throne. The memory of his soldiers' uniforms danced like flames behind her eyes. Could the wearing of those uniforms legitimize crimes committed in the king's name? Never. She'd not let the slaughter of her parents be forgotten. She'd not let their deaths be in vain.

She stared into the blaze until the searing heat dried her tears and cauterized her grief. Then she lifted her gaze, following the trail of glowing ashes skyward, her parents' final journey. She, too, was reborn, finding new purpose in a vow forged by the heat of their funeral pyres.

By the holy arks of Uhrth, if it took her the rest of her life, she'd see the king responsible for the deaths of her parents and for violence against a peaceful people removed from the throne. Xim and all his cronies banished, forever and ever.

CHAPTER ONE

THROUGH A SPYGLASS, General Uhr-Tao peered at a row of lookout towers whose sentries surely were looking back at him. The spires of the palace they protected glowed like newly forged spearheads in the glare of two suns. Four full cycles had passed since he'd last ridden inside those massive fortified walls to attend the wedding of his sister to the man who was now king. Then, he'd been in the company of only a few horsemen. Today, it was the thousands he'd earned the right to lead.

Though well defended, the eastern walls were not as thick or tall as the other three. He'd plan his breech there. Once inside, his army would overwhelm the home guard. The gates would open, and the city would fall.

But of course, none of that would be necessary. Tao lowered the spyglass, holding it to his chest. Satisfaction filled him knowing he'd never have to fight such a battle, and he reveled in it, realizing he could finally put away the mental trappings of war.

The spyglass went back in his saddlebag, perhaps for good. Even at this distance he could smell the city. Scents of incense and roasting meat mixed with the dust churned up by the men and beasts surrounding him. He breathed deep, remembering. Then, faintly, above the grinding and clanking of his army, shrill horns of welcome pierced the air, signaling the opening of the gates.

Home.

All told, he'd spent more than half his life away in the Hinterlands, battling the Gorr, going out on his first campaign before he'd shaved his first whisker. He'd never dreamed he'd see this day, his triumphant return home for good; he'd never allowed the fantasy of it to tempt him for fear it would have distracted him with hope in the face of impossible odds. But here he was, in one piece, all his limbs attached and working, a fate he owed as much to being in the right place at the right time as he did to blood and sweat. Or, he well knew, to not being in the wrong place as so many others were.

Thank you, Tao thought as the moment hit him, *for sparing my life when so many others perished.*

Uhrth rest their souls.

Then, a slow smile as he lifted his head. "Gentlemen!" he belted out. Blinding sunlight struck his helmet and leather armor as he raised a gloved fist high. "Today, we will bask in glory. Our victory, our peace. Final, decisive, hard-won. This is the last march of the last war, and we are the *last warriors!*"

The men's whoops and howls made his heart pump with joy. Their grins blazed beneath the shadows of countless helmets. Tao laughed out loud as Chiron pranced and blew, sensing the fever of celebration, long overdue. It had been a grueling slog from the blood-soaked killing fields of the Hinterlands, the days dusty and monotonous and the nights interrupted by tortured dreams. Not all battle scars were visible. Survival, however sweet, came with a cost.

Along the way, the army's depleted state had left them vulnerable to not only roving bands of Gorr stragglers but to the Sea Scourge as well. Burned in his mind was the memory of the Scourge's shadowy ships mirroring the progress of his army across the southernmost land-bridge. Part human, part Gorr, the treacherous pirates were the offspring of humans who'd mated with the "Furs"—by choice or by force, no one knew. Human at first glance, they were said to have inherited Gorish eyes capable of charming a man's soul right out of his body, if he was careless enough to stare.

Sea Scourge pirates kept the waters off-limits. This time, however, they'd stood down and let the Tassagons pass. Did they fear him, or did they approve of what he'd done to the Gorr? Perhaps it was a little of both.

Even after entering human territory, Tao had been forced to keep up his guard. The Riders of the sweeping central plains considered the grasslands theirs. They saw nothing wrong with stealing horses and leaving a careless Tassagon without boots or a mount on the open plains.

And then, there were the Kurel. The people living in self-imposed exile in the Barrier Peaks had allowed his army to use the passes through their mountainous home, saving many weeks of travel, yet they'd never once lifted a hand—and certainly never a weapon—to help stave off the Gorr. Not since their scientist ancestors in the days of the Old Colony had caused the near extinction of human civilization.

Not scientists. *Sorcerers.* Dabblers in the banned dark arts of science and technology. Many emigrated to the capital to live, serving his countrymen through teaching, tallying figures and writing, the tedious chores Tassagons either didn't want to do or couldn't do for themselves. But, they wouldn't join the army. Conscientious objectors? More like cowardly freeloaders. The Kurel accepted the benefits of the peace Tassagons won without being willing to pay. What did they want for that sham? A halo, claiming they were Uhrth's favored children.

Privately, Tao wondered if it were true. After all, the

fever that had killed so many in the capital had spared everyone in K-Town, even those who'd sickened. *Uhrth rest their souls.* He made the circular sign of Uhrth over his armored chest plate in memory of his parents, victims of the plague. It would soon be ten years since they had passed on to the other side.

He lifted his gaze to the brutal glare of morning once more. No matter the differences between the Tassagon, Riders and Kurel, they shared the most fundamental bond of all: they were of Uhrth. They were human. Any discord between them could cause their own downfall. The complete extermination of the human race had always been the goal of the Gorr. The furred muscular bodies, rows of needle-sharp teeth, the strange pale slitted eyes, designed to "charm" and then kill… Tao braced himself against an onslaught of unwelcome images. How many nights had he heard the Furs' eerie caterwauls upon their taste of first blood? How much sleep had he lost, wondering how many of his men would be killed in the attack? The idea of the Furs emerging from hiding to strike at the heartland chilled him to the core.

Tao set his jaw. *They will not. I have defeated them.*

Pounding hooves dragged his attention to a group of horsemen galloping to meet them. The leader brought his horse to a graceful and expert stop, raising his visor to reveal a relieved, if disbelieving, smile. It was as if

Tao's very presence and the circumstances surrounding it were a wish that not even the most optimistic of Tassagons had expected.

"General, Tassagonia welcomes you. *I* welcome you." Field-Colonel Markam seemed to hunt for the exact words he wanted, then finally shook his head, laughing. "It's good to see you, my friend."

Tao chuckled at the man's wondering expression. "Back from the dead, I am."

"And to a welcome worthy of your miraculous return. Wait until you see, Tao. It's completely spontaneous."

"That's the best kind of celebration."

"Most of the time." Markam turned his horse to head back toward the city with Tao. "Xim wanted to declare a national holiday—for *next week*—centered on him. Him giving speeches, him handing out a medal or two to you and your officers, him granting awards of land for your men, out in the countryside, where they can be put out to pasture with wives…but the citizens made their own plans, as you'll soon see. Xim's been stewing about it all morning."

When their beloved monarch, King Orion, had died unexpectedly three years earlier, leaving control of the realm to Crown-Prince Xim, Tao hadn't hesitated to give his fealty to the new ruler, his brother-in-law, despite his inner doubts about the man. It was his duty, his calling as an Uhr-warrior, to do no less. Still, it wasn't much of a stretch to imagine the king's petulant expression at not getting his way. Tao had seen it many times before on the younger, smallish boy he and Markam had known as children. But they were men now, the leaders of their people. Above such childish reactions. Or so they ought to be.

"I won him a war, Markam. *The* war. If he finds no pleasure in that, I can't help him." Tao shook his head, muttering, "Already I miss the no-nonsense laws of the battlefield, where a man says what he means, and there is no time for hurt feelings."

Markam's dark eyes twinkled as he rode at his side. "You haven't changed a bit. You still have no patience for politics."

"Never will!" Tao turned his focus toward the city. "Politics is the pastime for men who can't fight."

The rumble emanating from behind the walls became a wild roar of cheering as his army's point guard preceded him through the gates. Tao sat taller in the saddle. Pride swelled in his chest as he marched his army into their beloved capital city to the boisterous love of the crowds—and soon, he was certain, despite everything Markam had said, the thanks of the king himself.

"Uhr-Tao, Uhr-Tao…"

The incessant chanting. It had been going on since before sunrise. Elsabeth had dressed for her job as royal tutor while listening to it, the distant sound carrying into her parent's tidy row house next to their old clinic in the center of Kurel Town. The chanting had persisted like distant thunder all through her solitary breakfast, keeping her from concentrating on the book she'd intended to read with her morning tea.

At her front door, she stopped to sling a messenger bag over her shoulder and fill it with storybooks she'd purchased for the prince and princess: *Grimm's Complete Fairy Tales; Green Eggs and Ham; The Starry Ark*. As soon as she arrived in the nursery classroom, she'd lock them away as always. Having such things in the palace was her secret, and the queen's. Queen Aza had been adamant that Elsabeth not breathe a word of it to anyone.

Anyone meant Xim. In the capital, adopting Kurel ways could get a person killed by order of the king. No one was safe anymore. Not even his wife.

"Uhr-Tao…Uhr-Tao…Uhr-Tao…"

Before leaving, Elsabeth reached for a chunk of charred wood she'd kept on a shelf since saving it from her parent's funeral. Worn smooth over the years, the piece sat clutched in her hand for longer than usual. Today, especially, on General Uhr-Tao's homecoming, it paid to remind herself of her vow. Now that the general had spent himself slaughtering Gorr, would he cast about in search of new prey? What if Xim unleashed

Tao to finish what he'd begun—the violence, the raids, the Kurel arrested and never seen again?

I will not fear. I will never give up.

She replaced the piece of wood and left.

"Uhr-Tao…Uhr-Tao…Uhr-Tao…" The chanting grew louder the closer she got to the ghetto exit, where her usual morning routine would intersect quite inconveniently with the general's long-awaited arrival. The streets outside Kurel Town were packed. Never had she seen so many people gathered at once. The army kept pouring in from beyond the walls, thousands of soldiers. The city seemed too small to hold them all. Leading their slow, measured advance was General Uhr-Tao himself.

She slowed to see. For all his alleged exploits, he looked far younger than she'd expected, and storybook handsome. She had to agree with the Tassagons that the man fulfilled every expectation of what a legend should look like: his bare, golden arms corded with sinew and muscle, his thighs thick as tree trunks as they gripped the sides of his mount. Even the armor he wore across his shoulders and torso somehow fit him better than it did other, mere mortal men.

Look at him, so high and mighty on his horse, a man celebrated for the lives he's taken. Elsabeth wrenched her attention away. She'd been fully prepared to not like Uhr-Tao. Nothing about his flashy return changed her mind.

With the bag of books snug against her hip, she walked briskly out the ghetto gates and into the crowded streets of the capital.

ADORING CITIZENS LINED the road as far as Tao could see. The faces and voices extended in all directions, filling and overflowing the main square. A band of minstrels cavorted alongside him, singing ballads in his honor. Tao waved, soaking in the moment: the spontaneous celebrations, the music, the flowers and confetti flying, all under a sky empty of burning arrows and smoke.

A world finally without war.

A flower sailed up to him, thrown from a group of pretty women. He caught it and stuck the stem in his armor, causing them to shriek with glee. One tried to climb up to Tao's lap to kiss him. He laughed, making sure she landed safely back on the road. Her eyes were shining, her cheeks flushed, as if his mere touch were magic.

"It is safe to say you have reached god status, my friend," Markam said, grinning. Tao followed the sweep of his friend's hand across the throngs lining the road for the celebration of his victorious return. "Why, today even Uhrth himself would stand and offer you his chair."

Tao snorted. "Blasphemy!"

"The truth! Look at them. They worship you."

"They're celebrating our victory."

"*Your* victory, Tao. You're the most successful military commander of all time, a hero of mythical proportions."

"Mythical," Tao spat. "Ask my ass if it feels mythical after weeks spent in a saddle."

"They love you, Tao, and not their king. Just say the word, and the Tassagonian throne is yours."

The throne? Tao looked at Markam askance. The conversation had pitched off course as abruptly and perilously as a wagon with a broken wheel. "Your mouth is moving, but only nonsense is coming out of it."

"Are you sure of that? You have what Xim doesn't—the people's love and the army's respect. Two keys to lasting power."

"Legitimacy being the other key—the missing key." The implication that he'd use the momentum of victory to launch a coup was disquieting. Tao couldn't overlook the fact that Markam was Xim's chief adviser for palace security. To remain in such a position took Xim's trust—a slippery fish of a thing, Tao imagined—but it wasn't inconceivable that Xim had put Markam up to seeing what Tao's intentions were. "I can't tell if this is a joke, a test or a warning."

"Perhaps," Markam said, "it is a little of each."

A prickle of unease crawled down Tao's neck. He might not care much for politics, but he recognized its dangers. *Tread carefully.* Everything he said could go right back to the king. "No one need gauge my ambition. Once I've had my fill of feasts and parties, I'm stepping out of the public eye for good."

Tao conjured a favorite, infinitely pleasant dream of tending the ancient vines on his family's estate in the hills, and the simple satisfaction of adding his own vintage to the rows of dusty bottles in the wine cellar, a task he couldn't wait to steal from the hands of estate caretakers. He would grow old with his family around him. It was the kind of life his military father and grandfather had dreamed of but never lived long enough to realize. A life no one seemed to believe he desired. "I'll retire as soon as the king grants me permission."

"General Uhr-Tao—retiree? At *twenty-eight?*" Markam threw back his head and laughed.

"My officers had the same reaction. I'll remind you as I did them that a soldier's life ends in only two ways. Retirement is a far better fate than the alternative."

"Don't be so sure. Retirement requires a wife. If that's not life-ending, I don't know what is."

Just like that, they fell back into their usual banter in the way of men who'd been friends since practically infancy, as if four years hadn't passed since they'd last spoken.

As if he didn't just offer me the throne on a platter, Tao thought, squinting in the glare of the suns. "Life-ending? Only if one doesn't go about the process of selection properly. I simply won't settle for a female incompatible with my desires."

"The *process of selection?*" Markam lifted a skeptical brow. "Courtship you mean."

"That is how some describe it, yes."

Markam's teeth shone in the sun. "Since when did you become an expert on the subject, General?"

"Courtship requires a sensible plan and the discipline to stick to it. I'll acquire a wife the same way I've conducted my military campaigns—with logic, careful consideration and without emotion getting in the way."

Markam laughed. "Good luck."

A flash of long, bright coppery hair caught Tao's eye. A pretty young woman navigated her way through the crowds, a blue skirt flapping around her ankle boots, a bag slung over one shoulder. *Kurel,* he thought in the next instant, watching her devote more attention, and certainly no less distaste, to the steaming mounds of horse manure in her path than she did to him and his army.

Well, that's one female I can comfortably remove from any list of potential mates, he thought with an inner laugh.

As he rode past the simple Kurel gates, more of her kind emerged from the ghetto, their faces just as cold, wary, even downright hostile. K-Town was a city within a city, stretching out to the distant southern wall, a teeming warren of people and buildings that had for generations served as a haven for immigrants from the Barrier Peaks.

A people as frosty as their cuisine was hot, it was said. The biting spice of their cooking hovered in the air, a tantalizing whiff of foods he'd never tasted and likely never would, just as he and that woman would never speak. He'd visited nearly every corner of the known world, but he'd never once set foot inside K-Town. No Tassagon in his right mind would, lest they fall under a spell.

Shouts dragged his attention back to the streets. A pair of home guards on patrol blocked the redheaded woman's path. One was swaggering a bit as if to flirt with her while the other guard pulled open her bag for inspection, spilling a book as he rifled through the contents. She crouched to retrieve it, brushing off the cover as if the thing were more precious than gold.

More Kurel formed a bottleneck behind her. Their agitation made the air crackle with sudden tension, a needless escalation of the situation. Tao put his fingers to his mouth and blew out a quick, sharp whistle. The home guards jerked their focus to him, and he shook his head, motioning at them to move on. They had better things to do than pick on Kurel women, especially today, his homecoming.

The redhead's slender arms hugged the bag closely

and protectively. Her cheekbones turned pink enough to cover freckles that were a scant shade darker than her skin. Tao gave her a jaunty wave in advance of her gratitude at his aid. But the look she gave him contradicted all delicacy in her appearance. Those contemptuous blue eyes could have ignited stone.

"Are you all right?" he called.

She blanched at his attention and wheeled away without a word. Chiron clip-clopped along the same path, but the redhead kept walking, her attention fixed straight ahead as if he were a stray, possibly vicious dog she mustn't provoke.

He pulled Chiron back, setting the horse to prancing on the cobblestones, their enormous shadow looming over the other ghetto dwellers who had gathered around. As soon as they saw him looking their way, they, too, averted their eyes—as if afraid he'd single out one of them next. Ridiculous. He wasn't going to hurt them. Nor would his men. The idea of their thinking so annoyed him even more.

"The Gorr are the monsters, but in Kurel eyes I'm a monster," he snarled at Markam. "Distaste, I'd expect, but fear? Guards stopping innocents in the streets? That's not the way it was when I left."

Markam's gloves tightened around the reins. "Xim initiated a crackdown on K-Town as soon as King Orion was buried and you were back to the front."

"Your messengers mentioned nothing of the sort. Why?"

"Distract you when you held the fate of all humanity in your hands? I refused."

"Do you think I would have gotten this far if I didn't know how to prioritize?"

They glared at one another. Markam broke ranks first. "Xim fell ill, a fever. He refused treatment by a Kurel physician, fearing sorcery, and relied on a Tassagon healer. In his delirium, he fretted that the Kurel thought him weak, that they liked his father more and had therefore created a spell to make him sicken and die like so many did in the epidemic."

Tao clamped his jaw against an image of his parents' fevered suffering. "Go on."

"When Xim recovered, he said the current laws against sorcery were too vague and too lenient. He had the Forbiddance redone to his liking."

"The entire oral code?"

"Yes, all of it. He had everything transcribed into writing by Kurel and for them. Orders were given to shoot on sight any Kurel practicing the dark arts. Uhr-Beck's regiment was given the job of enforcement."

Old one-eyed Beck. Tao had sent him home five years ago, gravely wounded, never expecting he'd walk out of the Barracks for Maimed Veterans. But Beck had regained sight in one eye. Sidelined ever since, the old warrior chafed at having to serve inside

Tassagonia's walls, training recruits instead of fighting at the front. It was a valuable contribution to the war effort in Tao's view, but not Beck's apparently. He acted as if Tao had sentenced him to the worst kind of hell. The Uhr's resentment had turned into an obsession to prove he was still a potent warrior. Xim's handing Beck an order to quell Kurel would have been like pouring fuel on a long-smoldering torch.

"A few violent incidents occurred inside the ghetto gates," Markam continued.

"He sent his men inside?" Aghast, Tao wondered how Beck had convinced his green recruits to dare it. Even experienced soldiers were leery of risking a sorcerer's curse.

"Not very far inside, I assure you. A few Kurel came forth to reason with them. Stories vary. We'll never be sure what happened, but at the end of it, there were casualties. I did what I could to restore calm. There hasn't been a repeat, but the Kurel haven't forgotten."

The redhead's reaction to his homecoming confirmed it. Xim wasn't the man his sire was, anyone would agree, but it seemed the kingdom had fallen into the hands of a boy who didn't ponder the consequences of his deeds. Tao was only a few years older, but he'd acquired a lifetime of experience compared with the king. It was clear Xim needed support and guidance in a more sensible direction, but it would have to be done tactfully. Markam's insinuation that Xim had lost the respect of the public was a warning that others might see Tao as a candidate to usurp the king.

Politics. Was there no escaping it here in the kingdom?

"Ah, no frowning, my friend," Markam cried. "Not today. Look at the people. Feel the love. This is your day!"

Tao couldn't fault Markam for changing the subject. This moment of triumph had been many hundreds of years in the making. He was once again aware of the crowd crying out for him, but his thoughts inevitably returned to the angry Kurel woman and Markam's words. Had he returned from battle only to find war brewing in his own backyard?

CHAPTER TWO

"Uhr-Tao, Uhr-Tao…"

Chanting for the general chased Elsabeth all the way across the moat bridge and into the coolness of the palace, where servants hurried this way and that, carrying enormous trays of breads and fruits to tables already groaning under the weight of food set out for the banquet.

Her heartbeat hadn't slowed since the home guards had harassed her. She hadn't been afraid for herself. She'd been too worried that the books in her bag would be traced to Queen Aza. The Home Guard reported to Colonel Uhr-Beck, who reported to King Xim.

She worked to calm herself, lest she encounter anyone who'd notice her agitation. Her role in the palace was safe only because of her ability to keep from being noticed. Any nervousness on her part could very well be translated as guilt, and then it would be over for her.

"What's your hurry, Kurel?" the guards had demanded, wanting to search her bag—and more, had she not given them the reasonable expectation of a good fight if they dared try—all because she'd drawn attention to herself by failing to fawn over Uhr-Tao.

"Show the general some respect!"

Respect, when soldiers like Uhr-Tao won acclaim for wielding swords but wouldn't have the first idea what to do with a book or a pen, let alone proper eating utensils, or anything else associated with civilized human behavior. Respect, when every time she looked at a Tassagon Army uniform, she relived her horrifying race through the ghetto, only to discover she was too late, because her parents had already been shot like animals for no more crime than standing in the street. *Respect, when the soldiers responsible for killing them walked free, rewarded for their actions.*

Even now, three years later, her heart clutched with the memory of her parents' murders, and her vow to oust Xim for the crime was no less determined. She wasn't arrogant enough to believe she'd have gotten this far, spending her days within an arm's reach of the man, if not for discovering friends amongst her enemies. Some Tassagons were just as disillusioned as she was with King Xim, including the mutineer chief of his palace guards.

"There you are, Elsabeth." As if bursting from her very thoughts, Field-Colonel Markam stood in the entrance to the nursery, wearing dress blue-and-whites and gleaming boots. His features were too strong for him to be considered handsome, his nose too long and his chin too sharp, but with his sheer intensity and unfailing self-confidence, he attracted willing women by the droves. He gave them little notice, so devoted was he to his career.

Elsabeth planted two fists on her hips. "You couldn't have called off those battle-ax-wielding thugs yourself? General Tao had to do it?"

"It was the perfect way to introduce you as someone I wouldn't go out of my way to help. Just another Kurel."

Not one shred of apology accompanied his simple explanation, nor was the reasoning behind it something she could argue. No one must guess they were working together, or for what purpose.

Like a hawk folding its wings, he placed his hands behind his back and strolled the nursery, perusing toys and the other evidence of children with the same neutral observation she'd seen him use when inspecting troops passing in review. But it wasn't reflective of his true feelings. Whenever she saw his eyes light up at the sight of Aza, she knew that he cared for the queen and the children as much as she did.

He turned to her, grim. "He's afraid. Xim is. Thousands of soldiers have entered the city, loyal to their general, and none familiar with their king. I'm going to try my damnedest to reassure him, but this kingdom won't be big enough for the two of them."

"Would it be too optimistic to hope King Xim is the one who moves out?"

"If only it could be that simple." The tendons in his lean jaw worked. She searched his face, looking for clues. Any unrest would surely translate to action against her people. "Beck wants to take over as general of the army."

She swung to him. "You can't let him—"

Markam cracked a smile. "Oh, ye of little faith. Tao has confided his interest in retiring. I'll leave that to him to tell the king, but I've already suggested to Xim that the soldiers not be garrisoned in the capital proper. There's a region outside the western wall where they can settle, take on wives and farm. Xim likes the idea, but Beck, well, he won't want anything to do with that sort of life."

"His ambition would rust from disuse," she muttered. Markam seemed to have stabilized matters. Still, Uhr-Beck wanting to jump into Tao's place was worrisome.

"Until all this is settled, Tao must tread carefully. I need you to keep your ears and eyes open for any hints his safety is in jeopardy."

"Helping the man who never helped us." She found it hard to show sympathy for the general who ran the army that had murdered her parents. "He was off doing the king's bidding like a favored hunting dog. You're the hero, Markam. You stopped the violence in Kurel Town, not General Tao."

Markam spread his hands. "Tassagons see Tao differently than you do, Elsabeth. *I* see him differently."

A legend. A hero. Had he not proved it by shooing away her tormentors, a couple of thick-skulled bullies, in the midst of *his* homecoming parade, and doing it with a single flick of his hand? It had been a generous, unexpected deed.

You should have thanked him. The acknowledgment of her rudeness to the general came with a pang of guilt. Her parents wouldn't have approved of her behavior. They'd raised her to be tolerant, their silly liberal views preaching unity and acceptance, but every time she glimpsed a Tassagon Army uniform, she remembered her parents' brutalized bodies. If she scratched the surface, would Tao be any different from the rest of the thickheaded ax-throwers who populated the Tassagon Army?

Markam ignored her stubborn expression, his voice firm but patient. "We can use Tao. Turn him to our side."

"There's no guarantee of that."

"Perhaps not. But without Tao alive as a counterbalance, Xim will gain even more power. His ambition will know no bounds. He'll find excuses to send the army to destroy the Riders and Kurel. With Tao dead, the Gorr will no longer be afraid to regroup and attack. We'll be too weak to defend ourselves because we'll be warring human against human, blind to the coming danger, as is warned in the Log of Uhrth."

"I know what the prophecy says." She shuddered every time an elder read that passage from the precious volume. "If humans turn on each other, darkness will consume us and we will be lost to Uhrth forever," she whispered and narrowed her eyes at the spectacle outside.

Markam wanted her to help keep General Tao safe. Of all the Tassagons, he understood most what this promise would cost her. Inside these walls, the chief of the Palace Guard knew everyone's strengths and weaknesses. He had to. His life depended on it.

As now did so many others in the palace.

A glove belonging to Aza lay on a table. Elsabeth picked it up, savoring its softness between her thumb and index finger. Thick, sumptuous satin, such luxurious fabric was never seen in the ghetto. It held the woman's perfume, a whiff of fresh flowers. In the palace, the queen's presence was colorful and unexpected, like a beautiful, fragile flower poking up between the cold, hard slabs of a fortress.

Elsabeth turned Aza's glove over and over in her hands, then crushed it to her chest. "Damn it, Markam, if I'm caught doing anything that appears to protect

Uhr-Tao, if he suspects anything, Xim will blame Aza. He'll say she put me up to it, and he'll—"

"I know," Markam cut in bleakly, and with real pain. If he thought his unrequited love for Aza was a secret, he was a fool. He ran a finger along the inside of his collar. Beads of perspiration glittered on his furrowed brow as he regarded her. It was warm in the palace, but not that warm. He was nervous, a condition unprecedented for him that she could recall. "Can I count on you, Elsabeth? Will you put aside personal feelings about the general and stand ready to help if necessary, for all the reasons we've pledged ourselves to?"

To keep the darkness at bay...

She wiped suddenly cold hands on her skirt. "Yes. You can count on me."

A quick nod, a squeeze of her arm, and Markam strode away to complete more secret meetings with other collaborators, all of them treasonous by definition, and all of them at risk of discovery and capture with General Uhr-Tao's unexpected, utterly complicating return.

CHAPTER THREE

"UHR-TAO, UHR-TAO..."

The cheering was thunderous as the army entered Palace Square. Tao looked up in reverence. He could see this sight every day and never tire of it. The palace was a visual masterpiece, a fantastical creation built in much darker times, perhaps as a testament to the power of hope, or a way to show the Gorr that it wasn't as easy as they might think to kill the human spirit. Balconies festooned in carved stone ringed the lowest floors, the entire building narrowing to four towers where blue-and-white flags of the kingdom fluttered. Underneath, invisible to all, was an elaborate system of drainage pipes, many wider than a man was tall, to divert the deluge from the yearly monsoon. They emptied into the vast expanse of the moat, home to a pod of voracious, deadly tassagators, reptilian water creatures native to this world. The moat was the palace's best defense against Furs and humans alike. If a human were to actually survive a tassagator attack, the venom would kill, slowly and excruciatingly. There was no known antidote. No need for one, really. Anyone who fell in the moat was presumed eaten for dinner.

Before he'd been taken to train as an Uhr-warrior at age twelve, he, Markam and even Aza would explore the pipes on dares as children. They'd toss stones and the occasional dead rodent into the moat to attract the terrifying interest of the gators, then run, shrieking, into the deeper safety of the pipes. The humid and slightly sour air arising from the waters sparked memories of those carefree days.

My past, my present and my future, all meeting here and now.

He raised his hand to halt the army. As the men spent long moments soaking in their deserved acclaim, the royal family and various dignitaries awaited him across the drawbridge spanning the moat.

He let out a soft laugh of joy when he recognized his sister, her slender frame swollen with child, her bright gaze longing and urgent. *Aza.* A dazzling smile lit up her face when their eyes met, hers the vivid pure green of their mother's in contrast to his, the more hazel green of their father's.

Tao's combat-hardened heart softened at the sight of her. Too few moments in recent years had been spent together. That was about to change.

He dismounted and stroked a hand down Chiron's muscular neck. The great horse dipped his head, blowing softly. "Being put out to pasture won't be so bad, Chi," he told the beast. "You'll see."

He handed the reins to an aide. His armor was removed by his master-at-arms, Pirelli, his helmet given to yet another officer, his second-in-command, Mandalay.

"Sir, it's been an honor," Mandalay said, emotion in his eyes.

Tao glanced from Mandalay to a clearly moved Pirelli. "The honor's mine, gentlemen."

With emotion of his own swelling in his chest, he squared his shoulders. Standing tall, he strode across the drawbridge to the palace steps where the blessing ceremony would take place.

Although Aza smiled with love and pride and was as lovely as ever, up close he saw details he hadn't expected. Too-pale skin, lines where there hadn't been any before, tired shadows under her eyes. Where was the carefree girl he remembered? Palace life seemed to have sucked the spirit out of her as thoroughly as a Gorrish bloodsucker emptied a corpse. Two small children and another on the way—clearly his sister was exhausted. He imagined Xim was not an easy man to live with.

But it was Aza's duty to do so. Their family had always served the royals, from supplying commanders to lead their armies to providing beautiful wives for their princes.

Tao sought his brother-in-law's eyes and nodded. Pouting, as Markam had predicted, the man looked as though he'd swallowed a melon before finally acknowledging Tao with a reluctant lift of his brows.

Look within my soul, Xim, and you will see I have no interest in your throne.

As Tao approached the waiting priests, he tried to clear his mind of doubts, of hostile Kurel, weary sisters and impetuous kings, for he wanted to remember this moment for what it was. With all resentment purged from his heart and only the humility of a servant of the realm, he plunged to one knee.

The crowds grew hushed in anticipation. The hot breeze felt cool as it ruffled his hair. The picture of deference, he lowered his head in anticipation of Uhrth's blessing.

A priest sang as he dribbled holy water over Tao's head and neck. Liquid spattered and pooled like gemstones on the marble, a fitting nod to Uhrth's angels.

Born on their watery world beyond the sky, they journeyed across the mystical ocean of stars in great arks to the chosen lands of Tassagonia, thriving until the arrival of Gorr invaders. The two sides fought to near-extinction, until all the arks were destroyed on both sides, stranding the two enemies on Tassagonia forevermore.

They'd been fighting ever since.

Each shivering droplet reflected the sky. The holy

water used in the ceremony came from the only artifact to survive from the days of the Old Colony: the Seeing Bowl. It was said that within its waters the rightful ruler of Tassagonia could be viewed and the future revealed. Tao couldn't help but wonder what Xim saw when he stared into its depths.

"I DON'T KNOW WHAT to do, Elsabeth." The queen was pacing nervously after returning to her private apartments to change clothing for the banquet. Several handmaidens waited in her chambers next door for her to return, but she'd sought out Elsabeth in the adjacent nursery classroom as soon as the blessing was over.

The room was darkened with thick curtains, the children playing with their toys as naptime approached. "Xim is so jealous of Tao," Aza said. "He's always been. Since they were boys. Tao was always stronger, better at everything, but my brother is Uhr-born and bred, you see. Born to do battle." She swallowed hard, whispering, "Born to die for us, Elsabeth. But Xim, he was born for another path. Only, he's never been able to value what qualities are his alone."

"Hush, now. Sit." Elsabeth helped Aza onto a chair as a maid bustled around the room, pretending not to eavesdrop. The servant was Tassagon and not to be trusted.

"There." Elsabeth moved the queen's hand to her

rounded belly. "Reach deep for calm. Being upset isn't good for the baby."

Aza nodded, trying to slow her gulps of air. She took Elsabeth's hand and briefly squeezed it in hers. Once, years ago, it would have been an overly familiar, inappropriate gesture. By now it was automatic. They were friends across classes, across cultures, Kurel and Tassagon. But would Aza feel the same if she learned her children's tutor was a Kurel rebel with the goal of seeing her husband deposed?

"Miss Elsabeth. Pick me *up!*" Prince Maxim held out his chubby hands, and Elsabeth pulled him up to her hip. Drowsily, Max snuggled close, smelling of powder and milk. Little Princess Sofia climbed onto the queen's lap, to play with a strand of enormous pearls the color of her skin. *Oblivious to the danger swirling around them all,* Elsabeth thought, envying the babe's utter innocence. The maid left, but Elsabeth still could not relax.

"I didn't know the depth of my husband's jealousy at first," Aza said, absently stroking Sofia's golden hair. "One day, not long before King Orion died, Xim was in an awful rage. He told me that the king, his own father, loved Tao more. He recited a dozen incidents he thought proved it. At the funeral, he showed no grief, none at all. He seemed..." Aza's gaze drifted away, darkening. "Victorious. It was so odd, even horrifying, as if by dying, his father had lost and Xim had won. I wept that day for Orion, and I wept for my husband. I weep every day for him, Elsabeth. Hate is rotting his soul, Uhrth help me. It's putrefying his humanity like a dead body left out in the sun. I fear he'll do harm to my brother, and he'll do it without a care."

Elsabeth crouched next to her. "Please. The baby. Go, get dressed for your party, laugh with your brother. Don't worry about anything. Others will make sure the general is safe."

"Others will? Who?"

Wrenching hope glowed in the queen's anguished stare, making Elsabeth regret the words that had just spilled from her lips. She had to be careful or Markam would be executed, Tao would be captured or killed, the ghetto burned and Tassagonia would be no closer to ridding itself of its parasite king.

Elsabeth tried to keep her voice and words as neutral as possible. "Everything will work out, My Queen. You'll see."

Their eyes met, and a sort of understanding passed between them. Aza's shoulders lost some tension, and she drew her daughter closer. Whatever the queen had gleaned from Elsabeth's gaze was enough.

Elsabeth hoped the knowledge didn't kill the woman.

"Don't forget to come fetch me from dinner before the night nurse arrives. I want to see the children before bedtime."

"I will," Elsabeth promised.

The queen started to leave, then stopped. "And Elsabeth...?"

"Yes, My Queen?"

"You're a love for listening to me."

A pang of guilt. Everything Aza confided went straight to Markam.

The queen left to change gowns and prepare for the banquet. The children were carried away for their naps. Elsabeth remained in the classroom, pulling out a forbidden book and cracking it open to read, as she did many a quiet afternoon in the palace. After all, the children were still too young to endure long hours of learning. Often Aza would find her and ask for a lesson in reading, but always when Xim was far from her chambers. Elsabeth would fill the rest of the boring hours with her nose in storybooks, getting lost in other people's adventures.

Can I count on you, Elsabeth?

She closed the book and flattened her hand on the cover. The memory of Markam's request for help ended all hopes of reading. She should be living a safe life as a nice Kurel accountant's wife, spending the afternoon curled up in a cozy cottage with a favorite book and a cup of honey-tea. Instead she was biding time in a stone fortress, at risk of getting caught in a crime that could see her executed for treason.

At least she'd give them a reason for her execution. Her parents had given them none.

Yes, you can count on me.

CHAPTER FOUR

AFTER WASHING THE ROAD dust from his skin and changing into his formal uniform, Tao arrived in the banquet hall. The bracing days of winter seemed a long way off with such intense light and heat pouring through the windows. Servants had drawn heavy drapes against the suns, blocking out the light but holding in the dense air. A veritable army of other servants perspired as they operated giant cogs and wheels to spin ornate fans overhead, creating a much-needed breeze.

Savory scents made Tao's belly grumble and his mouth water. He'd eaten reasonably well in the encampments in the Hinterlands—plentiful game, fruits, nuts and vegetables—but it was a soldier's diet prepared by his men or one of the female camp followers, not palace chefs who'd outdone themselves preparing a boggling array of delicacies. Snatching a piece of pastry-encased roasted meat off an offered tray, he popped it in his mouth, chewing contentedly. Aza was at his side, cheerfully filling him in on the passage of time, the children, her hobbies, yet only the barest details of her marriage, keeping her arm linked with his in the endless crush of well-wishers at the party.

"Savior of us all…"

"Thank you, good sir."

Dancers spun close. "Warm your bed tonight, sir?" offered a dulcet voice.

"A scented-oil massage," tempted another with a glimpse of kohl-lined dark eyes.

"I expected gratitude," Tao confided to his sister, "but they're treating me like a demigod, for Uhrth's sake."

Markam overheard and chuckled. "I told you, Tao, but you wouldn't believe me." With a nod at Aza, he turned to leave them. "I will see you later, Tao."

"You can't escape, Markam," Tao said. "Not if I can't."

"Some of us still need to work for a living. You, however, are on vacation."

"Get back here and help me through this."

Aza pretended to be indignant. "You make my parties sound no better than going to the dentist."

"Both are a necessary pain, my dear sister."

Aza pushed at him playfully, her laughter sweet. It did his heart good to see her this way. He couldn't put a finger on it, but she seemed more relaxed than earlier. "Not to worry," he assured her. "I'm enjoying myself immensely."

Markam nodded at Aza, his smile for her gentle, then he strode away, careful to circumvent a troupe of musicians. The singers were belting out a ballad about Tao's exploits.

They were escorted to a table seating hundreds, Xim at the head, Aza at his right and Tao to the left. Down each side were Xim's loyalists. The banquet commenced, a circus of food and drink, marred by shallow conversation, overly long stories and competition for the king's favor amongst those retainers already favored enough to be seated in the hall. Platter after platter was presented, picked over and stuffed into hungry mouths. Limbs from roasted and smoked carcasses were ripped apart and slathered with gravy, and washed down with ale and wine. *The pointless excess of palace life,* Tao thought, while pretending to enjoy the event for his sister's sake.

Aza was in her element, making everyone laugh, while Xim alternately tore at his food and studied Tao. Hunting for malice in every word, every action, Tao was sure. As the evening wound down and the amount of wine consumed went up, the king grew more talkative. Out of the blue, he rested his weight on his arms and leaned forward. "Tell me, Tao. You've accomplished at twenty-eight Uhrth years what most men haven't at eighty. What does a man do when he reaches the zenith of his life at such a young age?"

Tao almost choked on the wine he'd just sipped. "I would hope my life is anything but over. While the days of racking up military victories are behind me, the years ahead promise much to look forward to."

"Like what?" Xim leaned back in his seat, his index finger curving under his chin. "You've driven back the Gorr and won me all the lands of the realm. What is left for you to do?"

"I'll settle on my family's ancestral lands outside the city."

"In the hills," Aza murmured, nodding. "We spent our summers there as children, to escape the monsoon. So lovely."

Xim scoffed at Tao as if Aza hadn't spoken. "I can't see you farming."

"My focus will be on the vineyards, overseeing the production of wine."

"And heirs," his sister put in with a wink. "I want many nieces and nephews to spoil. But first we'll have to find you a wife." She squeezed his arm lovingly. Her perfume enveloped them. "There is no shortage of lovelies in the kingdom, but how will I find one to enchant you long enough to commit?"

"I've already had this talk once today," Tao said. "Markam cautioned me against the hazards of marriage."

"Did he?" A funny look came over her. She shifted her attention to pushing food around on her plate with a crust of bread. She'd hardly touched her meal. "What does Markam know of that?"

Xim watched them like a brooding hawk. "A wine-maker," he sneered. "The Butcher of the Hinterlands, of all people."

Tao bristled at the slur as Xim lifted his goblet to the light of a chandelier to study the burgundy liquid. "I wonder, will your wine be sweet…or taste like vinegar?" He narrowed his eyes at Tao.

"My estate will never be able to produce anything to compete with what your sommelier has served us tonight, Your Highness. That is a certainty. Your wine is like silk on the tongue. In a word, magnificent." Tao lifted his goblet in a toast.

"Hmmph," Xim said.

Eyeing each other warily, the two men emptied their glasses. Tao's didn't have a chance to land on the table-cloth before it was refilled. He waited for Xim's to be poured before he reached for his. An intricate game, politics was, but in a tedious, manipulative, unfulfilling way. Tao preferred battlefield planning, where the aim was for the greater good, not to further one man's ambitions.

With dessert, the dancers returned to entertain them. Barely a shred of clothing covered their gyrating bodies. A curvaceous dancer, with her jeweled skin glistening and her eyes glowing with erotic promise, came spinning into his lap and kissed him.

Perhaps some bed sport was what he needed to re-acclimatize to Tassagonia. Indeed, followed by a long soak in a hot tub, a massage and the remains of a good bottle of wine, all to be enjoyed without having to worry about Gorr slipping past the defenses to strike while he wasn't looking.

Tao murmured in the dancer's ear, "Find me after dessert," and sent her away with a playful swat on her backside.

He stretched and leaned back in his seat, deter-mined to enjoy himself. As he inhaled, he detected a new scent wafting over him, as fresh as dawn dew, in contrast to the spicy aroma of the entertainer. He twisted in his chair to see a woman with distinctive copper-colored hair walk up to the king and queen.

Well, well. She who thinks me a monster.

She stopped in front of the royal couple, hiking up her skirt hem to curtsy, revealing a few inches of white stockings. As she dipped low, the bodice of her dress gaped just enough for him to glimpse the swell of her breasts cradled in filmy white cotton.

That modest peek did more to fan his desire than any of the dancers in their provocative, barely there costumes. He was utterly aware of this female, who alone amongst the guests in attendance paid him no regard at all, who treated him as if he were as compelling as an ant.

That was the Kurel for you.

She rose and released her skirt, ending Tao's casual appraisal of what was a very nice set of slender ankles.

"Ah, Elsabeth," Aza said excitedly. "I want to introduce you to my brother, General Tao."

Elsabeth's focus shifted to him. The expression on her face was typically Kurel, as impenetrable as a Barrier Peaks ice cave in winter.

"Hello, Elsabeth," Tao said dryly, with a hint of a conspiratorial smile. She'd be forced to interact with him now.

"He won't bite," Aza teased with obvious affection for the silent girl, "though sometimes he acts it." Her warning glance at Tao clearly said, *Be nice.* "Miss Elsabeth is the royal tutor. An extraordinary one at that."

"I believe it, Aza. We've actually met, this morning while Miss Elsabeth was on her way to work."

"Wonderful!" Aza clapped her hands together.

"Elsabeth was in a hurry. There was no time to stop and talk. But," he said dryly. "I hope I kept her from being late."

Everyone was listening now. Elsabeth's blue eyes bored into his for one brief, dismayed moment. And then she actually blushed. When was the last time any woman turned red around him? The camp followers certainly hadn't seemed capable, no matter what feats his fellow officers suggested they perform.

Elsabeth explained to the queen, "I was stopped on my way to the palace for a random security inspection. The general graciously shortened the process." She faced him. "General Uhr-Tao, please forgive my belated thanks. My gratitude is genuine."

Her cool eyes told a different story.

She returned her regard to Aza, and her expression warmed considerably. "Your Highness, I have come to inform you of the night nurse's arrival."

Aza started to rise. Xim's hand shot out and grabbed her wrist to jerk her back into her seat. His sister's swift, frightened gasp almost had Tao on his feet, ready to intercede, when her quick glance warned him not to. *It's all right,* her eyes said.

Tao's muscles remained coiled. It was not *all right*.

"Leaving, Aza?" Xim's smile was at odds with the tautness of his body. "The party isn't over."

"It will soon be time for Elsabeth to go home. I wanted to check on the children before the night nurse takes over."

"That worthless Kurel will go when you tell her to go."

Elsabeth stood with her eyes meekly downcast, but Tao wagered they were filled with fear and venom.

What terror had Xim roused in his own kingdom? What hatred?

"There's a sunset-to-sunrise curfew for Kurel-Town," Aza said quietly, "which *you* imposed, Your Highness. She cannot be out after dark."

Xim made a disdainful sound. "I suppose if we let one of them circumvent the rules, they'll all want to." He waved irritably. "Go then."

When Xim made no move to help his pregnant wife to her feet, Tao stood and moved behind the king's chair to reach his sister's, but Elsabeth had started to assist the queen at the same time. Aza waved him away. "I'm fine," she whispered.

"You're lying," he whispered back.

Stubbornly, she pressed her lips together, appearing more embarrassed by Xim's treatment of her than afraid. As a little girl, she'd been fearless. She still was, it seemed.

"I'll see you on the morrow, dear brother. Go, enjoy the wine." Her gaze darted to the entertainers. "And maybe a dancer or two." She bent down to Xim, taking his startled face in her hands, and kissed him on the mouth until his resistance melted into passion. To the delighted applause of those at the table, she smiled down at him. "Thank you, my husband, for this wonderful feast and for welcoming my brother with such generosity."

Her eyes flicked to Tao, willing him to remain, then

she walked away, holding on to Elsabeth's offered arm. Astounded, Tao watched her go. It seemed his sister was better at politics than he was, by far.

Aza's departure stole all the levity from the meal, and certainly from Tao.

"Help me up," Xim demanded of those who seemed to have no more purpose in life than to hover in the vicinity of their king. Aides who had ignored the queen now hastened to pull back his chair and brush crumbs from his clothes.

The king was unsteady on his feet as Tao followed him and the other revelers to the ballroom, scouring the area for Markam. First, violence in K-Town. Now, Aza's welfare. What else was his old friend keeping secret out of some misguided need to protect him?

Politics, Tao thought with renewed distaste. *Too many shades of gray here in the capital.*

On the battlefield, life was simple. Everything was black and white. Yes, and red. Memories rippled through his mind, the night shattered by screams…the stench of death, and of the Gorr…

Someone tugged at his sleeve, startling him. "General! I thank you. All in my home thank you."

A paper-wrapped cake was pushed into his hands as he blinked away the waking nightmare. Peacetime would take some getting used to.

"If not for you, General, where would we be?"

"Dead, I tell you," said another.

Adoring fans clustered around him, all hoping for a private word or simply a chance to touch his uniform. They pressed him for war stories, tales of heroism and combat with the Furs. What few questions he answered terrified them and only made them insatiable for more. A few even offered their daughters' hands in marriage, which would have pleased Aza and amused Markam, all while Xim alternately conferred with his cronies and glowered at him. In that moment, Tao would have traded life in the city for one more night under the stars in a Hinterlands encampment.

Firmly declining further pleas for his attention, he escaped the ballroom's thick, oppressive murk of perfume, sweat and smoky oil lamps, and went in search of fresh air.

ELSABETH CLOSED THE DOOR to the nursery behind her, pausing for a moment to search the shadows and gather her thoughts before leaving for the ghetto. The queen had acted both sad and determined, leaving Elsabeth certain her intent was to lure Xim into her bed tonight to distract him, insurance against potential harm to her brother.

Maybe it wasn't necessary. Tao wouldn't be alone tonight. The giggling dancer he'd played with on his lap would be playing in his bed before too long. Many more females would frolic on his lap and between his sheets tonight and in the nights to come. It was

rumored Uhr-warriors had sexual appetites as voracious as those of the beasts in the animal kingdom.

They couldn't help themselves, supposedly. It was
how they were bred and trained. Their lives were
destined to be short, men cut down in battle before
they had the chance to make a union proper, legal or
permanent.

She pressed her lips together. Why on Uhrth was
she even thinking about Tao in *that* way? Her curiosity
about the matter was disturbing.

The sound of men's voices approaching stopped
her cold. King Xim was striding toward the queen's
chambers, his hands behind his back, the half-blind
Colonel Uhr-Beck at his side, a gaggle of cronies following in his trail. It would not have been a sight for
a second thought, until she saw the expression on the
king's face.

Markam's warning echoed in her mind. *"Until all
this is settled, Tao must tread carefully. I need you to
keep your ears and eyes open for any hints his safety
is in jeopardy."*

She dove into an alcove outside the light of the
torches, flat up against the wall, holding her breath,
her pulse drumming in her ears.

The men paused outside Aza's chambers, so close,
but unaware of her presence. "Your Highness," Beck
said, "I don't blame you for not wanting to leave the
ballroom tonight. All the fuss. You'd think the man

would show a little humbleness, but he's lapping it all up like a kitt given a bowl of sweet cream."

Elsabeth strained to eavesdrop, as she'd so often done over the years.

Xim's expression wavered between uncertainty and annoyance. "He gets all the credit, when I funded everything."

"If only your subjects would see that."

Tinged with fear, Xim's frown made his young face look old. Beck's one eye narrowed, missing none of the king's unease. "More worrisome are all those soldiers, loyal to him. A dangerous thing, Your Highness."

"It's my army, not his!" Xim blurted this out in an indignant whisper.

"Yes, My Liege. But, beware. While the army may legitimately be your weapon, as long as Tao's hand is wrapped around the hilt, it's aimed at your heart."

OUTSIDE, BIG LUME WAS nearly out of sight, Little Lume following obediently in its showier companion's path, like two egg yolks dropped in soup. The first stars had already appeared. A half hour remained, no more, before all the Kurel would have to return to the ghetto, according to the new Forbiddance. Tao hadn't had time to hear the new code in its entirety, but confining all capital-dwelling Kurel every night was one of the more dramatic changes.

He found a vantage point by an open window to

look out over the city, including K-Town. The ghetto, as always, took on a strange, soft glow at night that didn't seem to flicker like typical candlelight, or lanterns. It was one more reason Tassagons were fearful of the place—and the people. Then there were the windmills, clusters of the spindly things, catching the stiff breezes coming off the plains. Also odd. What was life like behind those walls, where Elsabeth would soon return?

Woefully deprived of his company, poor girl.

Bah, she wouldn't know what to do with a man like him.

But perhaps he could venture across the cultural divide to teach her, spoiling her for all other lovers once she'd had a warrior in her bed. She wouldn't want to go back to her own pacifistic, intellectual kind once she'd tasted real Tassagon passion.

Behind him, purposeful steps on the polished stone floor ended in abrupt silence. He turned. Elsabeth was in the midst of catching herself from approaching any closer.

She backed away so swiftly and with such dismay that he wondered if she'd somehow seen his thoughts. His bravado of only moments ago turned into bashfulness, making him want to offer apology for the carnal direction of his thoughts. Was it a spell?

She must have come directly from his sister's quarters. "Aza," he began to say, walking toward Elsabeth, consciously controlling his stride so that it didn't appear he was chasing her down before she could escape—although he was. "How is she?"

"The queen is as well as can be. I left her with the children, and under the care of the night nurse." Clutching her blue skirt, she hiked it up to reveal her pointy, laced shoes, a clear sign she was about to run.

"Wait." She had information he needed. As exasperating as she was, he was determined to get it. He was also damn curious about her. In twenty-eight years alive, these were the most words in a row he'd exchanged with any of her kind. "My sister trusts you, and seems to very much like you. I want to know about her health and her state of mind, both of which you seem to care about more than her husband does."

Her lips parted slightly at his apparent criticism of Xim, her wary gaze sweeping the alcove for eavesdroppers before she answered him. "She needs to rest. The pregnancy has been hard on Her Highness."

"And King Xim? Has he been hard on her, too?"

"It's not my place to say, General."

She didn't want to forfeit her job, he realized, but her expression told him his answer. He wanted to squeeze Xim's scrawny neck in his hands. He'd come home expecting a quieter existence. It didn't seem he'd get his wish any time soon.

The drunken laughter of a large group of men

echoed from nearby. The tutor's jaw was tight. "General, I cannot stay here."

"We'll finish this in private," he decided. "My quarters. I myself have had enough wine tonight, but I can certainly offer you a glass." Fascinated, he watched her peach-colored freckles disappear one by one as a deep blush spread over her cheeks. *Did* Kurel drink? He didn't know.

"Or tea," he offered.

"General—" she tried.

"Tao is my given name. Both of us serve the realm, we may address each other as equals."

Her gaze flickered, that hooded, supercilious Kurel regard. He was the commander of a vast legion, and she just a Kurel girl; he was Uhr-born and bred, and she a daughter of sorcerers from the ghetto. Yet, it was clear that she considered herself the superior one, not the other way around, and certainly not his equal.

Hiding his irritation, he gestured for her to come with him. "This way."

"No. General—*Tao*—the curfew begins at nightfall. This means I must leave the premises." She enunciated each word with perfect diction, as if he were slow to comprehend. He was a general, damn her, the best strategist in generations, yet she treated him like her preschool charges.

"Do you think I'm so stupid that I don't recognize you can't be out after dark—?" He caught himself midbellow, dragging a hand over his face. No sense feeding her impression about Tassagon soldiers. "I'll see you escorted safely home afterward. Personally."

She shook her head. "It's against the law."

A shield had come down over her expression, but it failed to completely hide her stubbornness—and something else. Apprehension? He understood her dismay at missing the curfew, but he was the highest-ranking soldier in the kingdom; didn't she trust him to keep her safe?

Or, does she see you as the danger?

Of course, that was it.

The Gorr are the monsters, but in this woman's eyes I am a monster.

Frustration threatened to swamp him. For what had he fought so hard, when the peace he'd won meant so little to the rest of humanity? They were all on the same side. Couldn't they see? He'd barely gotten his army back from the Hinterlands intact. Men had died along the way, Uhrth rest their souls. Even those few survivors who didn't bear physical scars suffered from invisible ones that would haunt them the rest of their lives. And this Elsabeth, this Kurel, this mere tutor to children, dismissed all of it by dismissing him.

"Impossible is expecting your assistance, even after asking for help. Impossible is expecting help from any Kurel. Go on, run along, so you can sleep in peace night after night without any appreciation for the soldiers whose sacrifices are why your kind can lead safe lives in the first place."

"Safe." She spat the word as much as said it. Her fists closed in her skirt's blue folds. "Life for the Kurel in this kingdom is no longer safe. There are random raids by the Home Guard. People jailed and never seen again. Senseless killings." Her voice was low and passionate, and it echoed in Tao's ears. "Don't tell me you haven't heard."

"Until today, I hadn't."

Her eyes were dark, her jaw firm. "If you were as smart and capable as everyone says you are, you would have known what was happening."

"My hands were full battling the Gorr—"

"Chasing glory on a faraway battlefield—"

"Saving the human races from *extinction*. It wasn't my choice to be kept in the dark. I was being protected, apparently. By Markam. Away in the Hinterlands, I was dependent on messengers for my information."

"Even so."

They glared at each other, and he gave his head an uncomprehending shake. "Even so? Even so *what*? That I sent our mortal enemy running, tails tucked between their hindquarters?" Dumbfounded, he couldn't fathom how she could dismiss such a thing.

"By your own choice or someone else's you were insulated against atrocities at home. I have no patience for men who bury their heads in the sand, Kurel or

Tassagon. That kind of ignorance killed my parents."
Her anguished eyes misted over, and she turned her
head.

"Elsabeth," he started, in his shock unsure of what
to say.

"They went out to the gates to reason with the soldiers," she whispered. "I tried to get there as soon as I
heard. I knew what would happen. But I was too late.
Your army got to them first."

Bloody hell. "Those weren't my men. They were
Beck's."

She shook her head. "I have to go."

"Wait." The pain of losing one's parents he understood. He almost reached for her, but her glare stopped
him. She wanted no sympathy from him. "I'm sorry
for your loss."

"What do Uhr-warriors know of loss? Your role on
this planet is to destroy life, not create it."

Wincing, Elsabeth pressed her lips together, but
the hateful words were already out, her Tassagonian
blood once again overtaking her hard-won Kurel composure.

The general's face had turned hard. He wore the
veneer of good manners very well for a Tassagon, but
she saw how formidable he could be, if he ever loosed
the outrage he seemed to keep in check so well.

He spoke quietly. "Have you smelled the stench
after a Gorr attack, human corpses completely emptied

of blood? Have you ever tried to sleep after hearing the Furs' unholy jackal screams in the night, or the cries of your men being ripped apart?" His eyes narrowed against some inner agony. "No, you wouldn't know. Or of losing three brothers on the battlefield, one by one. Then my parents were taken right here in Tassagonia by a swift and stealthy enemy no weapons could fight off."

The plague. She wondered if he blamed her people for the epidemic as King Xim did.

"I thank Uhrth for my sister. She's all I have left."

Elsabeth forced herself to meet his eyes, seeing for the first time the man behind them. How could she possibly share anything in common with this Uhrwarrior, this *Butcher of the Hinterlands?* But she did. His family had been decimated, too.

"I would never have supported nor carried out atrocities against other humans," he finished.

He told the truth. She heard it in his voice. She saw it in his eyes.

She pushed loose hair off her face. "Markam told me that you had nothing to do with the violence. I want to believe him. I...want to believe you," she added grudgingly.

The general's hackles went down somewhat, but a powerful heartbeat pulsed in his throat.

"I apologize for implying Kurel own the rights to loss," she said.

"Grief and anger are close companions. Both have a way of overtaking reason. You are my sister's children's tutor. It says a lot about you if Aza trusts you. As for the actions against the Kurel, I will get to the bottom of this insanity, I swear to you."

The sound of beads tinkling and the swish of slippers cut short their tense standoff. The dancer from dinner swayed toward him, flicking a dismissive glance at Elsabeth. Her breasts strained against filmy netting that barely contained them. She'd applied fresh perfume, a come-hither musk, and it filled the air. Dark, painted lashes fluttered at Tao, her full lips curving as she dragged her finger across the bottom of his chin. "Good Sir, I do believe it is time for your dessert."

Elsabeth hoisted her skirt, her focus shifting to the dancer. "Stay with him until morning." The remark came as much to the woman's surprise as Tao's, making the dancer smile like a kitt that had just been thrown a whole fish.

It wasn't until Elsabeth turned to him that Tao saw she was serious. She stepped up to him, her voice a whisper. "Don't let down your guard tonight, even with her." She backed away from him quickly.

He swiveled his head to keep her in sight. "Explain."

"Just…do as I say." She took off in a dead run.

"Elsabeth!"

"Let her go." The dancer circled behind him and

slid her arms around his waist. Even as he felt his body react to her seductive touch, he took hold of her wrists and untangled her.

"You wish a Kurel over me?" She sounded stung.

It was true that he'd imagined teaching Aza's tutor a few lessons of his own, but she'd just revealed that he had unfinished business to attend to. Amorous play of any sort would have to wait. He pressed his chamber key into the dancer's hennaed hand. "I wish *you* in my bed, sweetling. Wait for me."

Tao strode after the tutor, but reaching a confluence of several corridors, he couldn't be sure which path she'd taken. Likely out the first exit and to K-Town.

Don't let down his guard? Why?

He suspected that no one had given him the full story since he'd returned home. How serious was the Kurel unrest in the ghetto? What drove his sister's unhappiness in her marriage? How likely was Xim to grant Tao's men land and wives when he seemed to view them as a threat? Or was only Tao the threat?

It was time he found out the truth.

CHAPTER FIVE

"DAMN THAT ONE-EYED bastard," Markam hissed.

As he escorted her to the palace exit, they spoke in low tones, their manner casual to anyone who would have observed, the routine of chatting at day's end no different from what they'd done for years, no matter that her heart was kicking so hard it felt as if it would leap out of her rib cage and draw attention to her treasonous deeds.

"Beck was very nearly mortally wounded at the front, left blinded in both eyes. But the hotheaded fool survived—and regained sight in one eye. Tao should have let the man fall on his sword when he became useless on the battlefield, the way it was always done."

Never had such open anger roughened Markam's voice. His temper was always under tight control.

"Always done?" Appalled, Elsabeth glanced sideways at him. "Where is mercy in all this?"

"To an Uhr, the circumstances of his death are as important as his deeds in life. A warrior must die honorably, even if that end is hastened at the hand of his fellow soldiers to speed the boarding of the angels' arks. But, Tao had Beck sent home to the Barracks for Maimed Veterans."

"Tao being Tao?" she prompted.

"His personal sense of honor is so great, he sometimes neglects to believe the lack of it in others."

"As in Beck…"

"Yes. Beck blames Tao for stealing his warrior's death."

"But Uhr-Tao saved him."

"Of course. But to Beck, Tao dishonored him in the worst possible way. Beck recovered enough sight to train recruits here in the capital, yes, but he doesn't see himself as serving a useful purpose—he sees himself as an object of shame, and Tao as the one responsible for his plight. Tao allowed a fellow Uhr the chance to resume being an essential part of the Tassagon army, but all he did was create a bitter enemy."

Tao being Tao. "Because his personal sense of honor is so great, he sometimes neglects to believe the lack of it in others," she said under her breath. Now she could see why Markam had described his friend that way. Her confrontation with the general had led to this conversation, and to something she hadn't expected: a revelation.

At the exit, Markam stopped, his heels clicking

crisply together as he wished her good-night. "Thank you for your help, Elsabeth."

"What are you going to do?"

"What I always do. Talk sense into young Xim and steer him clear of Beck's influence." Markam nodded pleasantly to a passing guard, then his expression turned serious again. "And hope I'm not too late."

MARKAM OWED HIM SOME answers.

At the guard barracks, Tao found a party in progress. The majority of his officers filled a balcony, whooping it up. The women hanging on their arms were just as inebriated. Uniforms were half undone, if they were on at all, and the pungent odor of alcoholic spirits was eye watering in the muggy air. Some sort of drinking game was under way that involved belting out awful songs.

Good on them. After all they'd suffered and lost, his men deserved a bit of fun.

"General! Why are you standing out there?" Mandalay cried. "Join us."

Sandoval, his armory captain, waved his arm so vigorously he almost lost his balance. "Surely you're not thinking of abandoning us for—" he belched "—royalty, are you, sir? Or better yet a willing wench. Not yet at any rate."

"We've whiskey aplenty here," Pirelli, his master-at-arms, called to him. "And I dare say a much better party than those stuffy upper-crusters."

They were right in that regard. This gathering beat the one he'd just suffered through. Tao joined the crowd on the balcony. A good number of the palace guards were there. "Field-Colonel Markam... Have you seen the man?"

"He's out on some business for the king," someone answered. "That's all he'd say." The man wore the trousers of a palace guard and a plain white jersey on top.

"Find him for me. Tell him I wish his counsel."

With an unsteady gait, the off-duty guard left to fetch his boss.

"Sir! Have a glass of ale, at least while you wait," Sandoval offered, thrusting a glass into his hands.

Tao took a long draught of the ale. It was ice cold and slightly sweet, refreshing and welcome in the stuffy heat of a summer that had overstayed its visit to the capital and seemed to have lodged inside the palace walls as a permanent resident. For a moment Tao forgot his worries, too glad to see his men acting without a care. They had won the chance to pursue a civilian life and, perhaps, even grow old.

"General Uhr-Tao!"

Tao tensed instinctively. He'd know that raspy voice anywhere. "Colonel Uhr-Beck," he greeted the one-eyed warrior.

The sleeves of Beck's uniform shirt were rolled up, revealing arms that, like the rest of him, were thick and solid without an ounce of fat. Tao knew Beck drilled his basic recruits without mercy, accepting no excuses for less-than-stellar performance. That quality hardened boys into men who could match the fierceness of the Gorr, a quality that Tao had welcomed at the front. It was a less desirable trait when training men to deal with their fellow humans, Kurel included.

Beck wasted no time with pleasantries. "They can't be gathered here, General Tao. Your men. It's the law."

"I know of no such law."

"As of tonight, sir, there is one." Shiny pale skin covered the socket of Beck's blind eye like a leather tarp stretched over a trapdoor. His good eye dared Tao to challenge him.

Tao was in no mood to bicker with the man. "Ah, let them be. They're enjoying themselves and causing no harm."

"Congregating of army soldiers in groups greater than three inside the capital is prohibited—by order of the king."

"Three?" Tao almost laughed. "How does the king expect to raise and maintain an army if no more than a trio of soldiers can be together at any one time?"

Tao's men snickered at that, winning a deadly look

from Beck. "Not other soldiers, General. It's your men he's got a problem with. Your army."

So. There it was again, the insinuation that the army was somehow his to use for nefarious reasons. He was no longer in the Hinterlands where his decision was all that mattered. At home, the commander of the army couldn't give the appearance of ignoring the king's orders, however nonsensical they were.

He turned to the officers. "As reluctant as I am to end the party, we'll have to break it up."

Sandoval and Mandalay nodded. "It's all right, sir. We don't want to cause you any trouble. We'll tell the men." Yet, neither looked eager to do so at the height of the party.

Tao couldn't blame them. "Gentlemen, if there were another other option, I'd take it, but there isn't. I'll see to this utterly insane law being struck out first thing in the morning."

"Utterly insane, is it? Is that what you think of my lawmaking, brother-in-law?"

Xim. Hell and damnation. The king stood at the entrance to the balcony, surrounded by his cronies and, at long last, Markam.

You've done it now, his friend's unhappy face said.

"Your Highness," Tao greeted, dipping his head, cursing his timing. If this were the battlefield, he'd be dead.

"It's not comforting to know my top military

commander holds such a low opinion of my judgment. Not only that, you've just encouraged your entire army to have the same attitude."

"Your Highness, my choice of words was poor. My aim was only to advocate a more lenient policy concerning my men—"

"I already know what your aim is, Tao. You've revealed your true colors. You declared your intent to overturn my law. Field-Colonel!" Xim scowled over his shoulder at Markam. "Arrest this man for treason."

CHAPTER SIX

MARKAM MARCHED TAO DOWN a curving staircase, through one fortified doorway and then another, leaving a pair of hulking guards by each, until it was just the two of them climbing down the stairs. The lower they went, the denser, colder, damper the air became.

I am descending into hell.

"Put me on house arrest and we'll revisit this in the morning when everyone's sober." Tao thought of the dancer waiting for him in the luxurious bedchamber he'd hardly visited since arriving. "Confinement to quarters works for me."

"You're to be held in the dungeon three days, after which the king plans on killing you."

Tao coughed out a derisive laugh. "Why three days? Why not just do it now?"

"He needs time for a trial with false witnesses and testimony." Markam's voice dropped. "Xim's not stupid. He knows the reason for your arrest is weak.

He'll simply find a stronger one, with the help of torture and truth serums."

True. Drugged, a man could be made to say most anything. "This is madness. Yes, I should have watched my tongue in front of my officers. I knew better. But treason? I gave Xim peace on a silver platter." Asking nothing for himself but the chance to fade away into the fabric of the precious lands he'd defended. "In thanks I get a death sentence." The aftertaste of betrayal was bitter indeed. "You can't let him go through with this."

"What can I do?"

Come on, Markam, think outside the box. Maybe there was a reason his friend had stayed behind with the Palace Guard and Tao had gone off to fight in the Hinterlands battlefields, where thinking unconventionally was a requirement for survival. "Help me escape."

"You'll end up living like an animal on the run, Tao."

"So be it. I have the survival skills. I'll go back to the Hinterlands. I'll disappear."

"And I'll be hanged for my role in it, leaving the madman in charge of the asylum. I can't, Tao."

Bleakly, Tao walked down the stairs, trying to think his way out of a dead end. He'd rather take his chances in the wild lands than wait for a mock trial, but he couldn't leave his best friend to be tortured and killed.

"Don't worry," Markam said. "By tomorrow, it will be as if you never existed."

Tao jerked his head up. "I thought I had three days."

The dungeon stank of rat feces and decay, the smell of hopelessness. Markam steered him into a cell and locked him in. Although it was arguably the best of the lot, inside the tang of urine was downright eye-watering. "Be patient, and you will see."

Tao gripped the bars. "You try being patient from inside a dungeon cell."

"Too many lives hang in the balance to tell you more. People I care about greatly. If things were to go wrong now, and you were hauled in for an interrogation, and you revealed…" Markam stopped himself. His angular face took on the appearance of stone, his eyes full of secrets.

"You want protection for your men." By Uhrth, Markam must have been thinking outside the box for years while Tao was away, if he had a network to protect. "In that case, I want protection for my men, also. Their service to the kingdom has been beyond the call. Beyond any crime blamed on me in a charade of a trial."

"Xim will need to placate them after getting rid of their general. There's enough land to go around, and a fair share of women, lonely from too many years of losing men to war. Knowing the alternative, they'll let Xim buy them out, I suspect."

Tao knew this was the unfortunate truth of a large fighting force. The average soldier didn't know him, the general, personally; they received their orders through the chain of command. His officers were the ones most at risk in this. Their loyalty and honor to him ran blood deep. Yet, if they moved to defend him, they'd be hanged for mutiny.

Weary, Tao gripped the bars. "I trust you'll look after Aza."

"Always," he said, his tone somber, his gaze flickering with something that gave Tao pause. It was more than just childhood friendship talking; Markam had feelings for Aza that transcended a palace guard protecting his queen.

I have indeed been gone from home too long. If Aza shared Markam's feelings, Tao prayed the pair knew enough not to take any chances and reveal it to Xim, and that a pointless dream of star-crossed love wasn't the motivation behind Markam's desire to undermine the king. But he bit back the urge to demand the truth. Any such knowledge could be wrested out of him and be used to hurt Aza.

Tao let his hands slide off the bars. "You'd better go." There was nothing more to be said, nothing more to do. Everything he cared about existed outside these prison walls. He was locked in a dungeon, and by to-morrow, according to Markam, it would be as if he'd never existed. *We shall see.*

"Good luck, my friend," Markam said. "To both of us, actually."

Then his oldest friend walked out, slamming the thick door closed behind him. The thunder echoed off the dungeon walls, the sound of boots hitting stone quickly faded and Tao was left alone with a chest thick with disbelief and a mind racing through a dwindling arsenal of options.

THE SUNS HADN'T YET peeked above the horizon when Elsabeth gave up trying to sleep and climbed up to the eaves to feed the pigeons. Her mother had always been the one to care for the messenger birds whose journeys could take them as far as the Barrier Peaks. Elsabeth had, by necessity, handed the running of the clinic over to others, but the aviary was hers to keep, in memory of her mother.

The interior of the roost was a simmering, cooing mass of gray and rainbow-hued feathers, bobbing heads, clawed feet and pecking beaks. "Hello, my friends."

Cuh-choo-coo, cuh-choo-coo—their melody greeted. She shook a tin can of dried beans, calling them to break-fast. As they ate their feed, she filled the water dishes and trough and added grit to the floor of the pen.

A loud fluttering of wings erupted at the landing outside. The flock scattered, noisily reacting, as a large blue male strutted inside, immediately committing himself to breakfast. "Prometheus! If you stay out all night carousing, you do it at the risk of being dinner for an alley kitt."

The bird strutted by, wearing a slender tube tied to its leg. *A message.*

A jolt went though her, sweeping her grogginess away. Her eyes opened wide. For most of the night she'd tossed and turned, suffering bursts of disjointed dreams, or had lain awake, worrying about Beck's treachery, Markam's plans, Aza's fears and Tao's return. Now, this message promised action.

"What do you have for me, little one?" She carefully unfastened the rolled paper and unfurled it. It was blank, and green.

"The green flag," she whispered. She'd been the one to think up the way Markam should alert her to an emergency so she would not be caught unawares. Red meant stay at home, and green—she crushed the paper in her hand—come to the palace as soon as feasible.

In her gut, she knew why: if Markam had summoned her, General Tao was in danger, if not already dead. She didn't want to analyze why she desperately hoped it wasn't the latter.

CHAPTER SEVEN

THE WEATHER HAD TURNED during the night, summer to autumn, the thick, humid heat of the past week replaced by the crackling air of harvest season. From the hooks behind the door she snatched a wool wrap and yanked it around her shoulders. She burst out her front door and ran around back to the medical clinic, where the current practitioner, Chun, slept with his family. The young physician, once mentored by her father, was trying to button a shirt with one hand as he answered her furious knocking at the door.

"Green flag," she said. "Don't know more. Tell Navi. Be at the Kurel canteen when Little Lume is straight up." The young accountant, Navi, also worked at the palace. At high noon in the mess hall, no one would think anything strange about the royal tutor deep in conversation with the palace accountant and guest healer.

A nod from Chun assured her he knew what to do.

She waited at the ghetto gates until the suns lifted above the horizon, slowly, like two old men climbing out of bed. Then she darted toward the palace, her mind considering a multitude of possibilities for the summons. The streets were quiet, most windows still shuttered after the festivities had gone on late into the night. The streets stank of stale liquor, manure and urine. On the palace grounds, General Tao's soldiers lay sleeping here and there, some with empty bottles clutched in their hands, others with women in their arms.

She hurried past them, her heart skittering, instinct calling out danger. Crossing the bustling upper bailey, she nodded to the regular staff, all the while pretending the green piece of paper hadn't been balled in her fist only a short time ago. A guard stood at the workers' entrance. Only his mouth was visible below the shadow of his helmet. Alarm twanged like the first pluck of a taut string. The entrance had always been unguarded before.

He waved her through. The only thing she could think to do next was to report to the classroom as normal and await contact from Markam. Before she'd traveled more than halfway across the grand foyer, Markam fell in step with her, his hands clasped behind his back. Shadows under his eyes proved he'd had no more rest than she.

"How do you do that," she half scolded, "appearing out of thin air?"

"You're simply not observant enough, Elsabeth. I was here the entire time." Very subtly, he scanned the area to be sure no one was listening. "It's begun. Xim arrested Tao last night. For treason."

Her heart dropped like a stone down a well. She'd cautioned the general not to let down his guard, fearing she'd revealed too much. Instead it carelessly had been too little. He hadn't retired to his chambers with that dancer; instead, he must have gone to seek answers after she'd refused to give him any.

Markam quickly summed up the events leading to Tao's arrest and the planned trial, the assured guilty verdict and the inevitable hanging. "Opportunity co-incided with intent. A single moment, a slip of the tongue and Xim pounced."

Poor Aza. "Is there no hope the king will grant clemency? The general's his brother-in-law."

"None. Xim must follow through. If he blinks, Tao looks all the more powerful."

"General Tao is a hero. Xim will have to convince the people the man they cheered yesterday isn't one, after all."

"Torture and truth potions will extract any con-fession Xim desires, all in front of so-called neutral observers and witness-scribes who will provide the testimony to the people. A death sentence will swiftly follow, before any real protests can form."

He sounded so certain. She blurted out, "You can't leave him to die."

"Of course not. He'll have been freed by then. Getting him off palace grounds isn't the problem. It's stowing the man where Xim can't find him."

Suddenly she didn't like the expression on Markam's face. "No." She shook her head. "Not Kurel Town."

"There's no safer place, Elsabeth. You know this."

"Tao's estate lands. He owns countless acres."

"Too predictable."

"In the countryside, then. The wilds. Not as far as the Plains or the Peaks, but far enough away from here."

"True, he could probably survive out there, for a time, while the weather is mild, but when winter comes where will he go? A hunter's cabin? A shepherd's hut?"

"The snows are months away. We have time."

"And if Riders find him? They've roamed wide since the drought. They'll steal his horse and leave him out to dry like a piece of jerky. Or, worse, enslave him."

Few in the capital had ever laid eyes on the elusive plainsmen, but evidence of their existence surfaced when livestock would go missing, especially in the late-summer months when the Riders occasionally raided Tassagon herds to pad their winter coffers. Maybe it wouldn't be so bad for the general to be abducted by the Riders. They were said to be a mix of Tassagon savagery and Kurel scholarship, and fiercely independent. But they could kill the general as easily as they could spare him and, in either case, he might never be heard from again. Her mind analyzed every alternative, even as she swallowed the realization that Markam was right. There was no safer place to hide Tao but where few Tassagons dared tread.

But General Uhr-Tao in the ghetto?

Dread coursed through her with the sense that this was a rash, even suicidal move. For centuries, only the Kurel had kept the fires of science and technology burning. Many of the precious, secret volumes that other humans had long forgotten, the last existing links to the origins of the founders of their world, were hidden within the ghetto. Within the Log of Uhrth was the very prophecy that directed her actions now. Yet, could she justify bringing a Tassagon Uhr-warrior within reach of that precious book?

She felt as if she were sliding toward a cliff, grasping for a way to stop her fall, but finding no way to keep from plunging over the edge.

"Let's not be rash." She made fists behind her back as if that would somehow contain her anxiousness.

"The army and also the common people love him. This could cause a spontaneous uprising. There could be violence in the streets, Tassagonian against Tassagonian, not just against Kurel." While she wanted Xim deposed, her Kurel sensibilities had always insisted a new king gain the throne in a nonviolent fashion. A peaceful revolution. The events now spinning out of control made her palms sweat with the dread of having to explain her role in any violence to the Kurel elders. "We need to be in charge of when and how Xim is removed from the throne."

Markam agreed with a firm nod. "Tao's escape will give the people hope. It will tide them over, and buy us time."

"And make Uhr-Tao a folk hero. Xim won't like it."

"Precisely. He'll focus on Tao instead of the army left in his possession. This buys us time, as well."

"All this buying of time," she snapped. "We're racking up quite a debt. At some point, we're going to have to pay what we owe."

"One always has to pay, Elsabeth. One way or the other." A chill ran through her with the fatalistic turn to his voice.

"An Uhr-warrior in the ghetto…" A hunter let loose in the midst of the flock. Her heart drummed a warning. Swallowing, she stared straight down the hallway to the classroom and pretended she didn't hear it. *Remember your vow.* "I'll have to let the elders know. If I'm caught harboring the king's number-one fugitive, there will be severe consequences, including banishment. And when I tell them, they may order him to leave."

"You'll advocate for him."

"It'll take more than that. He'll have to fit in. His commitment to following our ways will have to advocate for him." Elsabeth groaned silently, imagining the training this would require.

"Tao will cooperate," Markam assured her. "He'll understand the reasoning behind his asylum."

"In my home. He'll have to live with me." No other option existed. She had to be the one to take him in. By Uhrth, she would be personally responsible when she brought the Butcher of the Hinterlands to live amongst her people.

A Kurel bookworm sheltering a Tassagon Uhr-warrior.

Mercy.

Remember what you're fighting for, what all of us are fighting for. The fate of humanity seemed to be falling more and more squarely on her shoulders with every word they spoke. She took a steadying breath and turned to Markam. "I assume you've thought of the best way to get him out without anyone noticing."

Markam's eyes glinted craftily. "With a little pol-
ishing, yes." Together, they cobbled together the plan
to free the kingdom's most important prisoner. It was
outrageous, the idea of sneaking him out under *everyone's* noses—madly so—and it just might work.

CHAPTER EIGHT

TAO SAT HUNCHED OVER on the floor, his ears alert for the opening of the dungeon door as he hammered a metal button torn from his uniform with a chunk of stone. His fingers were bloodied, his concentration intense, as he fashioned a key.

He held the flattened piece of metal up to the pitiful light of a smoky torch. The button was relatively malleable, but it had taken hours to craft the correct shape. This was his second attempt, after having nearly broken the key by rushing. Spotting the bent seam, he went back to work, crouched in the play of torchlight on the filthy floor, dashing away the sweat dribbling in his eyes with the back of his arm.

He'd unlock the cell door, but leave it closed, and wait for a guard to come check on him. He'd surprise and disarm the guard, leave him hog-tied and make his way up to the next level's sealed door wait for a guard to open it, overcome the man, go to the next door and repeat. The part where he got out of the palace was still vague, but had a lot to do with changing into a guard's uniform and running like hell. Not the best-laid plan, but it beat sitting here until someone else figured out what to do. No matter what Markam promised, one didn't advance by waiting on the actions of others. Men made their own destinies.

After some chipping away at the edges, Tao deemed the sliver of metal ready for another test. He limped to the cell door on stiff legs, stretched his arm through the bars and contorted his wrist toward the lock, then slipped the key in and jiggled, trying to play it just right to unhinge the crude mechanism inside.

A scrabbling sound came from deep within the shadows at the opposite end of the dungeon from the door. Rats. Were they coming back to see if he'd been served dinner yet? "A waste of time, fellows," he said, hearing hoarseness in his voice. "No one's been by all day." No food, no water.

No Markam.

Tao worked the key, taking care not to snap the delicate piece. He wiggled the key the rest of the way into the lock and turned. The clank when the mechanism gave way was just about the sweetest sound he'd ever heard.

A distant sound like a heavy metal grate dragging over stone yanked his attention back outside the cell. That was no rodent.

The *twang* of a bow took him by surprise. Before

he could fully process what had happened, a wet rag had soared past on an arrowhead and doused the torch nearest him. Two more arrows extinguished the rest, plunging the dungeon into darkness.

With the memory of the Furs' eerie howls preceding an attack in his mind, Tao scoured the blackness for enemies. If these people had a way in, they had a way out. As soon as they came close enough for him to see how many he was dealing with, he'd make his move to take them. He'd have to be accurate, and quick. If he was captured and dragged back here, he was going to hang. Of that he was certain.

"Friendly, not hostile," a female voice assured him tersely, as any soldier would do coming unexpectedly upon another squad. "We'll get you out—if you're still interested."

"I sure as hell don't plan on staying here until judgment day." Blindly, he grabbed the bars. "If you've got a torch, light it."

"There's a certain way we have to handle this, General, and you being in charge isn't it. We'll get you out, but you must do exactly as I tell you to do."

He'd never taken orders from a woman before.

She apparently mistook his silence. "You must do exactly as I tell you," she repeated.

"Do you think me mad, woman? I will do as you say."

A lantern sparked to life. Two faces floated in front

of him. Tao squinted, trying to make out these strangers dressed in simple workers' clothing—driver's ware, roughly woven baggy trousers and shirts covered by black cloaks. One was a male, young, not much more than a boy, with dark gold skin and shaggy black hair. The other, most definitely female, with a pale oval face. Hair the color of a copper coin peeked out from under her cap. Like Elsabeth's hair.

Exactly like Elsabeth's. The tutor. "You do more than teach children," he observed.

"My job description is expanding daily." A key in her hand caught the light as she reached for the door.

"It's open." He walked forward and pushed on it. The two Kurel gaped at him, and he held out an open hand with the key resting on his palm. "Uhrth helps those who help themselves."

A small nod from Elsabeth, the tiniest glint of admiration. "We're going out through the spillway pipes," she said. "No guard will think we're that suicidal, to use what drains into the moat, and the tassagators. We'll end up at the loading docks. There we'll board a covered wagon. You'll hide in back. Now, come. Hurry."

They set off running. Running for his life—with two Kurel running for theirs as well. For his sake.

CHAPTER NINE

THE KUREL LED TAO INTO a passage that led from the dungeons to the very bowels of the palace, where the air was so dense he imagined it could be sliced with a blade. There was barely enough light to see the pair with their black cloaks as they sprinted and then crawled through the ever-narrowing passageway. Here the scent of dampness was strong, and yet familiar. The odor brought him back to childhood, when danger was excitedly imagined, never imminent.

Pipes, dead ahead.

The boy unlatched a heavy iron grate, lowering it carefully. Torn spider webs draped the opening. Light from the lantern penetrated the tunnel only as deep as the length of a man. Tao helped the boy replace the grate after they slipped through the opening. Then they were on their way, the lantern flickering as it swung from the boy's hand. The silence was as heavy as the air at this depth, the entire palace atop them, floor upon floor. The very thought threatened to turn him claustrophobic.

Inside, their footsteps echoed unimaginably loudly after all their stealthy silence. "It's slippery," Elsabeth warned. "The muck is like ice." She and the boy hesitated at a confluence of pipes, the boy holding the lantern high until Elsabeth found a marker they'd left and snatched it off the dank wall.

"Keep to the right." Tao knew the labyrinths of the drainage pipes as well as any formerly mischievous child raised in one of the noble families could. It had been years, but racing through the darkened passages, it came back as if it were yesterday. "I know the pipes well."

"That's what Markam said."

"So, you're in on his plan to free me. A Markam loyalist."

Her disdainful gaze sought him out in the gloom. "Markam is helping *me*—us. The Kurel. Any enemy of this king is an ally of ours. That's why I'm helping you." She looked him up and down, as if finding it difficult to absorb the very concept. "I also promised Markam." She seemed no more pleased with that promise than she did helping him to hurt the king. "I'm going to hide you where no one will look," she said. "The ghetto."

By the arks. K-Town. Markam had promised he'd disappear. The man had been telling the truth. "They'll come looking for me. Not too thoroughly in your ghetto, true, but Xim won't give up that easily."

"Let them come." The tutor's face looked paler in the shadows as they clambered in the wake of Navi's lantern. "We'll be ready."

He sensed her grit, and could believe her. Of all things, he'd just inherited a Kurel guardian, one who actually seemed credible in her willingness to wage a fight.

His situation was becoming more bizarre by the minute.

The boy threw glances over his shoulder at Tao, acting equal parts awestruck and nervous, but the tutor was cool, businesslike and in control, rather like he was when leading his men. If some Kurel could be this capable, why hadn't any ever signed up to fight?

Spongers, every last one.

Elsabeth said, "In case we get separated, head to the loading docks. Down by the kitchens. Do you remember where?"

How could he forget? They'd stowed away in the departing supply wagons as boys, never knowing what new places they'd see before being discovered by the drivers and shooed away. "Yes. I do."

"We can't dally. The kitchen staff returns at midnight." She lurched into a run. "Follow, Tassagon."

The boy was ahead of them now, keeping a breakneck pace. *Literally,* Tao thought with increasing concern. Several times the youth slid and almost fell, righting himself with a body that could bend and recover like a sapling. The lantern flickered with each crash, a bouncing ball of light. Tao could barely focus on the details racing past him. A wrong turn could put them out into the moat, where the pipes channeled the monsoon waters in season. Ahead was one such turn.

"Go right," he called to the boy. Tao had done this a hundred times, but never so fast and so dark. Here, the liquid under his boots was slicker and foul—algae, affording little traction as the spillway pipe angled steeply downward.

The Kurel boy fell to his rear, bumping along the pipe's inner ribs in an effort to slow down and make the turn. Ahead the outlet yawned like an open mouth. He was slowing, but not fast enough.

"Navi, go right," Elsabeth warned from behind Tao.

"Right—*now*," Tao yelled.

Navi's heels finally caught, but the sudden deceleration pitched him forward. Straining, clawing for a handhold, he fought to stay in place, but gravity had other ideas. He crashed into the grate, hands first. For a heart-clamping moment Tao thought the grate would hold for the boy, but the force of his palms jarred it loose.

"Navi!" Elsabeth skidded to a stop next to Tao, both

of them sucking in air as they peered out, just above the misty waters of the moat.

Somehow the youth hung on as the grate swung open like a door, but as it bounced off the stones on the exterior of the castle wall, he lost his hold and fell for only seconds before they heard the splash of his landing.

"*By the arks*. He's in the moat." Elsabeth whirled to Tao, panic etched on her once-composed face. "The tassagators—"

"Stay put."

Tao dove in after the boy. Hitting the water was a cold explosive shock. Within the depths of the moat, crushed by the weight of the black water, he knew his imagination was playing tricks when he sensed the twitch of awareness of untold primitive minds.

Bubbles streamed past his face until he slowed his descent and reversed his course with powerful kicks. Was the motion in the water ahead of him the churning wake left from the boy's plunge? Or was it the stirring of a powerful, reptilian tail? Eyes wide open, he saw only waving fronds of underwater plants in the dim moonlight. Then, ahead, the dark form of Navi struggling upward in slow motion.

Tao grabbed him. He surfaced, explosively, shoving the boy toward the grate, the lowest rungs still several feet above their heads. "Climb," he gasped. "Go."

Navi clambered up the hanging grate. It swung

crazily. Tao reached up to hold it in place to muffle any noise and keep from drawing attention to the moat.

Elsabeth snatched the boy's hand, and they disappeared inside the pipe. Tao scrambled up after them, hoisting the full weight of his body out of the moat up with his arms.

Rung over rung… His battered fingers closed over cold slippery iron, each grab hauling him higher. With his strength flagging from a day of no food or water, his waterlogged boots weighed him down like anchors.

This is nothing compared to that Furs hunt in the Sarcen Swamps. They'd slogged through mud up to their necks, Gorr all around them, while fighting off clouds of ravenous sting flies. In the end, it had been a major victory, finding and destroying three heavily populated dens, but it had been hell to get there. *But you did.* With the thought to spur him on, Tao pulled himself higher on the grate and away from the water to keep the beasties from having a taste of him.

He threw one arm over the lip of the pipe opening, then the other, his weight on his elbows and forearms, his legs pedaling in the air. Elsabeth and Navi grabbed at him, almost frantically, trying to drag him the rest of the way inside.

A splash, a spray of water shooting across his back. "Come on, come on," the tutor urged in a whisper. "Hurry. *Hurry.* They're all around you."

A larger splash. Something hit him. In the legs. *Hard*. It yanked him out the pipe, but he caught a rung with one hand, stopping his fall. For a second he felt nothing at all below the waist. It was if the entire lower half of his body had departed. Then, a blow of pain rammed into him with crushing intensity, roaring up his body like an out-of-control fire so hot, he was sure he was being burned alive.

Gator bite.

CHAPTER TEN

TAO UNSCRAMBLED HIS thoughts enough to figure out he still had a grip on the lip of the drainage pipe, while his legs were consumed by pain so severe he almost screamed.

The water was churning. A dark form swept past, as large as a warhorse. And another. Blood in the water: prelude to a feeding frenzy. Like hell if he'd take credit for defeating humanity's greatest enemy only to end up a forgotten morsel for moat pets.

Up. He had to get higher. He had to get inside that pipe.

The Sarcen Swamps were tougher. He chanted the thought, silently, as his breaths hissed loud in his ears. Rung by rung, he hauled himself up the rest of the way, vaguely aware of the two Kurel reaching for him, attempting to drag him farther into the pipe.

He was in. His burning legs wouldn't support his weight. The side of his face lay on the cold curve of the pipe, the stink of the seeping runoff water strong, his awareness narrowing to encompass only the gator bite, a blinding, blistering sun of agony.

"Tao. Nod if you hear me. *Tao*." The press of a cool, smooth palm on his cheek. "The noise. People may see. You have to move out of sight."

Hands pulled at him. With their urging, he low-crawled a few yards and collapsed again. His pants were soaked with water and blood. He felt himself going into shock, staying conscious only because of his battlefield experience. He was burning alive, his flesh popping and sizzling while imaginary saws dug deep, back and forth, flaying the seared flesh—it was so bad a part of him wished he would black out. Inside he was screaming, screaming until his voice had shredded away to nothing.

"Get up…Tao… Can't stay here."

He heard her voice. *Elsabeth*. Pulling…pulling him out of a dark place where he sensed he ought not venture…

"General. On your feet. Do it now!"

Tao jerked back to awareness. Another ragged breath and he remembered why he was there.

The loading docks.

His escape.

The Kurel were helping him up to his feet. He leaned heavily on Navi, who was surprisingly wiry and strong.

"That's it. You'll be all right. Hold him, Navi! Walk, Tao. Walk."

Tao focused on the fierce female voice directing him, following it like a torch in the dark. "Step, and step. One more. Keep going. We're almost there."

A loss of consciousness in a battle meant almost certain death. This might not be a battle like he was used to fighting, but it was war all the same. He'd been betrayed by his king and now was in the hands of Kurel, who viewed his people as little more than savages.

Any enemy of this king is an ally of ours. That's why I'm helping you, Elsabeth had told him, revealing in her tone a very real determination to see Xim dead. He'd remain a recipient of her aid only for as long as he continued to be of use to her. The thought struck him in between waves of agony. He'd long ago learned to think his way out of situations in spite of trauma to his body. He would do whatever it took to survive to see his sister and his kingdom safe, even if it meant giving the Kurel temporary control of his life.

He staggered, pausing every few breaths to crush the urge to scream, to fall to his knees. To die.

"Keep going. You'll be all right." Elsabeth's voice again. "You're going to live."

The pledge of a sorceress. "Swear?" he rasped.

A pause. "Yes. I swear."

Good. He'd hold her to it.

THEY PLOWED OUT OF the pipe into the muggy haze of night. A pair of bored mules jerked their heads up from grazing. The air smelled of manure and waste-water, and crushed late-summer grass. "Chun, *help*, he's hurt," Elsabeth said, Tao's weight descending on her as his legs folded yet again.

Chun vaulted off the wagon, his expression both alarmed and determined, a competent young physician knowing what to do.

The general's nose was bleeding, his hair matted with dirt and sweat. Lacerations and welts crisscrossed his quivering hands and arms, and his knuckles were scraped raw. His face was so streaked with grime his gold-green eyes appeared to glow like embers in his agony. She'd seen few people in worse shape in all the years she'd helped her parents in the clinic. "Gator bite," she told Chun.

"Great arks. Why were you in the moat?"

"Navi went for a swim."

"I fell!" Navi protested in a loud whisper.

"He did," Elsabeth assured Chun. "He slipped. It could have happened to any of us. The general went in after him."

Chun took her place under Tao's arm, and the two men walked him to the covered wagon. The general's lips pulled back over his teeth, as he seemed to be fighting the urge to writhe or yell, obviously aware they'd made enough noise already. Tassagator splashes weren't unusual, but on a night like tonight, they couldn't risk *any* notice.

Her ears strained for telltale noise coming from

the kitchen. The docks were still deserted, but with each fleeting minute their escape window shrank. The kitchen staff would arrive at midnight, clanking pots and pans, lighting the fires as they prepared the kitchens for the morning meal.

"Let's go, get him in," she urged. Chun jumped in first, pulling the general into the wagon after him. Straw covered a wood floor. Empty produce crates and high wooden sides provided cover from passing Tassagonians. A tarp was thrown over the open top of the cargo area.

Navi nimbly jumped into the driver's seat, then held his arm out to her. She grabbed his hand, and he hoisted her up to share the hard bench. A snap of the reins and they were off, the brims of their caps pulled low over their faces. A small lantern swung from the front rail and provided just enough light for Navi to steer. Then, laughter.

She jerked her gaze up. On a balcony high above, revelers partied, appearing blessedly ignorant of the fact that the general had escaped. Nor did they seem too concerned about their hero rotting in jail. *Xim's loyalists,* she thought, sickened by their disregard for anything other than their own personal advancement. The lives of anyone outside the palace, let alone in the ghetto, meant nothing to them. News of her parents' deaths had probably dropped into the muddy puddle of their ignorance with nary a ripple to account for it. It made stealing Tao from under their noses suddenly more satisfying, the first measurable victory over the king since she'd come to work at the palace.

And not the last.

She turned narrowed eyes back to the moat bridge ahead. "Easy, Navi. Not too fast." The urge to cross it at top speed was almost too fierce to resist, but it would draw too much attention. Curiosity was the last thing they could afford. If they were caught, Xim would have their heads, and quite likely everyone else's in the ghetto.

Across the bridge they rolled, as fast as they dared. The waters below were as smooth and opaque as a piece of charcoal silk. A leaf broke free of a tree and floated down to the water. A small splash as a fish rose to investigate, and Navi's filthy hands shook. "You all right?" she asked.

He hung his head guiltily. "Sorry about what happened is all." His eyes slid sideways. "And thankful."

She rubbed his arm. "Me, too. I thought we lost you."

"I mean, I'm thankful for him—the general. He saved my life."

"I know he did."

It seemed the people's hero was now theirs, too. Tao had jumped in to save Navi with no hesitation, an act of raw heroism. It was obvious, looking at the man, that war had hardened him on the outside, but she now understood his toughness reached inside, too.

Navigating the pipes with gator venom in his blood, something described as being burned alive by the few who'd survived to tell about it, would take a superhuman strength of will. That kind of inner strength was likely the reason he'd survived to return home from the Hinterlands in the first place, surprising all of Tassagonia,

Especially Xim. She tightened her jaw, remembering her vow to see the king deposed. Tonight, she'd come one step closer by rescuing Uhr-Tao from his clutches.

Yet, as much as general's feats kindled a burst of awe, they served to remind her that he was used to taking charge without consulting others, as willing to risk his life for the Tassagonian Kingdom as he was to save a young, insignificant accountant from the ghetto. Admirable, yes, but not when it was *the general's* life on which everyone's future balanced so precariously. He mustn't risk that life to save anything—or anyone—other than the kingdom. And the Kurel.

How was she going to be able to control such a man? She had to. No question. General Uhr-Tao's life was no longer in his hands; it was in *hers*.

CHAPTER ELEVEN

THE WAGON ROLLED OUT the palace gates toward an old, rutted merchant road. They approached Kurel Town via the growing-fields and orchards along the capital's southern wall. While Navi drove the wagon at a deliberately normal pace, Elsabeth crawled over the driver's seat to join Chun, ready to assist with the general's medical care any way she could.

The physician's skilled hands hunted over Tao's body. "Bite wounds left thigh…and the right calf," he said, having already sliced open the shredded trousers with bandage scissors. The punctures and gashes on Tao's legs were deep, discolored and seeping fluid as the angry, ragged edges swelled. "Without antivenin he'll lose his legs."

Tao went rigid. "No, Kurel. Don't you take my legs."

"No one's going to take your legs," Elsabeth blurted out. Whether it was true or not, she didn't know, but she knew they weren't going to keep the warrior in this wagon if they threatened him with the loss of his limbs. "There's antidote in the clinic."

Chun reached into his medical bag. Made of black leather so worn it felt like the softest cotton, it had been her father's. Doc Ferdinand's satchel. Every time she saw it in Chun's possession, it brought tender memories pierced with a poignant sense of loss, and bitter anger. Always that.

The physician went to work cleansing the general's wounds. Sweating profusely, Tao was panting, almost too fast, his great fists opening and closing with each wave of pain. No man should have to endure such misery, even General Uhr-Tao. "A strap," he gritted out, seeing her crouch down next to him. "Get me one."

"A strap?"

He squeezed his eyes shut. "Between the teeth."

Mercy. The man wanted to bite down on a leather strap to blunt the pain. It probably wasn't the first time, either. Primitive, when there was real pain medicine. Sad. "He's suffering," she told Chun. "Do something."

"I will, Beth. Hold on."

Navi hit a pothole in the road. The wagon rocked. Tao grunted harshly, his first real expression of discomfort. Instinctively, she grabbed hold of his hand as she had for countless patients in her younger years. "I'm sorry. Chun has something to ease the pain."

"Had worse." Tao panted some more. "Took an arrow once. In the shoulder. Went straight through. Compared to that, this is like a fleabite."

"If that's the way fleas bite in the Hinterlands, I hope none rode back with your soldiers."

That drew a ghost of a smile, although his palm was sweaty in her fingers. If bravado helped him, so be it, but it was inconceivable that anything was worse than the horrific effects of the gator bite.

Another sharp jolt. Tao grimaced, his teeth bared, his hand clamping over hers. "Navi, please," she said over her shoulder, pitching her voice just loud enough to be heard through the tarp. "Try not to hit every bump in the road."

Chun told Tao, "Give me your arm, and hold it still. It's hard enough to keep my balance in this bouncing wagon, let alone get some medicine in you."

Tao's expression was instantly suspicious. "Why my arm? It's my legs they got."

"The medicine has to go in your arm to reach your leg," Elsabeth explained, and he made the sign of Uhrth over his chest. *The Tassagons fear us as much as we do them.* "You can trust us, or you can lie here and suffer your fleabite—" The wheels hit another pothole and they bounced hard.

"Navi," she scolded in the general direction of the driver's bench.

"Do it." Tao's expression was resolute. "Wherever it needs to go."

Chun cinched a band around Tao's forearm. Into a bulging vein he emptied one syringe, then another, taking pains to stow both out of sight in his pocket. Such items were preciously guarded. Possession was considered evidence of sorcery, a charge that carried a punishment of death. "I gave him drowse with some mondosh," Chun told her.

Sedative and painkiller. It would act fast. "Better?" she asked the general, gently.

Tao's wary but surprised eyes found hers. In them she read clear relief, telling her the medication had helped some. "A magic potion."

If only magic did exist. She shook her head. "Medicine."

Tao's eyelids drooped. He was too wrung out and now too drugged to argue their methods. "Elsabeth," he whispered thickly, his speech slurring, causing her to move closer. It seemed jarringly intimate, her face this close to his, their hands so tightly clasped—this man, this stranger, this enemy of her people who was also to be their savior, if all went as planned. "If I die, watch over Aza. Don't let her fight Xim over this." Swallowing, he closed his eyes. "Over me."

"I will," she whispered. Just as she'd promised the queen she'd protect Tao. Her life was becoming a web of promises; sticky and overlapping, they could very well entrap her.

Only then did Tao surrender to the drugs, his fingers relaxing in hers. A conscious decision to let go.

Maybe he trusts me.

It would make everything easier.

She sat back on her haunches, hanging on as the wagon bounced along. He'd looked so very noble in the homecoming parade, dignified and confident with his broad shoulders, perfect posture and lean athletic build. Even now, stripped of all the trappings of his profession, he looked no less noble lying on hay in muck-covered tatters.

No less a warrior.

"He's got a lot to learn if he's going to impress the elders," she admitted to Chun. "Asking for straps to bite. Calling a painkiller 'magic.' He knows nothing about our ways."

"You're a good teacher. He'll pick it up fast."

She sighed. "He'll have to."

Both of them fell silent, their minds full of what they'd done. Tassagonia's greatest war hero lay wounded in the back of a mule-drawn produce wagon driven by a Kurel, sleeping off the effect of drugs he considered sinful. In all of history, nothing like this had happened. Not only was she witness to it, she was participating in it. She'd even instigated it.

When she was a child, she'd hungered to be like

the characters in the stories she loved, always out on another adventure, a circumstance far removed from the reality of the dull, quiet, studious life at which she'd constantly, secretly chafed.

How things had changed.

She'd wanted excitement. *Well, Beth, now you've gotten it.*

CHAPTER TWELVE

UNDER THE COVER OF THE predawn darkness, Elsabeth and the men helped Tao sit up in the back of the wagon. Despite his wounds and the sedating drugs, he was able to walk. Again, his sheer force of will kept him going when others would have given up.

Tao became more lucid out in the night air, taking in his surroundings, the congested but squeaky-clean warren of shops and homes populated by people with an age-old, blood-deep distrust of Tassagons. He made no comment until she began unlocking the plain entrance to her parent's house.

"Is this where I'm to hide?" he asked, as she opened the front door and turned on a light, revealing the cozy interior.

Perhaps he'd been expecting a hospital or a cell. "My home, yes. You'll live with me."

His eyes found hers. No longer drowsy slits, they flickered with surprise and then speculation. She'd seen that look before when men in the palace sized up potential bedmates. No Tassagon had ever pondered her the way the general was now doing, but he clearly fancied she'd be his lover for the mere fact that they'd be sharing the same living space. Were Uhr-warriors truly that indiscriminate?

"With no chaperone?" he asked, confirming her suspicions. Any valued Tassagon maiden had to be chaperoned, lest a warrior deflower her at the first opportunity. Kurel knew no such barbarity, so no Kurel maiden required a chaperone.

Elsabeth almost laughed at the idea. "If anything, I am *your* chaperone in Kurel Town."

"Our staying alone together won't cause a scandal?"

Was he actually concerned he'd sully her reputation? Or were his doubts about his ability to control his impulses around her? Rumors about Uhr-warriors and their appetites aside, gut instinct told her the general wasn't a man to take a woman by force. He had more honor than that, and this conversation proved it. "Your very presence in Kurel Town is scandalous. Whose home you occupy makes little difference."

They made it inside without rousing any of the neighbors. With shuddering relief, Elsabeth leaned back against the closed door, her hands flat against the cool dark wood, and inhaled the sweet scent of her living room.

The detached row house had only one main living

area, one bedroom and a tiny loft where she'd slept since childhood, tucked under the slope of the roof. The bedroom had belonged to her mother and father. No one had slept in it since their deaths. A Tassagon warrior wouldn't be the first. "We'll need an extra bed," she told the men. "He can sleep here, in the living room."

She pushed away from the door to help. Some furniture rearranging allowed a bed to be brought from the clinic next door, and soon they had the general settled in a corner of the living room. A screen blocked a direct view from the front door, should anyone drop by unexpectedly.

Chun approached the bed. Several needles and sutures sat in a sterilized pan. "Healer," Tao mumbled. "Remember, you are not to take the legs."

"And if the choice is between death and amputation?"

"When isn't that the choice?" The general turned his gaze to the ceiling, and Elsabeth's heart went out to him. "I will make my decision if I am required to. Until then, you will treat my legs as if I'm keeping them."

"You have my word." Chun emptied another dose of mondosh and drowse into the man, knocking him out to administer the antivenin.

While the general was stripped of his soiled uniform and washed by the men, Elsabeth climbed up to the aviary and lit a small lamp. *Cuh-choo, cuh-choo-coo*. Rustling and cooing met her as she cut a small square from a piece of green fabric. "I need a volunteer. Who will carry this to the palace? Where are my best night fliers?"

Prometheus strutted by, tilting his head at her, one black bead of an eye searching hopefully for a few grains of feed. She cupped him in her hands. "Of course it's you." With the green flag rolled and tucked in a tube fastened to the bird's leg, she released him into the night. A flutter of wings, and he was on the way to the palace aviary. *The general is here and safe.*

By the time she'd washed up and returned to the main floor of her house, Tao was cleaned up, sutured and tucked in bed with an IV of antibiotics. The sheets were pulled midway up the general's bare chest. His shoulders and arms were brown from the suns, the smooth skin marred here and there by puckered scars. The souvenirs of battle, she thought and shuddered. She hoped they'd given him pajama pants to wear. A Tassagon warrior in her living room was one thing. A naked Tassagon warrior was entirely another.

But embarrass herself by expressing such a ridiculous concern? Clearly she'd gone soft in the years since Chun had taken over the clinic. After so long assisting her parents with patients, what Tao wore—or didn't— shouldn't concern her.

But it did somehow.

After setting a pot of stew on the stove to simmer for breakfast, Elsabeth stood over her unexpected houseguest's side while he slept. A dark brown strip of leather circled his neck, threaded through a slender, polished silver rectangle. It was an odd item of jewelry, showcasing a piece of metal that hadn't been crudely extracted from a mine and melted by a smithy, but created instead through advanced technology millennia ago on a world countless light-years away. Nothing she'd expect a Tassagon to own. Such pieces were usually remnants of the destroyed arks of old, but it was rare to find any traces larger than a pebble. A war prize, perhaps, removed from a Gorr corpse or found in some distant glade in the Hinterlands, one more item attesting to the fact that this man had roamed farther and wider than she'd ever have the chance to go, except in her imagination and in the stories she read.

The charm rose and fell with his steady, quiet breathing. "He's going to be all right," she said.

"Yes. I think so." Chun was at the sink, pumping well water into the basin. He and Navi would need to leave soon for their own homes, so they could begin their days as if nothing had happened during the night. "The problem was the venom, but the antidote is very effective."

Elsabeth held a lantern closer to Tao. Here was a gravely wounded man, too young to die, his utter vulnerability rendering him somehow incapable of the terrible things she knew he'd done. Yet, despite his unexpectedly boyish looks, the creases on his sun-tanned skin had been carved by stronger emotions, she knew. They, along with his many scars, attested to the viciousness of his years in the Hinterlands, a life that had very clearly taken its toll. She set the lantern down and crouched by his side. "You're as much of a victim of Xim as any of us are," she murmured. "You don't deserve to die."

She caught a glimpse of green under his heavy lids, and it almost looked as if he'd smiled.

"Good morning, sunshine," he murmured. His voice was soft, playful, sleep-roughened and completely un-nerving. She almost gasped at his audacity, shooting to her feet.

"Sunshine?" Navi asked, trying to hide a smirk.

Tao was already back asleep. "The general is drugged," she said. *Sunshine. My.* What would it be like hearing *that* every morning from the pillow next to her? She cut off her imagination before it went any further. "He doesn't know what he's saying."

Navi shrugged. "It seemed like he did."

Chun listened as he washed his hands. "Agreed. Mondosh has no effect on reason, and the drowse just makes him sleepy."

She frowned at them, saying under her breath, "If he knows or he doesn't, just pretend it didn't happen and continue on with proper etiquette." Clearly, his warrior's thoughts fell into well-traveled grooves, like the mule wagon did on the merchant road. That's why reacting with a nonreaction was best. Simple, neutral serenity. "Eventually, he can be trained to behave like a Kurel, and he'll think he's learned it himself."

"Rather like a dog."

They all jumped at the sound of Tao's voice. Elsabeth winced. His eyes might have been closed, but the man behind them was very much awake.

Elsabeth's face burned. She'd underestimated him. Worse, she'd insulted him. Again. "I didn't mean to imply that you were like a dog..." The rest of her sentence was lost when she turned to face him and saw how intensely he was concentrating on her, despite the mondosh in his system. It was as if he'd decided he'd will away the effects of the powerful drug as he had the agony of his injuries, dismissing them as mere fleabites. "Not at all like a dog."

"But stupid, yes?" Tao's jaw was hard. "A brute."

"No. I don't think you're stupid." It was true, she didn't. "Or a brute."

"So she says, in an effort to salvage her credibility and my trust."

"My credibility isn't in question. I got you out of a prison tonight. And of course, I want your trust."

"Want it, or need it?"

"I need your trust. Are you satisfied? All of us do."

Chun warned her into silence with a frosty look in her direction. *No arguing with the patient.* He was right. She was supposed to offer sanctuary to the general, not bicker with him.

Swallowing her pride, she again dropped to her knees at Tao's bedside. *Remember your vow. This man will help you achieve it.*

"Here is your first lesson in the ways of my people," she said, softer. "Kurel don't say those kinds of endearments to a woman they don't know in front of others. I felt embarrassed. It was easier to pretend you didn't know what you were saying than to accept that you did. But, I didn't need to point out your unawareness with such disrespect."

A satisfied sound came from deep in his throat. He murmured, barely audible, "It seems we have something in common. I have as much to learn about your ways as you do mine." He tried to hold his sagging eyelids open, but the effort proved too much. After a moment, his breathing deepened. It seemed this time he was really asleep.

She rose, wiping her hands on her skirt, awkwardly meeting the men's eyes. "He appears to be open to learning, at least."

"You, too," Chun said. Before she could retort, he told her, "I'll be back after first light. Two and one?"

"Two and one," she repeated, confirming their coded knock for the door. "Navi," she pressed a note into the accountant's hand, "deliver this to Elder Gwendolyn's mailbox." His brows lifted. "It says we've rescued a high-ranking Tassagon from the king's clutches, and that he's here, injured and under watch. I'll be in touch with all the elders come morning regarding the request for sanctuary." Elder Gwendolyn was one of the most junior of the ghetto's ruling council, but as Elsabeth's great-great aunt, she was family and thus was more likely to consider her appeal. "At the very least I hope they let him stay on humanitarian grounds until he's healed."

The men left. She walked past the niche housing the chunk of charred wood saved from her parents' funeral pyre, pausing to brush her fingers over its polished surface, then she plunged, exhausted, into a chair in sight of the bed. The house was finally silent but did not feel empty. General Tao filled the entire space with his presence: his scent, the sight of his unmoving bulk under the quilts, the unavoidable realization that he was *there*. Not just physically, but something else she could sense but not define. Whether washing the night's grime from her hair or making stew, she'd felt it.

No one had said this would be easy.

A cup of cooling honey-tea sat on the lamp table next to a book she had no intention of opening. For once, real life was providing far more twists and turns than anything she could possibly encounter on those pages.

I did it. The enormity of what she and Markam had achieved finally sank in. An Uhr-warrior in Kurel Town. The concept boggled. It could very well be the first occurrence of its kind since the Old Colony, when all the peoples of humanity had lived as one—before the Gorr invasion, before the near annihilation of both species, before they'd been reduced from the possessors of powerful, star-reaching arks and stunning weaponry to a bedraggled group of survivors, defending the last of humanity with little more than sticks and stones.

The self-appointed first Tassagon king had banned advanced technology forevermore. The first Forbiddance had deemed it wicked, blaming technology for all the ills that had befallen the colony. Leaving those "responsible" with no choice but to leave and set up their own colony in the Barrier Peaks.

Now the descendants of those outcasts had Tassagonia's future in their control once again. Like the suns at summer solstice, Xim had reached his peak. From this point in time, from this moment in Colony history, he'd shine less and less until the day he was finally extinguished.

Elsabeth returned her gaze to the sleeping form of Tao. So why did this feel more like a beginning than an end?

"ALL HANDS! ALL HANDS!"

The guard's panicked cry pierced the foggy dawn air, rousing even the drunks scattered and sprawled across the bailey—those not lucky enough to have found a mattress inside and a willing wench.

With a green square stuffed at the bottom of his pants pocket, Markam met the guard. "What happened?"

"He's gone," the man said, trying to catch his breath. "General Tao. He escaped."

"How the hell did that happen?"

"Don't rightly know, sir, but I found this." In the guard's white-gloved hand was a flimsy shard of metal.

Markam examined it. "The man fashioned one of his buttons into a key. That accounts for the cell door, but the barrier doors, were they not guarded?"

"Guarded and intact, sir."

"How did he get out, then? Through the walls?"

"Sir, all I know is that he wasn't there when I brought him a pot of gruel and a cup of water."

Markam paced, a finger pressed crossways under his chin. "There is access to the spillway from the cell block, a small opening, although I don't believe it leads anywhere but into the moat."

"If he was desperate enough, sir…"

"That's what I'm thinking." Markam glanced over at his second-in-command. "Bowers, sound the alert.

All guards are to assemble in the barracks. Then send them out to scour every inch of this palace and the city. We'll find Uhr-Tao. He can't have gone far."

Across the bailey Markam spied Beck storming in his direction. He turned back to Bowers and said, "One more thing, the palace is off-limits to Kurel workers until further notice—security reasons."

"Do you suspect a Kurel role in the general's escape, sir?" Bowers asked.

"The Kurel? Turning aggressive, actually plotting and carrying out a dangerous extraction mission to save an Uhr-warrior?" Markam laughed.

Bowers snickered. "I guess you're right, sir."

"Now, go deal with Beck. I'll be with the king." Markam set out in the direction of the royal residences to put himself through the particularly unpleasant experience of having to rouse Xim—from Aza's bed.

CHAPTER THIRTEEN

Tao was underwater, swimming to the surface glimmering above him. For all his effort, he could swim no closer to it. He kicked harder but his legs seemed to be caught in mud. He'd drown unless he got free. Running out of air. He swept his arms, powerful strokes, but his left was caught—an eel had tangled itself around it!

He jerked awake, dragging in air, his heart slamming like a broken door in a windstorm. Something was tangled around his left arm like in the dream, stinging, like a bee bite—a clear vine. He tracked it to where it dangled from an upside-down bottle all the way back to the inside of his elbow. The head was buried under the bandages. And in his flesh!

He yanked it out. Liquid and blood sprayed.

"Don't!" Elsabeth was there, a cloud of red hair and wide, angry blue eyes. Hands flat on his shoulders, she pushed him back down to the pillow, her hands warm on his bare flesh, her sweet scent intensified by the sweep of her hair against his jaw. "You pulled the IV out."

"IV?"

"Yes. It's short for intravenous. It sends medicine directly into your bloodstream."

He drew the circle of Uhrth in the center of his chest to ward off bad luck. "Sorcery."

"What you've been brought up to believe is wrong. We Kurel don't practice sorcery, or magic. We practice medicine."

"Science—" he started to say with distaste then stopped. *Keep your head.* His response had been automatic, like a reflex. Was it any different than the way the Kurel glared at his army? He and the Kurel might be aligned in their fight with Xim, but sanctuary or not, he was in their custody and at their mercy. Best to give the appearance of behaving and gain their trust.

In case he needed to break it.

Elsabeth snatched his wrist to peer at his arm. "You're bleeding," she scolded.

"I was having a dream. An eel was wrapped around my arm..." It all sounded silly now.

"Science, not sorcery, is the reason you're alive this morning—with both legs still attached."

The tassagators. His legs. Instinctively, he went hunting for them, taking inventory. Two complete limbs. "I'm indeed whole." He let out a quick amazed laugh. "They seem utterly insufficient words, but thank you, Elsabeth."

"Thank Chun. It's his handiwork." She smiled, though, at his sincere words.

He wondered if she was aware how much her rare smiles transformed her face. Capable of taking a man's breath away, they were. But he held his tongue rather than tell her. Getting to know a Kurel woman required an entirely different protocol than what he was used to. "I am in his debt. And in yours, despite what you say."

Xim's suspicions were accurate about one thing: the dark arts were thriving unchecked in the ghetto. But whatever had been done to Tao, magic or otherwise, it had left him in remarkable condition. His wounds should be throbbing, swelling and have him wracked with fever by now. Every major injury he'd ever suffered came with the sweats. It was expected.

But not here in K-Town.

He couldn't help thinking of how the plague had roared through the capital like a deadly wildfire, taking so many lives, including those of his parents, but no Kurel. These IVs and potions were the reason. But did the benefits justify the crime?

"I have to treat the wound, Tao." Holding on to his biceps, the tutor sat down on the mattress, pressing gauze to the crook of his arm. "Hold still."

He certainly wasn't going to run away. Not half-dressed with a very pretty woman sharing his bed, sitting so close he could feel the heat radiating off her body. Her sheer proximity—her scent, her curves, her mouth—commanded his attention, to say the least. But her intentions weren't sexual. Not even remotely. Her entire focus was devoted to a break in his skin to which he'd not have otherwise spared a second thought.

Her ivory skin was scrubbed and clean—not like the dancer at the feast with her face paint and heavy lashes, or like the females who frequented the encampments, hard-worn and jaded from having visited too many men's beds. Nor was she like the daughters of the king's men or older officers, his father's contemporaries, who had been introduced to him during his brief returns to the palace over the years. None had conjured in him more than a passing interest. All were now lost in a blur of stilted, boring conversations made while sipping expensive liqueurs and wearing stiff ceremonial uniforms.

In his defense, he'd been at war and focused on war during those visits, devoted to service to his kingdom and fairly certain he'd not be alive to see the end of it. He hadn't been looking at any women as marriage candidates, or perhaps he might have viewed them differently, considering each as the possible woman to whom he'd be faithful for the rest of his life, the woman who would share his bed, her body, their children.

Thoughts of the vineyards filled his mind, the

sprawling white house with a ribbon of smoke rising from the chimney, the lush gardens, sounds of song and laughter cascading through the serenity of the hills where he'd live, surrounded by family.

Never going off to war again.

The idealistic stuff of daydreams, perhaps, but such dreams had kept him going for countless years through hellish experiences no human should have to suffer, offering solace on the darkest of terrifying nights, when there was none.

When there were no women like Elsabeth to offer him comfort—or to pluck him from the jaws of death. No woman he'd known would have risked guards, arrows and tassagators to save his sorry ass, nor possessed the courage to try.

Now she was dabbing ointment inside his elbow. He'd spent less time on a dislocated shoulder. "I am fine," he assured her as she continued to fuss over him.

"The smallest wound can kill if infection sets in. I can't let you die. I won't. Too much hinges on your life now."

Her concern would have been flattering in any other situation, but he knew she only desired to use him to seek vengeance against Xim. He took the gauze from her fingers and tossed it to the table in contempt. "I will not be part of an ill-thought-out power grab."

"It's not ill-thought-out. It's been three years in the making."

"Whom do you hope to install on the throne in Xim's place?"

"You," she said with quiet urgency.

"What? No, Elsabeth."

"Ask Markam. He agrees."

Tao remembered all too well the strange conversation he'd had with Markam at the homecoming. The man had been feeling him out, gauging his interest. "Perhaps not ill-thought-out, but just as potentially destabilizing, Elsabeth. For all your passion, you're hopelessly innocent about the consequences of what you and the other rebels aspire to do." He girded himself against an onslaught of memories: the screaming in the night, the corpses in the morning. The lingering, nauseating musk. If humans were the enemy instead of the Gorr, the violence would still be nightmarish. And then the Gorr would come, ready to exploit the human civil war.

He waved away her attempt to wrap a bandage around his elbow. The Kurel and her gratuitous nursing. "I'm fine."

She pushed up off the bed, taking the bottle of liquid off its hook and placing it on a low table, stopping the incessant dripping from the end of the tube. The I.V. "Chun warned me you'd be a terrible patient. You'd want to be up and about before you're ready."

"In the Hinterlands, if you weren't up and walking quickly, you'd slow down the others."

"Weren't there camps for healing? Hospitals?"

"If there were, they'd be Gorr bait. The Furs could smell an injured human from miles away. Their ability to smell blood was one of their most lethal traits."

"What were they like, the Gorr? No one will ever talk about them." She dragged a footstool next to the bed and sat on it.

"Pray you never have to know. That none of the people here do."

Her jaw was harder. "The real answer, Tao. You've lived outside the walls, and I..." A lantern on the bedside table illuminated her face, her slender neck. Almost bashfully, she hugged her knees and confessed, "I've only dreamed it. I want to know what it's like out there. And not a made-up version. I can get that from a book."

Books. Not only did potions abound in the cottage, but also books and more books. They lined the shelves and were piled on tables, more of every size and color tucked into nooks and crannies everywhere he looked. It was insanity. "What do you do with so many books? What does any Kurel?"

"We read them. I'll teach you."

He dismissed the idea. "I've read a book before."

"You," she said. "You read a book?"

"And can't see the point of doing any more of it.

One of my men found one of the things and brought it to my tent." Tao had sat alone with the old battered book as night fell, rifling through the pages, looking for enlightenment in the indecipherable marks and finding none. Yet, a Kurel like Elsabeth wasn't satisfied with one book; she required hundreds. "Have you read them all?"

"Many of them. What ones I haven't gotten to, I will one day."

"Elsabeth, you'd be better off getting out and experiencing what the world has to offer than burying your nose in paper."

"There are whole worlds between those covers. Entire universes." Her eyes grew so dreamy he could almost believe it—if he hadn't already tried it for himself.

"What more can be gleaned from ink on paper that a man can't learn with his own senses?"

"You tell me. You've been out there. Tell me. What lies beyond the walls?" Her voice dropped as she leaned forward, her hair falling forward over her shoulders. "Tell me about the Gorr."

He'd never met a female with such interest in venturing outside the walls for no other reason than excitement. The camp followers were with the army, true, but to them it wouldn't matter where they were as long as they could eke out a living by serving the soldiers.

"They resemble us in the body, but that's where any

similarities end. They're covered with fur like a dog's, and they're driven by a lust for blood in a mindless, soulless way we humans can't understand." He told her of how they preferred to travel in packs and live in caves or in dense brush—their dens—where they hid their young. "Only the alphas in the pack are clever enough to strategize and plan above and beyond basic survival, and they're the only ones who can breed."

"Why would anyone raise young in a war zone?"

"They saw the Hinterlands as their lands, their home, and we the invaders. To us, a war zone. To them, their home. All a matter of perspective."

"To bring children into that kind of world is unconscionable."

Tao held his tongue. How the Gorr felt about their children had been immaterial to him.

Apparently, not to Elsabeth. He could hear the dismay in her voice. She kept talking in the face of his silence. "Since the Gorr don't differentiate between the helpless and the combatants, I take it your army didn't, either."

"We had to take out the dens. Pups and all."

She recoiled. "Are there no rules in war? No laws of decency?"

"I have no sympathy for these creatures, Elsabeth, as harsh as that seems. They were monsters. Hell-bent on our extinction. The young were just as dangerous, even the smallest pup." The disconcerting howls in the night came back to haunt him, countless pairs of glowing orbs up in the trees, Gorr waiting, ready to pounce and strike. "Maybe ten percent were alpha, no more, although there seemed to be more of them at the end, after we'd killed off so many of the lesser Gorr. They'd taken up a last-ditch defense of their kind, but it was already too late. If it weren't for their eyes, we'd have defeated the damned Furs long ago."

"Why the eyes?" she asked, hugging her knees.

"The eyes… They charm you. Be-spell you. If you let them hold your stare, you'll lose your mind. Many of my men who were killed dropped their weapons willingly and all but asked to die."

Her disturbed gaze lingered on his for a moment longer. "Mercy," she whispered, her expression part horror but more fascination, as if he'd just shared a particularly scary bedtime tale.

It's not real to her. Despite Elsabeth's insistence that she wanted a real answer, to her and to everyone at home it was the same: the Gorr were the stuff of nightmares and old soldiers' yarns.

She rose, wiping her hands on her skirt. "I imagine you're hungry. I made stew."

The abrupt change in subject sent awareness of his empty belly careening into him like a fully loaded weapons cart. Why hadn't he noticed that the cottage was filled with a savory aroma, heavy with spices that all at once smelled foreign and made his stomach growl with hunger? Whatever the Kurel had pumped into his body had done nothing to quell his body's need for food.

Elsabeth left his side for a kettle bubbling on an iron stove. Stirring the contents, she lifted a spoon to her lips to taste. "Just right."

Long, curling strands of hair hung down her back as she prepared to serve the meal. He fancied he could wrap each lock around a finger and it'd hold its corkscrew shape. Then he pictured that fiery hair tangled and damp from their lovemaking, spread out on a pillow—and her, warm and lush and spread out under him. His loins tightened at the thought.

A wasted thought. No matter what her ulterior motives were for wanting him healthy, he was certain her hospitality wouldn't extend that far.

He pushed up to a sitting position, his head still swimming, and instinctively noted several escape routes—a front and rear door as well as windows—four in this room alone, two pairs of them. A ladder went up one wall. To the roof? The scrape of the spoon against the sides of the kettle mixed with the distant, muffled sound of doves or pigeons. The soft, mournful sound magnified the silence. It was nearing morning, but the ghetto was still asleep.

Crutches were propped against the wall closest to his bed, but he'd soon be walking without aid. He had to be. Those he'd left behind in the palace needed him as much as Xim needed some sense knocked *into* him. For the king to think that he—a man he'd known since childhood, his top military officer and his brother-in-law—lusted after the Tassagonian throne, to believe it enough to have him killed, it was madness.

So much for Tao's dreams for a quiet retirement.

Elsabeth carried two bowls to his bed, one for him, which she placed on a tray in his lap, another for herself. She sat on a footstool dragged close to his bed. "The elders will have to be told you're hiding here. It's up to them to decide if you can stay. If I keep your presence a secret, I could be banished." She paused in the middle of stirring her stew. "I've invited the elders to dinner. Tonight."

"I'll be ready."

"You have to make a good impression."

"Don't worry. I will." Tao glanced around for a crust of bread, or a hand-plank with which to shovel the stew into his mouth, but a delicate little spoon was all he had at hand, the same kind Elsabeth was using. He picked it up, pinching it between his two fingers. "Silly thing. Almost useless."

"It's a spoon." She said it as if she thought him unbelievably backward for questioning it.

"I know. But look at it. How can a man expect to get enough to eat?"

"Our men do just fine eating with utensils."

"Your men read books and work with numbers—and

treat wounds with potions. They don't expend enough energy to need more food than they can eat with… this." He scowled at the little spoon. Still, he could not afford to be put outside the ghetto gates, or cause Elsabeth to suffer the same fate. *I must learn to adapt to the ways of my hosts.* He dredged the utensil through his stew, only to find her watching him attempt the feat with a sort of repulsed yet enthralled curiosity.

He'd show her.

A sinfully small amount of the stew fit on the spoon. It was chunky and brimming with meat and vegetables. He sucked some into his mouth, and was halfway to digging up more when he was hit by an explosion of heat. It set his tongue afire and shot up his sinuses. "What in all Uhrth," he croaked. "Water…"

Elsabeth jumped up, returning not with water but with milk. "Goat's milk," she said. "Drink it down. It'll quench the heat."

He chugged all that was in the glass and expelled a gust of air. "There's enough spice in this stew to burn a village. I thought you said it was 'just right.'"

"It is." She was trying hard not to laugh at him. "For a Kurel. Our food is considered spicy by some."

"Some?" He was wiping his eyes, his mouth still on fire. That won him another smothered laugh. Could he not maintain his dignity around this woman? "I thought you were a peace-loving people. This is a dangerous weapon. You promised Markam to keep me

alive. Where's your sense of responsibility? Where was the warning?"

"I can arrange for you to be fed baby food—bread and milk…"

"Bah!" Like grabbing hold of a sword for battle, he lifted the spoon. "If I am to live like you, that means eating like you." Pausing to say a prayer, he then wolfed down mouthful after burning mouthful until he'd cleaned the bowl. Eyes and nose tearing, he sat back in bed, sweating—but not from fever. From breakfast!

"More?" she asked.

"Yes, please," he rasped. "I haven't eaten in days, and by Uhrth, I won't let a little spice stop me."

After he'd eaten his fill, his eyes and nose watering, Elsabeth cleared the dishes and returned with two cups of tea to her perch on the bedside footstool. He lifted the impossibly little cup to his nose. It smelled like mint and grass.

"It's safe," she assured him.

He snorted. "'Just right,' I suppose." It did taste pleasant, but what he really craved was a glass of chilled ale. Who knew when he'd next have the chance? He was, for all intents and purposes, dead. A general without an army, corralled by people who refused to fight. A Tassagon Uhr-warrior stuck in the heart of K-Town with a woman who'd rather be anywhere else on this world but in his company.

Tao wondered if Markam was at the palace laughing at that fact? Probably. It would be just his friend's sense of mischief to set him up like this.

Except the reality of the matter was sobering. He was a fugitive, his sister, Aza, was at risk if she dared protest the king's actions against him and his army was in danger of being used as a weapon against other humans, his officers executed if they refused. Frustration burned in his gut at being so stymied.

Consigned to K-Town, he'd be able to do little to help the kingdom from such an awkward fallback position—let alone help Aza. But he wouldn't stop trying. He'd survive to see his sister and his kingdom safe.

He had no time to devote further thought to ale and tea; he had a meeting with the elders to prepare for. But Elsabeth's attention had shifted outside, gauging the amount of darkness left. "I'll leave for the palace at suns-up," she said.

"You will be my conduit of communication with the palace. Between Markam and I. Also Aza. Bring back everything you hear. Everything you see."

She only lifted a brow at his thinly disguised orders.

"No different from what I've been doing for the past three years. I give information to Markam, and he does the same for me." She paused to contemplate him as he emptied his cup, holding it out for her to pour another.

"How long have you worked with him?" he asked.

"Since the day I accepted the position as royal tutor." The candle on the table sputtered. She straightened the wick with deft fingers, her expression growing sober. "Something he set in motion before I ever knew of him—because he knew of me. After my parents were slaughtered, I tried keeping their clinic open in defiance of the violence, just as I'd vowed at their funeral. So they'd know they didn't die in vain." The candle flame danced in her darkened eyes. For the first time he could see the full measure of her grief. Like him, she kept the pain of loss hidden. It could be misconstrued, after all, as a weakness.

"But for all their brilliance in medicine," she said, "they overlooked their financial matters. They'd spent all their coins on the clinic, leaving me with nothing. If not for donations from the neighbors, I wouldn't have been able to eat, let alone run a clinic. How could I restock medicine if I couldn't afford enough tubers to fill a pot? I had no aptitude for medicine, no real skills to speak of—aside from a love of books, a knack for organization and an unfettered imagination." She cracked a self-deprecatory smile. "If one can consider that a skill and not a liability. I let it be known I needed employment, but the only offers that came my way were of marriage."

"And you couldn't decide amongst the many men?"

"Actually," she replied, a hint of pink tinting her cheeks, "when I thought of the depth of love I saw in my parents' relationship, I decided none of the men who came forward had even a trace of that potential. Accepting any of their offers was out of the question."

"Not even to improve your circumstances?"

"Especially not for that reason. I knew I'd achieve my goal another way."

"But you would have married, if you'd found your so-called true love?"

"Yes. I would have."

Sighing, he shook his head. "Love will get you only so far."

"Don't you ever plan to marry?"

"Of course. But I'll expect whomever I choose to be able to ease my retirement, to work at the vineyards with me, providing womanly comforts, bearing my children. That will take a deliberate effort more than it will love."

She almost choked on the tea she'd just sipped. "You want to grow old with a woman who sees being with you as a *deliberate effort?*"

"I hope she'll enjoy my company, but yes. Much like a successful battle strategy, marriage requires endurance."

"But not love."

"Correct."

She wore the same expression of revulsion as when he'd told her about the Gorr. As if his beliefs on such things as love and marriage were equally horrifying, and distressing. "Is that how it was between your parents, Tao?"

"My father was gone at the front more than he was at home. My mother raised us. They seemed to enjoy each other's company when he was there, they treated each other with respect, but the point of the matter is that she was the right mate for him. My father chose her because she'd be strong and loyal. And independent. A warrior's woman, not a weak-willed female afraid to face life alone. When it comes time, I'll find an equally compatible female using the same logical, carefully considered methods with which I've conducted my military campaigns. Emotion will play no part in it, this flighty idea of 'true love.'"

Her luminous blue gaze radiated at turns abject pity, intense curiosity and flat-out doubt. She started gathering their cups to put away.

"What?" he said. She'd gone silent, but not for the lack of an opinion. It was suddenly important he know what it was.

She spun to face him. "I hope, for your sake, you find a woman who'll love you so powerfully, so completely, that she'll render every ridiculous belief you just expressed completely and irrevocably wrong."

He fell back against the pillows. Gooseflesh tingled on his arms, as if a window to his soul had been thrown open to let in a fresh and bracing breeze—which threatened to blow all his carefully arranged viewpoints off the table.

He slammed that window shut. He'd spent the past fifteen years plotting out the remainder of his life, should he ever get to have a remainder of his life. No one's whimsies would disrupt his carefully made plans, especially not a Kurel's—although her skeptical reaction did bring to mind Markam's comment from the homecoming: *good luck*. But then, his friend had always given too much weight to Aza's fantasies of true love.

Elsabeth carried the empty cups to the kitchen. Gruffly, he said, "You were telling me how you came to work with Markam. Finish the story." He blamed the healer's potions for allowing the tutor to sway him so far off course. The wizardry was as dangerous to his judgment as a Gorr's eyes, fooling him into letting down his guard.

She appeared entertained by his discomposure as she pumped water into a basin. "As the clinic was failing, the palace announced there was an opening for a royal tutor. Just like that, out of the blue, when nothing else was going right. It was the perfect job at the perfect time, and I was the perfect applicant. Coincidence?" She shook her head. "That opening was meant for me alone. Markam masterminded my hiring to get me in the palace. He convinced Aza of the need for a tutor even though the children were too young for one. Xim, of course, wouldn't have seen the need for a tutor at any age. But I was the poor orphan of the first two casualties of the crackdown. The two people who were probably the best friends you Tassagons had in this ghetto." She pressed her lips together, her expression darker. "Markam never said so, but he must have known my bitterness would make me eager to work against Xim. He was right."

She started scrubbing dishes as if she could just as easily wash away the anguish and anger of her past.

"So, I came to work at the palace, and did just as Markam hoped—I became attached to the queen and the little ones. I grew to love my job. I grew to love *them,* Tao. Teaching the prince and princess while working for their sire's overthrow, it tears me in two. But Markam must have banked on this, too, when he hired me. He'd wagered that the loyalty I'd develop for the queen and the children would keep me from endangering them unnecessarily. Markam wants their fates considered separately from Xim's. He wants to see them safe. And so far he has."

"You don't resent the manipulation?"

"I don't fault him for any of it. He may have lured me here for his own purposes, but he gave me the means to fulfill my vow to my parents."

"To oust Xim," he said with a snarl, shifting position to ease the pull of his stitches. "You have no idea what you risk by doing this."

"I know what we risk in doing nothing," she said with quiet certainty. From where she stood, a rebel positioned incongruously in a kitchen, she met his hard stare with determination, but he could also see the exhaustion in her face, the residual fear. "Xim wishes to force all human tribes under his rule. In our scriptures, the Log of Uhrth, it's warned that if we humans turn on each other, darkness will consume us and we will be lost to Uhrth forever."

"No one needs scripture to tell us the mistake in fighting each other," Tao snapped. "Our weakness emboldens the Gorr. Division amongst us will lure them out of hiding. And back to war we'll be."

"You can stop a future war, Tao. You can stop Xim."

He recognized the look in her face and folded his arms over his chest. "No, Elsabeth. No more campaigning for me to be king. The throne isn't mine to take. I'm not in the line of succession. My nephew is the legitimate heir. By the arks, what am I saying? Xim is still the legitimate king!" He paused. *Keep your head.* "If not the ideal king," he qualified.

"He is more than a less-than-ideal king, Tao. He's treacherous, demonstrating it with his cruel deeds. You could rule until Crown-Prince Maxim comes of age.

Use King Martin as your model. He was the one who invited the Kurel to immigrate here, to the capital."

"But he forced you to live apart."

"That was our choice," Elsabeth said. "Just as we chose to leave the Old Colony."

She was rewriting history as he sat there, listening to her rubbish. He'd long believed the Kurel were lost in their own little world; this proved it. "The Kurel were exiled to the Barrier Peaks for crimes of sorcery."

"We left on our own." Wiping her hands, she walked closer, standing above him, her skin fragranced with the sweet, fresh scent he'd come to associate with her. He could detect it even with the heavy spice of the cooking in the air, much the way her appearance had stood out on that crowded street the day of his homecoming. "General Arakelian wasn't yet king of Tassagonia when he first called science a crime, blaming us for the bad end to the war. We may have made the glove, yes, but ours wasn't the fist that was in it when it threw the punch."

Tao blinked at the play of words. He'd never thought of it that way.

"Arakelian and his warriors needed someone to blame after they'd destroyed everything they had in their arsenal, everything they threw at the Gorr. The Gorr weren't any better off, but he couldn't see it, or he refused to. No different from now, with King Xim blaming us—Kurel Town—for his woes. So the Kurel left, a great exodus to save civilization. We were the teachers and researchers, the scientists, physicians and writers, the drivers and mechanics of the arks. We took the knowledge from our birth-world beyond the stars with us for safekeeping. If not for our daring, the legacy of Uhrth would have been lost. Both our people's legacies, Tao, and the Riders', too."

He took a moment to absorb the vast amount of information she'd divulged. "How can you possibly know all this?"

"It is written," she said.

Written, he thought. In books he could not decipher.

"Where are these books and what do they say?" How did he know this so-called Log of Uhrth wasn't a fable, meant to teach the Kurel the virtues of being passive? Even if it was a description of actual events that happened so long ago, without being able to see it, he could not tell for himself.

"Only the elders know," she said mysteriously. "But they exist. I've seen the Log," she trembled, "when I was a little girl. At my Reckoning."

"What Reckoning?"

"It's when we learn where we came from. All of us. When we're told the story I'm telling you now."

"Story. See? Not real. A fairy tale."

She shook her head. "No. I saw it—the Log. I saw

what it was. It's the one copy left of the original in the Barrier Peaks."

"A log... A book?"

"And more." She turned her back on him to resume her work in the kitchen.

He exhaled. There would be no more Kurel secrets revealed.

According to Elsabeth, the Kurel had left the Old Colony on their own accord rather than dig in and defend their beliefs, their science. Why? Because they thought they'd lose? What happened to taking a risk for an uncertain reward? That leap of faith was the spice of life for him. Or did their voluntary exodus demonstrate exactly that—a leap of faith? A grand risk. If preserving Uhrth's legacy had indeed rested on their shoulders, then they'd managed something extraordinary. They'd given up their personal safety, their home, for the greater good. Altruism was one of the basic values of the Uhr ideology.

He'd long thought the Kurel incapable of such grand deeds, and had pitied them for it. They were wizards who practiced the dark arts and thus belonged behind the walls of this ghetto. But what if there were more to their pacifism than cowardice or convenient morality? What if as the guardians of knowledge they held the last links to Uhrth in their safekeeping? Whether or not the rest of humanity agreed with it, they'd put that responsibility above all else.

And thought themselves superior for it. Uhrth's favored children.

Perhaps deservedly so.

He gathered his folded arms close.

"Are you going to share the reason behind that frown?" Elsabeth asked.

He managed a smile at her probing, though a small one. "I can't help think of Tassagonia's shunning of the technology you claim you saved. A knee-jerk reaction based on a war gone bad? A weak leader looking for a scapegoat? If so, we followed such teachings blindly for all the centuries since, never questioning." He thought of the plague, all the deaths. Could they have been preventable? "Did my parents die for nothing?"

Are we Tassagons really as ignorant as the Kurel think?

"We have to hope they didn't, any more than mine didn't die for no reason," she said quietly. "We have to hope we can conquer the ignorance that led to their deaths."

Starting with those who perpetuated it.

Xim.

Tao dragged his hands over his hair and exhaled with weariness. "I returned home believing I led the last warriors, that ours was the last march of the last war. I believed, truly, that I'd won peace. But there can be no peace unless a king understands the consequences of war. Xim is too rash. Too selfish.

Shortsighted. I was too long out on campaign to realize the extent of his failings as a ruler."

She tipped her head down, her expression as soft and kind as he'd ever seen it. He had the oddest thought of cupping that sweet face in his hands to kiss her. "Do you know what Markam told me about you?" she asked, quieter. "He said your personal sense of honor is so great you sometimes neglect to believe the lack of it in others."

"An oversight all the same," he said gruffly. He couldn't afford any more mistakes like that. "But am I Xim's replacement? No. No more campaigning for me to be king. There's another way, and we will find it."

We. The word might be misconstrued as evidence he was throwing support to the rebels. But these humans were playing a very dangerous game. Aligning himself with them was premature.

"Oh, dear." She threw a worried glance outside at the coming dawn. At least she shared the same concerns of what might happen in the palace as soon as the empty dungeon was discovered. "I have to get ready."

She quickly went into the one adjoining room. He listened to the sounds of a woman dressing for the day, familiar from his youth, unfamiliar from his years at war. In minutes, she returned with her hair pinned up, wearing a blue skirt much like the one she'd worn on the day he'd first seen her—one, no, two days ago. By Uhrth, had he spotted her during his homecoming parade only the day before *yesterday?* She knew more about him now than any other woman, including his sister.

She spoke quickly, hurrying about as she tidied up, putting the entire room back in order in a dizzyingly short amount of time, finally slowing down enough to pick up her messenger bag. "No one will much be in the mood for learning, and I'm in no mind to teach, but my absence will be more noticeable than my presence."

He caught her wrist in his hand. "If the truth of my situation emerges while you're there, you won't be allowed to leave. You can be sure two escapes in a row through the spillway won't happen."

She looked away from him. "At least I would be confined with Queen Aza and the children."

Tao didn't like that option, either. He hated that Aza was in danger, but if Elsabeth were there, too, then damn it to hell, she'd also be in danger. The tutor was courageous but she was no trained warrior; she could not protect his sister and the children. She would only share in whatever fate befell them.

Of course, harboring him in her tiny home put her in danger. She risked banishment, or worse, simply for helping him. The idea rubbed like a pebble in a boot. He, known as humanity's greatest warrior, was endangering a woman. *Not for a minute longer than necessary,* he vowed to himself.

Cuh-choo-coo. Cuh-choo. The sound of pigeons suddenly swelled in volume. Then a commotion of bird wings came from the roof. "Prometheus is here," Elsabeth announced.

She hurried away from the front door. Tao tensed and looked for anything in his reach that could be used as a weapon. The crutches could make decent clubs. "Who is Prometheus?"

"A messenger," she said. "With news from the palace."

CHAPTER FOURTEEN

ELSABETH TOOK HOLD OF one of the rungs on the ladder up to the aviary. Her hands shook. A message, just as it was getting light. She'd have to see it before she left, which was no doubt Markam's intent.

Something has happened at the palace.

Tao stumbled out of bed, grabbing a crutch on his way, and hobbled after her, bare-chested, tugging on the waistband of a pair of baggy black pajama pants.

She gave her silent thanks to Chun for his consideration in not leaving her with an entirely naked man. "Tao. Get back in bed."

"I will hear the news."

"There won't be anything to hear. Prometheus is a pigeon. He will have carried a message back. I have to go up and get it."

He almost dropped the crutch. Swearing, he tucked it more firmly under his arm, trying to pretend his freshly stitched wounds didn't hurt as she knew they must. Yet he was eyeing where the ladder ended above his head as if he were actually considering the climb.

"You're not coming. Back under the blankets."

"It's better for healing that I stretch my legs. I'll wait here." He leaned jauntily on the crutch.

He might think she didn't notice the tightening of his abdominal muscles to brace against the discomfort of his wounds, but she did, and frowned at him. "Your legs will swell."

"You'll work your Kurel magic and fix them."

"Medicine can't fix everything. That's why it's not really magic, or sorcery, like you Tassagons think."

"I was joking, Elsabeth—"

"It can't cure every sickness. It can't overcome any injury. It won't bring people back to life, no matter how innocent they are of any intrigue." She stopped herself, biting her lip.

"I know," he said, gentler. "I'm worried about her, too."

They exchanged a look of concern for Aza.

He hunched over the crutch. "I'll wait in bed."

"I won't open the message until I come down."

A staccato knock at the door. "That's Chun," she said. "Shall I give you a few seconds to hobble back to bed before I let him in?"

"The man saved my legs. I owe him the appearance of obeying him, at least."

"And me. I went through a lot of trouble to get you back here."

Tao dipped his head. "And you, yes." Stiffly, the wounded general, in all his godlike, half-naked magnificence, returned to bed.

She let Chun in. The physician's energetic steps and purposeful expression gave no hint to the night he'd spent treating Tao after they'd fled from the palace. His brows lifted quizzically at the sight of the general sitting up on the edge of the bed.

By the time Elsabeth returned with the tube carried home by Prometheus, Chun had examined Tao and told him what the soldier already knew from far too much experience with wounds: his legs were healing. "I'd rather you stayed off your feet today," he advised before he left them to start his routine day.

Elsabeth could tell by the exasperated look on Tao's face that he had little intention of complying. "He saved your legs, remember?" she said, sitting down on the footstool.

"What about when the elders come?"

"You'll greet them from this bed. You're hurt."

"I will not lounge abed to meet these elders."

He was tossing out commands like a general again. "A chair, then," she conceded, but in the same no-retreat tone. "As long as you're off your feet."

"We'll discuss the matter later." He flicked a finger

at the small brown tube she held in her fingers. "What does it say?"

"It probably won't say anything at all. To be cautious, we send what we call flags to each other, colored squares of cloth with nothing written on them."

"Markam can't write, anyway, or read."

"Actually, he can and does."

"Markam?" Tao seemed stunned.

"Yes. Aza, too."

"My sister reads books?"

"Simple texts. She's still learning."

Tao's brows drew together and his frown had returned. It was as if he were ashamed. "Open the message," he said curtly.

What troubled him so much about knowing how to read? It was nothing to be ashamed of. In fact, for any Tassagon, especially a Tassagon soldier like Tao, to be literate was considered a rare and wonderful thing, in her people's view.

"I sent him a green flag last night to let him know you were safe." She upended the tube and spilled the contents into her palm. Crimson filled her palm like blood.

Her terrified thoughts spun like leaves caught in a cyclone. Clearly Xim knew about the escape already, but had he guessed the Kurel role in it? Would she be arrested? Would soldiers be unleashed on the ghetto once more? To fire their arrows inside the gates at innocents?

"Red." Tao narrowed his eyes at her.

She bit her lower lip. "Red means danger. He must be telling me to stay away from the palace."

"Then you will, until we know more. You'll remain with me."

Without hesitation, and with the kind of confidence born in a man, Tao had assumed protection of her, and it hit her what an advantage it could be having a warrior here to defend her. And the ghetto.

More pounding on the door, no code this time.

"I don't know who that is." Elsabeth stepped back as Tao jumped up. This time, he didn't hide the pain it caused him to put his weight on his injuries. "You're going to rip open the wounds if you keep getting up. You're not in charge here. I am. Stay in bed." She reached up and pushed on his shoulders, a sizzling second of contact with smooth skin and hard muscle. Down he went down to the mattress, almost taking her with him. A part of her wished he was badly behaved enough to do it.

She straightened, stepping backward as she held up a warning finger. "Stay."

His brow went up, his eyes dangerous, his slight smile even more so. "Like a good dog."

"No. Like a good general."

More knocking. Who could it be at this uncivilized

hour? *Please, not the elders.* There was one good thing about not going to the palace—it gave her more time to get Tao ready for their scrutiny, and she'd need every minute of it.

She smoothed her hair and skirt with nervous hands before opening the door. Navi stormed inside. "I was on my way to work when they told me," he said. "The king closed the palace to Kurel, even palace workers. None of us can report for our jobs today." The accountant marched past her and around the screen to speak to Tao. "Out in the capital it's crazy. A massive search is under way for you, house to house."

"Furs." Tao spat the name of his enemy like a curse as he dragged a hand over his head. "Has any attempt been made to come inside the ghetto?"

Navi shook his head. "So far, no."

"We'll hide you in the crawl space if we need to, Tao," Elsabeth assured him. "You'll be safe."

"It's not me I'm worried about! It's all of you. My presence here brings risk."

"I told you, I'm not afraid."

Navi puffed out his chest. "Nor am I."

"What of everyone else? The other Kurel. Those who don't raid dungeons in the middle of the night, or pull warriors out of moats seething with tassagators? If guards come into the ghetto and start killing, I'll have a hard time taking cover like a coward."

Her heart flipped at the thought of him giving up

and turning himself in, returning to an almost-certain death. "You'll have to. Everything hinges on you staying alive."

"Everything…" Tao crossed his bare, muscular arms over his chest to ponder them, no less the intimidating war hero for being confined to his sickbed. "Like Xim's demotion?"

"Humanity's future," she insisted.

They exchanged stubborn, challenging glares.

Clearly skeptical of his individual value in the rebellion, Tao shifted his focus to Navi. "How long will the palace be off-limits? Did they say?"

Navi shook his head. "None of us wanted to ask the guards and provoke them."

Elsabeth threw the empty messenger bag off her shoulder. "This is the way we've lived ever since King Orion died. Like sheep in a pen. We can do no more but wait for something bad to happen to us."

"You didn't wait," Tao pointed out. "You took action."

She stopped, a fist on her hip. "Yes, I did. I'm going to keep doing so. This won't stop us. Those who work in town can pass us information on what's going on inside the palace."

"I tally the books for a baker and blacksmith," Navi volunteered. "I'll see what I can find out."

"Wait for the turmoil to die down," Tao cautioned. "To do otherwise is to court danger. Markam will keep a tight rein on his men, but Beck's Home Guard is a young and inexperienced force. No telling what they might do."

She knew this better than anyone. Tao was right. They had to wait for the storm to pass. "We'll use the time to our advantage. To rest—" she shot Tao a pointed look "—and to prepare for dinner with the elders."

"That's right—it's tonight." Navi gave Tao a sympathetic shake of the head. "That's not good news—for you." Then to Elsabeth, he muttered, "Or you."

"*Navi,*" she whispered through gritted teeth. "Hush."

"I just meant the general could use all the practice he can get."

"*Navi,*" she whispered again. "Hush!"

"No. Navi's right." Tao's mouth curled with the kind of smile that broadcast he wasn't at all intimidated by the prospect. "Since we have nowhere to go today, we're going to use the time to teach this Tassagon dog a few new tricks."

CHAPTER FIFTEEN

TAO LEANED ON A CRUTCH, submitting to Elsabeth's inspection. She stopped, folding her arms over her stomach, taking in the sight of him dressed in his borrowed clothes: a collarless white long-sleeve shirt, with buttons beginning halfway up the front, loose brown trousers over work boots. Traditional Kurel clothing.

She had to say that no man she'd known had ever quite filled out everyday work clothes as the general did. His need of the crutch humbled him, made him more approachable, more human, but he was still a strapping, supremely self-confident male in his prime.

"How do I look?" he asked, stopping short of preening. He still had a long way to go, though, to truly adopt the Kurel value of modesty in appearance.

"Like a general disguised as a Kurel."

"Then no one can say we're trying to hide anything. Honesty is a prized Kurel virtue, you said. It will be good if I look like what I am."

She hoped the elders would see it that way. "You missed a button." It had been hard for him to get dressed himself. She'd helped him only in order to keep his wounds from being unduly stressed. Not for this intimacy.

She felt his eyes on her as she buttoned the shirt, felt the stir of his breath. Already, the fabric smelled like him, a masculine scent of clean, warm skin and the soap from her wash basin. The summer-weight linen of the shirt was so fine that his suntanned skin showed through. In her imagination, she saw her palms sliding over the cool fabric, her fingers opening the buttons, not closing them, until she could pry the shirt wide enough to slip her hands under it, exploring firm, hot skin.

A wave of warmth made her flush. She pursed her lips, stepping back. *You silly fool*. Her inexplicable physical attraction to the Tassagon general wasn't anything she wanted him to know about, for he was probably game enough to try anything she might ask of him. He hadn't turned out to be an immoral beast today when it came to being alone with a woman, contrary to what the Kurel believed about Uhr-warriors, but his behavior with the dancer at the palace left little doubt in her mind that he'd willingly lay down with her if she revealed her secret, wholly inappropriate appreciation of his body.

"It won't be easy tonight," she said. *On so many levels.*

He watched her with bemused eyes. "Don't be nervous. I'm dressed like a Kurel. I'm eating like one—or trying at least. And I haven't once reverted to calling you sunshine all day."

"Or I, to calling you a dog."

Their shared smile faded quickly. "There's more you need to know," she said. "Maybe you should sit down."

"I'll be in a chair all evening. I'll stand."

He did seem to be getting better, still moving as if sore, but no pain cramped his features when he did. "The elders are our senior statesmen, twelve in all, and also our moral compass, sticklers for tradition. They are…not exactly friendly to outsiders. Half of them are so old they were born in the Barrier Peaks. It's like they never thawed."

"I've been through the Barrier Peaks many times, moving my army. Cold, inhospitable… And then there are the mountains."

Laughter at his joke would indicate disrespect for the elders, but she almost did. It would be serious business soon enough. "Farouk is the eldest, and the leader. You'll know him by his height—he's taller than you, but very slender and supple, with a bushy head of white hair. Like a marsh reed in spring, my father used to say. He's the one you'll want to impress. My great-great-aunt Gwendolyn is another to know. She's plump and as short as Farouk is tall, almost bald. She's the conscience of the group, the heart. They all act as if she's too young to pay much mind to, but what she thinks they all eventually do."

He was nodding, absorbing her words. "I am ready to do battle." Then he tipped his head down. "Pardon my Tassagon words. I'm ready to make peace."

She hoped so, for nothing less was at stake but the unity and the salvation of the human race.

ELSABETH HAD DICED AN alarming amount of what Tao now recognized as hot chilies, folding them into a mixture of mutton, grains and butter that she covered with a layer of dough before sliding the pan into an oven to bake. Even she'd sniffed as she'd chopped the peppers, dabbing at watering eyes with the knuckles of one hand.

Tao observed the process with mounting dismay. "What is it?" he asked.

"Sumsala. My grandmother's recipe."

"It smells delicious." The spicy scent made his nose itch ominously, though. How he'd eat tonight without weeping openly at the table he didn't know. He forced himself to swallow his doubts and said nothing, but he cast a grateful glance at a cold pitcher of frothy goat milk she'd set in the center of the table.

Chun and Navi arrived, their presence demanded

by the elders. All the "guilty parties" were now here. Tao was ostensibly the one being judged, but he knew failure tonight would endanger his rescuers' futures as well.

With some banging of crutches and stiff legs, Tao let Chun help him into a chair at the table. "Remain seated when they arrive," the physician advised. "The elders will expect no less, knowing of your injuries."

Finally, the formal knock at the door. Four pairs of uneasy eyes met then diverged. Elsabeth straightened her spine and walked to the door, looking as if she'd whispered a prayer before she opened it. The front landing was crowded. The glow of the room's lights illuminated the ancients' crinkled faces.

"Greetings, Elders," Elsabeth said, her head dipping with respect. Tao followed her lead, lowering his chin, but he kept his eyes on those who would judge him. They filed in, some using canes, another in a wheeled chair, but all spry and alert. "Elders" was an apt term. He'd never seen so many humans so advanced in age who were still upright and moving. Tao marveled at them. How old were they? How much history had they lived? Few Tassagons reached a ripe old age without succumbing to disease first.

Potions. That was the reason for Kurel longevity.

Yet, these elders were the leaders of the community. In Tassagonia, those who held sway over the people were the ones with the most physical strength and power, not experience.

Tao pushed to his feet. Chun frowned at him, but it seemed disrespectful to sit while these fragile souls stood. With his weight heavy on the crutches, he bowed his head fully this time, trying to assume the respectful stance that came so easily to Chun and Navi.

The elders gave him a wide berth, gathering a safe distance away. It was as if they thought he might suddenly decide to strike at them. Maybe it would have been better if he'd stayed in his chair.

"He doesn't look Uhr, dressed like that," a small woman remarked, sounding more admiring than disapproving. Her white hair was drawn so tightly back from her face that she looked bald. Elsabeth's great-great-aunt, he guessed.

"A wolf in sheep's clothing," whispered the wizened old crone next to her. That one definitely disapproved.

Tall, dour and fragile looking, one of the men marched forward and rapped his cane against the floor, inches from Tao's borrowed boots. Unruly white hair sprouted on the top of his head. *A marsh reed in spring.* "Sit."

Sit. Stay. Did all Kurel assume warriors only understood these one-word commands? The one thing Tao refused to do was beg.

Elsabeth swooped in. "Dinner is ready. Please. Sit down."

So, even the elders were not safe from Elsabeth's plain orders—although for them, she'd added "please." Tao hoped the humble dip of his head hid his smile.

As the twelve regarded Tao with cool wariness, she circled the table and served each of the elders their dinner, doing so with such reverence that it seemed more of a religious offering. Yet, when she took her seat next to him, no one blessed the food the way he was used to doing as a Tassagon. No thanks were given—not to Uhrth, nor for this bounty. They simply began to eat.

For all the bold flavor of their cooking, the Kurel made for lackluster tablemates. There was no conversation other than a few murmurs exchanged. Yet, the more he observed, the more he saw that the meal was indeed being enjoyed—a quiet savoring rather than loud appreciation. No slurping or unruly shouting. No chunks of bread being dredged through the juices and shoved into mouths, true. No eating with hands, either.

Farouk's fluffy white brows lowered over his black eyes when he noticed Tao hadn't touched his meal.

With dread, Tao faced his plate. A part of him wanted to trade it for the sting flies and muck of the Sarcen Swamp.

A small part. He could do this. Easily. A matter of mind over…sumsala.

He chose a fork as if he were choosing a blade and used it to break through the crust. Steam burst forth. The aroma was intoxicating. Masking the toxicity of the contents, he was sure. A taste, a cautious taste. His tongue caught fire. A cough rose in his throat and he stifled it with crushing self-control as he felt the elders observing him. Did they find his attempt at adaptation entertaining? He'd like to see them try to hold their own in the chaos of a Tassagon meal. They wouldn't be so judgmental then.

The elders consumed their food with surprising speed. Elsabeth had hardly touched hers, and he felt as if he were dying slowly of starvation. Goat milk and slices of crispy flatbread did not a warrior's meal make. He was going to have to get a full meal in his belly soon or he'd be forced to bribe Navi to bring him something less spicy than Elsabeth's cooking.

"Ferdinand's daughter, our Elsabeth, has spoken for you, but I want to hear it from you—why are you here, Uhr-warrior?" Farouk demanded.

Tao put down his fork, relieved to trade sumsala for interrogation. "I come seeking sanctuary until I can safely return to my people."

"Our palace workers are barred from pursuing their livelihoods. Now you want to stay here and further inconvenience us," Farouk challenged.

Tao resisted the urge to retort with an unflattering remark about knowing better than to expect help from the Kurel. He'd spent the day fighting to set aside such lifelong prejudices. Elsabeth, Navi and Chun had proved to him that not all Kurel refused to help Tassagons—at least not when it would benefit their people.

Elsabeth had emphasized, over and over, the Kurel preference for almost brutal frankness. That was one trait he could admire. If only Markam had been more frank in his communications these past years... But this was not the time for regrets. This was the time to win the Kurel elders' approval. Brutal honesty, he could do. "There's more than inconvenience at risk, Elder. When they don't find me in the city, they'll come here next. Uhr-Beck and the Home Guard."

Farouk's face darkened. "No Tassagons will find what we don't want them to find."

"They could harm innocents trying."

The elder let out a quick, hoarse laugh. "Are you trying to convince us to let you stay, or to make you leave?"

"Neither. I'm stating the facts to allow you to make the right decision for your people."

The elder acted dumbfounded that Tao would volunteer reasons for the man to deny him asylum. They expected as little honesty from a Tassagon as he expected help from a Kurel, apparently.

"He's right," another elder said. "His presence here brings much risk. Put him out the gates."

"And sentence him to die?" Elsabeth protested. "He'll be arrested on sight."

"His arrest could have been a hoax orchestrated by Xim to get Tao into our midst," the same elder proposed. "We don't know."

Elsabeth shook her head. "Markam's been helping us. For years."

"Markam is Tassagon," Farouk reminded her sharply.

"Elder Farouk, Markam is an ally," she insisted. "He trusts us to keep his friend safe."

"We don't have to give the general back to the king. We can put him outside the city walls completely," another elder suggested. "A few day's food, water and leave him to find his own way."

"What, no weapon?" Tao said in a deceptively helpful tone to hide his sarcasm. "I'll need a bow to shoot my dinner."

Farouk narrowed his eyes, considering this. Young Navi broke in, "No, Elder Farouk. General Tao helped us. He saved my life."

"It wouldn't have needed saving if you young rebels weren't meddling in Tassagon affairs."

"*Their* affairs?" Elsabeth asked. Tao could almost feel her anger crackle. "Their king's crimes have certainly been *our* affairs. Xim brought violence to Kurel town. He allowed my parents to be slaughtered in cold blood. He sanctioned it; he even rewarded the killers. What about those arrested for suspected sorcery? Gorski's wife and Lars, all the others, never heard from again. Murdered, too. Xim is a monster who deserves no less than the same cruel fate."

Several of the other elders coughed nervously. Tao lifted a brow at Elsabeth's bloodthirsty desire for vengeance. Doing actual harm to Xim was something he still hoped to avoid.

An elder with a broad white streak through her black hair sniffed. "It is clear that the least violent path is to turn the general over to the Tassagons to appease the king."

"Xim won't be appeased until he learns who was behind freeing me and smuggling me into K-Town. Turn me in and you risk Elsabeth being caught and put to death. Chun and Navi, too."

The lines bracketing Farouk's mouth deepened. "We Kurel believe that the needs of the many outweigh the needs of the few."

Was the elder serious about exchanging Elsabeth for safety for all of K-Town? The thought of her in Xim's hands—Beck's hands—shuddered through him like the sound of a Gorr's howl. "We Uhr-warriors share your views of altruism. But every belief worth having comes with the responsibility of common decency, Elder Farouk. Risking the lives of your bravest, most

selfless citizens to settle an old score with the Tassagons falls far short of that."

Elsabeth folded her hands on the table. "I would
gladly die to keep General Tao alive if I knew it would
assure Xim's downfall and peace for our people," she
said softly.

Several elders audibly gasped, but Farouk acted
unruffled as he addressed Tao. "You have won the
loyalty of our Elsabeth, I see."

Elsabeth's quiet pledge had struck Tao deep. That
she would trade her life for his…personally, he did not
think he could bear it. But as a general, he recognized
her words as being those of a warrior. "Miss Elsabeth's
loyalty is a worthy prize if I have indeed won it. I hope
to earn the trust of all the people of Kurel Town. Know
this—our peoples must not battle each other. As we
speak, the Gorr are scattered, demoralized, running
scared, but if we go at each other's throats, they'll
sense the turmoil as swiftly as they do the scent of
our blood. And then they'll regroup, motivated by the
damage that human has done to human, emboldened
by the way we've weakened ourselves, and they'll
finish us, once and for all."

A few of the elders recoiled. Others turned colder,
repulsed by his frank words. Tao wasn't sorry. Only
fools glossed over the realities of war then stumbled
right back into it for their folly.

"Elsabeth tells me that your holy book, the Log of

Uhrth, warns of the danger of divided human tribes. With your asylum or without it, I'll do everything in my power to keep the peace." His voice grew quieter. "So I can get back to what I came home to do—retire, work the land and, yes, grow old. I'm weary of war, Elder Farouk. Let this be its end."

Farouk set one clawed hand on the table. "You present yourself as a man of peace, but you led countless men into battle to achieve your victories. What if one of them refused to fight?"

"My men knew what they were there to do—and why."

"We have heard of stories of soldiers who refused to pick up a weapon."

Tao frowned. "That was rare."

"But it happened," the elder prompted. "What did you do to them?"

"I had them flogged for dereliction of duty or for disobeying orders, depending on the circumstances."

"And if that didn't work?"

"That, too, was rare. Very rare."

"General…"

"They were put to death by a firing squad."

The elders breathed a collective gasp of dismay. Tao gritted his teeth at their shock. Elsabeth had warned him. To the Kurel, any spilled blood was horrific, even that of an enemy. This line of questioning was leading them away from the important issue. The only issue.

How to prevent Xim's paranoia from pitting human against human. Without vanity, Tao knew he was essential to that cause, and so it was also essential that he make these elders understand.

"War is an ugly thing," he said evenly, "but not the ugliest of things. Worse is the person who has nothing for which they're willing to fight. Who finds nothing more important than their own personal safety. Cowardice or desertion can't be rewarded. If a soldier runs when he's being counted on to protect his comrades, he's as dangerous as the Furs themselves. The Gorr were a known, deadly threat, but a coward amóngst us? That was an unseen, unpredictable threat. Far worse to find an enemy where you expected an ally."

"Like General Tao discovered when he returned home," Elsabeth said. "An enemy in his king. Elders, I once again humbly request sanctuary for the general. He has put himself at our mercy. His presence here is no trick. I stake my reputation on it, my standing in this community. I've already staked my life."

Leaving her powerful statement to linger in the silence, she sat back in her chair. Only her bloodless knuckles gave any hint to her inner strain. The elders turned away to confer, grumbling amongst themselves.

Tao waited. His fate was up to these Kurel. And in the hands of Uhrth, if he were to look at the far bigger picture. Still, men made their own destinies. If he were to be turned out, he'd stay alive and survive to save his sister and his kingdom. And if Elsabeth, Chun and Navi were turned out with him?

At his side, his three rescuers waited in tense silence. If they were banished for his sake, he'd honor their sacrifice by not forsaking them as they continued the fight to restore sanity to the throne.

Finally, Farouk turned back to their group. "First, we elders have made a decision regarding the palace ban for Kurel workers. We will not be split apart at the whim of the Tassagon king. We will not be separated into classes, those who are under suspicion and those who are not. All Kurel will remain in the ghetto until the ban is lifted. A messenger will be sent to the palace in the morning to deliver the news."

From Elsabeth to Chun, there were collective gasps of surprise. Tao could imagine the effect the elders' decision would have on Tassagonia's citizens, not having the Kurel around to do the myriad chores they couldn't or wouldn't do. Passive resistance—the Kurel had just reaffirmed their expertise at the practice.

Would it give Xim new appreciation for these people or convince him of his apparent desire to subjugate them?

"As for General Tao…"

Tao lifted his gaze, slowly, to meet Farouk's. When the elder issued his verdict, it would be done looking into his fellow human's eyes.

"He will be granted conditional asylum in Kurel Town."

A powerful release of tension in his body made him realize how much he'd been bracing for bad news. Elsabeth gave his thigh a quick squeeze under the table.

His heart leaped at sharing the victory with her, until he remembered that the only reason she was happy was because she was one step closer to avenging her parents' deaths. Kindness had nothing to do with it. It was as much a self-serving gesture as when she'd saved his life. She needed to use him against Xim.

"If the general agrees to adhere to our ways, to abide by our laws and refrain from influencing any Kurel to commit acts of violence," the wheelchair-bound elder added.

Tao set his jaw. Elsabeth was their greater worry when it came to that.

Farouk held his gaze. "Any violations will result in immediate banishment."

"I will comply, Elder."

"Thank you, Elder Farouk," Elsabeth gushed. "Thanks all of you."

The elders prepared to leave. "Take care around him," the old woman with the white streak warned Elsabeth.

Gwendolyn nodded. "Your own mother is not here to warn you, so I will. Dependent as he is on our generosity, he is what he is. An Uhr. You have heard the tales."

Tales? Tao caught Elsabeth blushing so fully that her ears turned pink. He was dying to know what these tales included.

"I can control him, Auntie," Elsabeth said, pointedly ignoring Tao's near-silent snort.

White Streak bounced a disapproving glance off Tao. "But, can you control yourself? Beware your mixed blood, Elsabeth. It may lead you down unwanted paths."

"Marina," Gwendolyn exclaimed. "Are you insinuating my Elsabeth's sensibilities are in doubt because she's a halfie? Any Kurel girl would need to take care. Any human girl."

Elsabeth was of mixed blood? This paragon of Kurel virtue? He knew even less about her than he'd thought.

Tao folded his arms over his chest as the women discussed him and his apparent threat to women— or his apparent temptation to women; he wasn't sure which—as if he weren't there.

"It will be more difficult for her, yes."

He could only hope.

"Pash," Gwendolyn spat. "She'll be stronger for that Tassagon blood. You'll see."

"Elders, please." Elsabeth sounded mortified, insulted. Angry. "I won't be led down any path I don't choose." The tone of her voice left no doubt of that in Tao's mind. He wondered what kind of path, exactly, she feared to tread with him.

"Which is precisely what I worry about," Marina muttered.

Farouk's cane tapped on the planked floor.

"Good night, all. Elsabeth, the sumsala was every bit as good as your grandmother's."

Tao's stomach rumbled. The mention of food reminded him how empty his stomach was.

Goodbyes were said, leaving him alone with Elsabeth.

"We did it, Tao." Her eyes shone. "You have sanctuary here."

Conditional sanctuary. If he didn't comply with the terms, he was out. How hard could that be, pretending to be a Kurel? "A victory," he agreed, longing for a little chilled ale with which to toast their success.

"Markam will be so relieved. Now we can plan. We need to reestablish contact with Markam, and keep that channel of communication with the palace open. Damn this confinement. How will I see Aza now?"

Her focus on what steps they'd take next drove home the point that her excitement at saving him had nothing to do with him as a man, and everything to do with her plans to oust Xim. She'd told him as much in the pipes. He had to give her points for sticking to that damned Kurel frankness.

Elsabeth rose from the table in a whirlwind, cleaning up the disarray left in the wake of the meal. He grabbed a crutch and pushed to his feet. "Surely there is something I can do to help," he said. "I've had to clean up around the cook fire while out on patrol." As if that qualified him somehow to assist Elsabeth with her kitchen chores.

"Not until you're healed."

He grumbled at that. "I'm not a cripple."

"But you will be if you don't get off those legs." She rolled her sleeves up and sank her arms into soapy water, elbow deep, and gave him a warning glare when he sank back onto the chair at the table. "Not there. In bed."

His stomach rumbled again. He was so hungry he felt hollow. "Elsabeth. I need food."

She paused, water dripping in soapy rivulets down her slender arms. Her blouse had gotten damp in spots as well, clinging to her curves, parts of the proper white cotton now allowing a near-transparent peek at the flesh underneath. "You're still hungry?"

Unfortunately the kind of hunger he had in mind was the furthest thing from her mind. "I've not stopped being hungry. I need food. I need to eat…a lot more than this." A lot more than the men in her experience did, obviously.

"There's some leftover sumsala…"

He supposed he could eat it, now that the elders

weren't watching him. It wouldn't matter so much now if he sneezed and wept.

"Wait. You're still acclimating to the spices. I have a better idea." She went out back with a basket, returning in moments with it filled, unloading the contents on the counter. "This was in the cool box in the clinic. Chun won't mind. Bread, butter, eggs, cheese." She threw a chunk of the butter in a pan, set it over the fire, and soon it was sizzling. Beaten eggs splashed in next and were covered with thick slices of cheese.

His mouth watered as he inhaled the aroma. Within minutes, she was sliding a large platter of food toward him to eat. He took in the sight of a mountain of scrambled eggs and melted cheese surrounded by thick slices of buttered bread and tried to remember the last time he'd consumed a full, uninterrupted meal.

Too long ago. Years, really. Battlefield fare, usually consumed while discussing war plans, had been followed by the political machinations of a formal palace dinner. He tore off a piece of bread and dredged it through the scrambled eggs, scooping them up and into his mouth. "Heaven," he mumbled, going back for a second pass.

He looked up to compliment her cooking, but the look on her face made him freeze, his hand halfway to his mouth. A hard gulp, and the mouthful went down like a stone. He reached for the fork. "I wouldn't want to violate the terms of my parole the first night."

And then he was filling his belly the Kurel way. He'd never tasted food so satisfying. Was it his hunger over so many days, or the fact that Elsabeth had made it personally for him? That she'd understood him, at least in this.

He felt her eyes on him, her curiosity. "What exactly do they say?" he asked, swallowing. "About Uhrs?"

"Excuse me?"

"The elders, the two women, they warned you about Uhr-warriors. What do they say about us?"

"It's not relevant." She pushed up from the table and returned to the kitchen.

"Indeed it is. If I'm to adhere to your ways, I'd best know what they are."

She was scrubbing dishes with vigor now. "If you really want to know, it's said that Uhr-warriors have insatiable sexual appetites. Like the animals in the forest."

He realized he was still shoveling in food like a ravenous beast, and she was watching. Drawing parallels? He paused, dabbing his mouth with a cloth with as much civility as possible. "We're compared to animals…in bed?"

She nodded and stacked another washed plate on the growing pile. "It's all right. They say you can't help it. You were bred for war."

"I *trained* for war. An honorable profession. To say I was bred—for anything—does make me seem like a beast." He frowned, his fists resting on the table. "If their implication is that I'd force myself on you—"

"*I* don't think that."

"Then what are they worried about?"

Her expression closed as she grabbed a cloth to dry off her hands. "Marina brought up my mixed blood to insinuate I have no control over my actions."

"Rather like a Tassagon."

His tone was almost playful, but hers wasn't. "Exactly like a Tassagon, yes."

"Who was the Tassagon, your father or mother?"

Her mouth twisted, making it clear the subject made her uncomfortable. Was she ashamed of this "stain" on her past? "Mother was Tassagon, but she was born here, in Kurel Town, raised as one of us. She considered herself Kurel, and everyone saw her as one. Her mother was a Tassagon, a runaway, and died soon after giving birth to her. We don't know who her family was—or is. No one ever reported her missing." She muttered, "No one seemed to care."

"The Kurel couldn't save the woman?" He'd begun to see their methods as infallible.

"She sought treatment too late to save herself. But at least we were able to save the baby."

"She sought out the Kurel?"

"Yes." Elsabeth pondered him. "Tassagons do, you know. They come to us even knowing it's against the law." Then she whipped her head around and bent to the task of washing, her hair swinging loose. "But that's a story for another day. If Marina thinks I'm controlled in some way by my Tassagon blood, she's wrong."

Elsabeth's shame and distrust of her Tassagon blood was obvious and, perhaps, in some ways understandable. But, she was in need of a little education on his kind. He cleaned his plate and downed the glass of water she'd left for him then he pushed to his feet, ignoring her dismay as he limped into the kitchen with his dirty plate.

"Shush," he said softly as he dipped the plate in soapy water, sparking her protest. He washed it and added it to the stack. "You will get to know this Uhr-warrior," he assured her. "In the name of understanding between our peoples."

He limped back to the table to retrieve his crutches, while feeling the tutor's startled, curious and even intrigued eyes on him all the way to his bed. A beast from the forest in her home? He cracked a private smile. Perhaps.

But not for her first time.

ELSABETH PRETENDED TO be busy within the protection of the kitchen while Tao got ready for bed. A splash of water from his washbasin, heavy masculine footsteps, sounds long absent from this home. She'd tried to insert a wedge between them, thinking she was so superior with her Kurel blood. But the more she was with the general, the more she saw she had more to learn about honor and sacrifice than he did. And graciousness.

If not table manners. How he'd wolfed down the eggs, throwing all etiquette to the winds, consumed with pleasure, not holding anything back...until he reeled himself in. Was that how he was with a woman?

If she wasn't careful, her curiosity about the matter would get the better of her.

And prove Marina right.

CHAPTER SIXTEEN

ELSABETH TURNED DOWN the light, leaving only enough illumination to let her cross the room without tripping over the newly arranged furniture. The long, trying day was almost over. She felt as if she could sleep for a week straight. But first, putting the injured general to bed was on order, making sure he had all the meds necessary for a comfortable night's sleep. She'd nearly starved the man by accident, almost lost him to a tassagator before that. If she wasn't careful, he wouldn't survive to see her goal realized—taking the reins of rule from Xim and thus fulfilling her vow to her parents. As to what would happen after that, she didn't know.

For so long, she'd been single-minded, so focused on her goal that thoughts of her own future faded away. Ironic that in contrast, this warrior who hadn't expected to live to see his thirtieth year had his entire future mapped out in every way, including what kind of wife he'd acquire. She remembered when she, too, would ponder what kind of man she hoped to find and fall for: a kind, like-minded bookkeeper or pharmacist, she'd assumed. She'd hoped to spend her days snug and safe in their tidy home, wiling away the hours by reading about the adventures she'd never have. If not for Tao's rescue, she'd be reading at this very moment, in fact, curled up in her tiny loft bedroom, her nose buried in a book.

"Elsabeth, you'd be better off getting out and experiencing what the world has to offer than burying your nose in paper," Tao had told her.

She crossed the room, took Tao's crutches to stack against the wall as he eased himself onto the bed and stretched his arms over his head. His shirt had been unbuttoned for comfort. It gaped open as he slipped his hands behind his head. Around his neck, the pendant glinted in the dim light.

"Where did you find that? That piece of metal you wear around your neck?"

"This?" He touched his fingers to the piece nestled in the hollow below his throat. "I found it in a place we called the Glass Sea, far in the north."

"The Glass Sea..." Savoring the sound of it, she scrunched down on the footstool. "Tell me."

His mouth edged up, smiling at her eagerness. "First the Gorr, now my talisman. I may have to start trading for the telling of my tales."

"All right." She agreed without hesitation.

"All right?" Tao asked, lifting his head to look at her in the lantern light. "You'll give me whatever I ask in payment for another tale?"

"I don't have anything worth bartering. Some ill-mannered pigeons. Leftover sumsala…"

"I would disagree, Miss Elsabeth." He smiled slyly.

The heat in his eyes made her heart pound. "Just tell your tale and remember who broke you out of prison. That's quite a debt you've racked up, General Tao."

"I saved Navi. Doesn't that account for something?"

"That debt's his. With me, you've got quite a few more stories to tell before we break even."

She waited with hushed impatience for him to begin.

Chuckling, Tao tried to find a comfortable position. As all wounds tended to do, the pain from the gator bites had worsened with the coming of night, although that mattered little now that he was the center of the tutor's attention, this little fireball of a rebel who'd won him asylum in K-Town. "We were out on patrol," he began, "farther afield than we'd ever been…"

"The Glass Sea," she filled in for him.

"Yes. But it was an illusion."

Perched at his side, her lips parted, she was un-ashamed to show she was hungry for more, a reaction he'd like to see for another reason. Pulling back from a kiss, hungry for more…of him.

"Keep going," she demanded.

"We were up in the north, a region of high desert, where no one lives. I didn't know to what extent the Furs had established dens. Scouts had returned from the area with tales of having walked on water, a vast plain as slick and shiny as liquid, but as hard as the ground, a place they called the Glass Sea. I decided I wanted to see it with my own eyes."

"I would have wanted to, too. I envy you those sights," Elsabeth all but whispered.

The girl, he decided, was crazy. Here she was protected. But out in the Hinterlands… He cut off the accompanying grim thoughts. "It was a sea only at first sight. As soon as you put the weight of your boot on it, the surface crackled like ice. I walked out on it, a great gash of glass across the land." He still remembered the loud *crack* of fissures shooting out from his footsteps, where the glass was a mere crust suspended over the dirt in the few places not yet shattered from years of being exposed to the elements. "We had never seen anything like it. Halfway across or so, I noticed something that looked like a frozen soap bubble, about this size…" He formed a curve with his hands shoulder width apart. "The top had long since shattered. It was open to the elements, filled partially with grit. The suns shone though the walls, like the underside of a great wave…" He stopped himself. "Elsabeth, you have never seen an ocean." And the sight of sunlight piercing through the top of a cresting wave.

"I have in books," Elsabeth said.

"You have books with drawings of the ocean?"

"And much more."

"I'd like to read books like those." With pictures in them. Things a man could appreciate, as opposed to a mash of marks.

"The glass bubble," she prompted.

"Ah, yes. I saw something shining inside, and reached in. And found this." He unfastened it and placed it in the palm of her hand. "It was such a curious thing, Elsabeth. I'd never seen metal that well crafted. See the line, near the bottom. That isn't a crack; it's etched into the surface in a way that can't be duplicated. I tell you, for months after I had my smithies and armorers try to continue the design, but to no avail. The metal was too hard."

"Was there more of it?"

He nodded. "At the end of an enormous furrow, a great silver wing thrusts out of the sand. It's taller than ten of these buildings, stacked one upon the other. For all our trying, we couldn't cut off a piece. We scoured the Glass Sea and the area all around it, far and wide, looking for more metal like it, smaller pieces we could carry back with us. The weapons we could have made, Elsabeth, the armor… We didn't want the Furs getting hold of any for that same reason." He watched her turning it over in her hands, her look one of wonder.

"We must tell the elders," she said. "This could be wreckage from the *Discovery*. The mothership, the great ark, that brought our people here from Uhrth."

He pushed himself higher in the bed to listen as she shared a tale of her own, in her mind a true story. The *Discovery* was presumed lost, sacrificed in a last-ditch effort to repel the Gorr invasion. "Something so important to humans to be lost without a trace, it was tragic," she said. The crash caused intense heat that flash-melted the sand, forever erasing the existence of the *Discovery*, which had carried 3,032 colonists to this world. "She was never meant for battle," Elsabeth finished somberly.

Then she spun her own ending to the tale. From far, far away came an Uhr-warrior with a fragment of the *Discovery* hung around his neck as a souvenir from his travels. Something that caught his eye, and his imagination. It seemed meant to be that it was returned to the people who could appreciate its true significance. Except it was already back in his callused, warrior hands, returned by none other than the fiery-haired tutor who had no love for the Tassagons.

Tao reacted with a quiet, slightly skeptical snort. He couldn't verify that any of what she'd told him was true, that it was anything more than a much-loved sorcerer's fable. He knew only what he could confirm with his hands and his eyes. "I knew it was a special find, Elsabeth. I've kept it with me ever since. For luck."

He refastened the charm around his neck. An amulet from an ark, an ark of the gods, no less. Good luck indeed. No wonder he was protected.

He'd had doubts about its effectiveness since, however. In less than three days he'd plunged from the top of the world to utter hell. But with the elders agreeing to let him hunker down in K-Town to wait out Xim's tantrum, maybe the piece's good luck was returning.

"Our relic," she said. "Your talisman. What makes you believe it protects you?" Her eyes were luminous as they searched his face. The room was so quiet he could hear the rustle of her clothing, her quick, quiet breaths as she awaited his tales with such appealing anticipation.

I promise you, before I leave your care, you'll be anticipating more than my tales. Like the taste of his lips on hers, the stroke of his hands on her body.

The faintest hint of pink colored her cheeks. Had she guessed his thoughts? That she didn't jump up and flee gave him hope he had a chance with her.

"I have to save something for later," he said.

"Something?" She sounded a little hoarse.

"More tales of the Hinterlands. Dramatic escapes. Adventure."

"Oh. Yes." She gave an embarrassed little laugh.

"Of course." Yawning, she stood, drawing the fabric of her skirt into her hands. Her hair hung over her shoulders in long coppery ringlets. "Is there anything else you need before I go to sleep?"

Well, there were a few things he'd like—her slipping under the quilt to lie with him. His legs ached so badly that the thought of falling asleep with her warm next to him would be enough. Perhaps, naked and warm next to him...

"You're smiling," she observed.

"Imagine that," he said, keeping his thoughts to himself. "Get some rest, Elsabeth. Uhrth knows we have not had much."

She extinguished the oddly glowing lantern. He sensed her standing there awkwardly for a moment in the dark. She really didn't know what to do with a man, did she? How to react, what to say? "Good night," she said.

Then he heard her hurry away. What exactly was she fleeing? The attraction they couldn't explain? He didn't know quite what to do with it, either, except how he always would have handled it in the past with a woman. Into bed, first thing, and be done with it.

Like a beast? Feeding her clichéd opinion of an Uhr-warrior? Hell, no. This woman would require a different approach. He was up to the challenge. "Good night, sweet Kurel girl," he murmured under his breath. Sweet...and smart. Focused. She needed him for a greater purpose than bed sport. She needed him for revenge.

He needed her, too, in order to survive to save his sister, his officers and his kingdom. Their goals ran along parallel courses. They may have come from far different beginnings, but for now they were fated to travel this road together, not knowing where it would end.

"UHR-TAO, DEAD? ARE you sure?" Xim clutched the scraps of fabric in his fist, pounding it once against the armrest of his throne. He'd hoped to see Tao twitching on the end of a hangman's noose by now. Instead, that pleasure had been stolen by a creature with the intelligence of a kernel of corn.

Markam replied, "Being that it is from the general's uniform, dredged up from the moat in the search, I would say, yes, it indicates the general died in his escape attempt. But, we have no body to show as proof."

"You found a body, did you not?"

"Pieces of a body, Your Highness. Several bodies, actually. The moat cleaners collected bones from what appear to be numerous skeletons of various ages, picked clean."

Beck's chuckle was raspy. "Apparently the gators dine better than we knew."

Xim scowled at the colonel, whose chuckles died

quickly. "I don't see the humor in this. The general has been missing more than an Uhrth week—*a week*—and now pieces of his clothing turn up in my moat." He threw the scrap aside. "Priest! Could any of those body parts be Uhr-Tao's?"

The Tassagon healer-priest glanced nervously at the others gathered in the throne room. "I will have the bones cleaned and burned immediately, and the cracks interpreted for clues."

"I want the results the moment you are done, day or night." Xim turned to Markam. "Do you really think he died in the moat?"

"The probability is high. He hasn't shown up any-where."

"Anywhere we have looked, Markam. There's still the ghetto."

Markam clicked his heels together. "I'll dispatch a regiment to K-Town."

"That's a Home Guard mission," Beck broke in.

"It's all yours, Uhr-Beck," Markam said with a mocking dip of his chin. "I don't care to go in there. But don't forget the last time your Home Guard tried to help, they shot two of them. That week there was an outbreak of fever in our city that killed a family of six. That's two Kurel for six Tassagons. Now you want your Home Guard to go marching in, looking for a fugitive who's more than likely sitting half-digested in a gator belly. Do we want to spur an epidemic here?"

"Absolutely not," Xim said sharply, breaking out into a sweat. "Hold off on searching the ghetto. We'll see what comes of the interpretation of the bones."

"Speaking of the Kurel, Your Highness," Markam continued, "complaints are coming in from all over the city. Administrative work is piling up. Everyone wants the Kurel back."

"I didn't ban them from the city. They did it to themselves."

"In response to banning them from the palace."

"I don't like being blackmailed, Markam. Especially by Kurel."

"I'll go round up a few magicians," Beck rasped. "To keep in the dungeon for sport."

"The fever comes on quickly I hear," Markam murmured to the one-eyed warrior. "A slight headache, achy joints. Within hours the lungs fill with fluid as the fever climbs. Your innards bloat and cramp. You can't hold down food, or water. The hallucinations are said to be so terrifying, you're happy when the angels finally arrive to take you away on the ark."

Beck's throat bobbed and, although his expression was unrepentant, he said nothing.

"So go on, Colonel," Markam coaxed quietly. "Make your arrests. Incur the Kurel's wrath."

"Enough!" Xim glowered at them, his dismay even more pronounced than Beck's. "I hereby rescind the order to bar Kurel workers from the palace. They can come back, all of them. Better to keep the charlatans happy and busy than to have them bored and concocting curses and spells. Markam, send out messengers. This will take effect at suns-up." The king dismissed his men with a careless wave of his hand.

THE DAY DAWNED COLDER and overcast, the strongest hint yet to the waning of summer. Elsabeth had donned a dress of soft, well-worn wool the color of rust, pinning back only her bangs to allow the rest of her hair to flow freely, an informal style she'd never worn to the palace. She double-checked her appearance in the mirror before climbing down to the living room, giving her cheeks a pinch for color, biting her lower lip to add more plumpness, tucking away a stray curl only to release it to soften her look. She frowned at her reflection. For a girl who'd given nary a thought to primping her entire life, she'd certainly become preoccupied with it.

Downstairs Tao was getting ready for the day. His shirt stretched taut across his back as he leaned over a basin. His belt dangled, unfastened. His charcoal trousers ended in bare feet. To her the floor was too cold to prance around with no stockings. The general was made of stronger stuff when it came to discomfort, having become accustomed in his years living in the wilds.

"Good morning, Elsabeth." His smile flashed in the

mirror. No shame filled her at being caught watching him. It had happened too many times already.

She smiled back, smoothing her dress as she saw him sweep his admiring gaze over it. "Good morning." She set a kettle to heating on the stove and pulled out plates for their morning meal.

"Will we have another day with no news?" Tao grumbled, using a towel to blot moisture from his freshly shaved jaw. "Surely Markam realizes he's our only source of information."

The chief of the palace guards was alive and well—there had been several sightings of him on horseback, patrolling the streets of the capital, as reported by lookouts in the spy nest on the ghetto's tallest windmill—yet Markam had sent them nothing since the red flag. *Stay away.*

That information was not enough for Tao, apparently. "It's been more than a week," he said, his impatience obvious. "What kind of game is he playing? Have you checked for messages yet?"

When he got like this it reminded her that he didn't want to be here. He wanted to return to his people and the life for which he was destined in the capital. A life where he'd not have spared her a second thought outside perhaps a stray compliment or two about her hair, which she knew he admired, or a passing acknowledgment that she was the palace tutor. He wasn't a pet to keep close for companionship and protection like the

Tassagon "dog" she'd once accused him of being. He was a man with responsibilities, most of which she'd foisted on his shoulders when she sprang him loose from the dungeon.

You have to give him back once you're done with him.

"I'll check." She left a pot of rice and chicken breakfast congee simmering on the stove and climbed up to the aviary under the eaves.

The ladder shook beneath her. "I'll join you," Tao said.

She stopped. "But the muscle cramps..."

"An aftereffect of gator venom. Gone. No spasms last night and all day yesterday."

True, he was healing so quickly he'd all but stopped limping. There'd be no more persuading him to stay at ground level now. She had a new warrior in her household, one who had the strength to do anything he cared to try. "Come on. You can learn the care and feeding of our valiant messengers."

They climbed up to the snug area under the roof. Tao had to bend over slightly to fit.

Cuh-choo-coo, cuh-choo-coo.

The pigeons were clustered in a boiling mass of rustling, feathered bodies, making her and Tao the focus of their red-rimmed, black-bead eyes. "Shake this," she said, reaching for the can and handing it to

Tao. The dry peas inside rattled. "A couple of times will do."

He reacted with a curious smile and gave the can a brisk few shakes. More pigeons roosting out on the roof flew in with a loud flapping of wings, jumping into the fray. "You've trained them to know the sound, obviously."

"Everyone's voices and whistles are different but peas in a can—always the same, no matter who shakes it. Otherwise, if someone new were to take over their care, and everything changed, it would upset them. The birds might not eat, and sicken and die." She reached for the bags of feed and grit. She turned to the birds. "Who's hungry?"

"I am," Tao said hopefully.

She'd thought his appetite would have leveled off after his body caught up from the deprivation of his first days back, but apparently he had the strenuous march home to account for, as well. He'd been eating her out of house and home, but she knew he wouldn't be if he sensed it was a hardship. Chun had been craftily accepting donations of food and steering them her way. "Be glad you're not a pigeon. The food can't collect on the floor of the aviary—it will soil, a sure source of illness—so I'd feed you only what you could clean up in about ten minutes."

"I take no more than five minutes to eat," he boasted. "Even with your tiny spoons."

"Pigeons can't be fed before a flight. It makes the birds heavy and lazy, and prone not to return promptly."

"Much like soldiers."

"I put grit in with the feed to aid in digestion."

He laughed. "That's where the differences between pigeons and soldiers diverge. Grit was a staple of our diet in the Hinterlands—but I never noticed any benefits."

Cuh-choo, cuh-choo-coo.

"They sound like the hill doves," he said, seeming to fall into a memory. "In the vineyards. I always liked the sound. Mournful…"

"The sound reminds me of my mother. The morning after she was killed, I had to come up here and do what she always did, as if nothing had happened." As if her quiet, predictable, happy life hadn't been upended, everything destroyed. "Every morning and night, I'd come up and shake the can—during the grief, after the funeral and so on. To the birds, I was just another shaking can, calling them to feed. Perhaps this shaker took care of them a little differently, a little less confidently, but nothing that upset them. That's when I learned the true meaning of 'life goes on.' Even though it was a lesson I didn't want to learn at the time."

"It does go on," he agreed. "It's both the hardest and the most welcome aftermath of loss."

She threw him a look. Why did it always surprise

her that this warrior could have deep, introspective feelings about the loss of life? *Because it makes it more difficult to accept he's spent years taking other's lives.* "My mother tended the aviary for all of Kurel Town, so I couldn't skip even one day."

"For what purpose—messages to and from the palace?"

"Uhrth, no. In those days we didn't speak to the palace at all. It was all between us and the Barrier Peaks."

He peered out the hatch in the wall at the first sun rising over the distant, jagged mountains. "That's a week's worth of hard, steady travel."

"As the bird flies, mere days."

"What kind of information do you exchange with the guardians of the passes?" His green eyes were vivid, searching. She felt the sudden, keen interest of the battlefield general, instinct driving him to uncover useful intelligence.

"Anything of importance," she said vaguely, and saw his mouth tighten in reaction. Hadn't he expressed the shared desire for an alliance between their people? Hadn't she agreed to help? "For instance, we knew when your army was on the way home long before the palace did."

"We employ messengers on horseback, but these pigeons would have saved me time and men." His brow furrowed. "But pigeons easily fall to hawks, or a hunter's snare."

"Didn't any of your messengers ever ride too close to a Gorr den? Or wind up stranded by a horse with a broken leg? The birds are very reliable. Few have ever failed to deliver their messages. But we do send out pairs, mated pairs, on the longer journeys."

"Hmm," he said. He was thinking, plotting, coming up with ways her pigeons could benefit his army.

Be careful, Beth, or he'll exploit all your peaceful ways for use in war.

"What's that powder you're mixing into the water?" he asked.

"Vitamins—nutrients—to keep them healthy and strong—and antibiotics. Even when the aviary is kept scrupulously clean, they're prone to infection."

"Potions and spells, even for your pigeons."

She spun toward him, the water jug in her hand sloshing, only to see a look of mischief: sparkling hazel-green eyes and the hint of a boyish grin. But he was only half joking. He still distrusted Kurel methods.

"But unlike me, they can come and go as they please?" he asked.

She filled the water dishes. "Except in foul weather, when rain or snow is likely to blow in, I lower the wooden flaps."

He reached over to one of swinging boards, rapping

it against the outside wall. "By the arks, Elsabeth. That's what I've been hearing at night when the wind picks up. This, hitting the side of the house."

"One of the dowels broke in the last storm of winter. I never got around to having it repaired." She'd been consumed with the disappearances of several Kurel charged with sorcery, and then, midsummer, news of Tao's returning army had kept her preoccupied. "There's been no time…"

Now the flap leaned against the house like a drunken old man, scraping the wall in an east wind, as it had last night. "I woke three times last night, thinking an intruder had come inside the boundaries," Tao said. She thought, just maybe, it sounded as if he was sharing some secret.

"Boundaries?"

"We'd keep a ring of torches blazing around the encampment to keep the Gorr away." He moved the flap back and forth, testing the flexibility. "It wasn't a hundred percent effective."

She couldn't imagine the strain of years on end of closing your eyes at night, never knowing if you'd wake to the sight of your killer's eyes. A strain that apparently still robbed him of sleep.

But Tao had moved on, preventing her from questioning him further, as she'd noticed he often did. "All these men around you," he said, "and yet no one to fix what is broken in your house?"

"None offer."

"That's what happens from eating with spoons. I'll fix this," he said in a no-arguments tone. "Is there a place I can procure the supplies?"

"The market."

"Consider it done."

Much like releasing a pigeon for its first flight, she worried about Tao venturing out in Kurel Town amongst those who'd see him as the enemy. "Chun or Navi will go with you, and show you what you'll need."

A brilliant blue bird strutted by. Slowly and smoothly, she raised her hands above the bird and then swooped them downward, bringing both hands together over the creature. "This is how you can catch them, even if they try to take to the air." She settled it in her palm; her thumb and fingers encircled the body. "Meet Prometheus, my best flier. He's made many trips back and forth to the Barrier Peaks."

"Do you know all of them by name?"

She laughed. "You sound the same way as when you asked if I'd read all the books in my library."

"Do you?"

"Yes. But I have only twenty-six pigeons, and hundreds of books. You do have to get to know each bird, their individual fears, their quirks, to help them overcome them." Her free hand smoothed over the pigeon's folded wings. "Never frighten a bird in its home. Never

trick a bird—it will never trust you again." She soothed
Prometheus until he'd utterly relaxed in her palm. "For
instance, trapping a bird while it's eating from your
hand. And never handle a pigeon roughly, or it will fear
you always." Tao's eyes followed her hand, stroking
Prometheus as she murmured, "You want them to learn
that you're their friend, that their food, water and all
their comforts will come through you."

The bird's lids were blinking shut. "It works well,
this technique of yours," Tao said, smiling gently as
she met his eyes. "In a short amount of time, I've come
to rely on you for all my comforts, Kurel girl."

She didn't expect the shiver his quiet tone sent
through her, nor could she hide the fact that it did.
Damn if his smile didn't turn smug.

She released Prometheus. "That concludes your
first lesson in the care and feeding of our messenger
pigeons. Breakfast?" Wiping her hands on her apron,
she'd all but fled to the ladder when a tremendous
beating of wings called her attention back to the hatch.
A white-and-ginger-colored female she hadn't seen
in weeks had arrived—with a message secured to
its leg.

CHAPTER SEVENTEEN

ONE DAY AFTER THE PIGEON had brought a green flag from Markam, the Home Guard patrolled the streets, providing an ominous escort for the Kurel leaving for their jobs in the city, released to do so by the elders who had relented when the king lifted his ban, and only because he had. It marked a victory for the ghetto after too many years of defeats, albeit a psychological one.

The guards called out and stopped several groups of workers, delaying them with silly demands in the name of security that were meant only to harass and slow them down. Uhr-Beck himself trotted by once, his eye sharp, searching the crowd. *For Tao.* Elsabeth kept hidden in the midst of others destined for the palace, doing her best not to look nervous.

Navi was at her side. She couldn't have shaken him if she'd wanted to; Tao had given the accountant strict orders not to let her out of his sight until they reached the palace. Even then, the general had not liked the idea of her reporting to the classroom alone, despite their receipt of the green flag.

"The queen has no need for an accountant," Elsabeth had tried to convince him. "It will draw too much attention. Navi has to do his duties, and I mine."

The memory of Tao's stonelike, disapproving face, his muscled arms folded across his chest as she'd ducked out the door remained with her. He was upset that he couldn't provide protection. But he had to accept that she'd been doing rebel work long before he'd met her. When she returned later with worthy intelligence gleaned from overheard palace conversations, hopefully he'd feel better about her working. He had no doubts about her courage and capabilities after the escape and the elders meeting. His reservations had more to do with her jeopardizing her safety. She'd have to prove she was essential to their plans, not just capable.

A line of Kurel had formed on the upper bailey. "The bastards are checking each one of us," said Leif, a royal supply clerk and rebel with a disturbing desire to see the rebellion turn violent. It was why she'd not chosen him for the dungeon mission. "What do they think—that we've got the general hidden in Kurel Town?"

Her laugh sounded false but he seemed not to notice. Tao had stayed close to home the past week and out of public sight. To heal, they'd agreed, but to her that was only part of it. The man she'd begun to consider a friend her neighbors would view as an enemy.

Elsabeth kept her eyes down and her ears tuned to danger until she finally reached the entrance. A couple of palace guards stood watch, armed and solemn. Their crisp white-and-blue uniforms reminded her how much she missed Markam. There was no sign of him. Bearing the crushing weight of his dual roles, he'd had to make himself scarce, she imagined.

A Home Guard soldier stood with them. Beck's man. Wrapped around his fist were the leashes of three, straining, muscular brown dogs. "Next," he said.

She stepped forward and submitted to the guard's scrutiny and the dogs' glistening, twitching noses. Did they smell the scent of a Tassagon on her Kurel clothing? Were they able to sense her lies and the treachery of her actions against their king? Could they hear how hard her heart pounded against her ribs? She nearly sagged to her knees when the dogs were pulled back and she was allowed to pass.

"Thank Uhrth," she murmured, entering the grand foyer without incident. She expected Markam to appear out of nowhere as he always did. "I'll look for you in the Kurel Canteen," Navi said.

She nodded. They'd return to the ghetto together as well.

Still no sign of Markam as she pressed on toward the nursery classroom. It felt as if it had been a lifetime since she'd last navigated these hallways of marble and plaster, since she'd last slid her fingers about the lever to open the classroom door and let herself inside.

The pleasure of familiar smells was immediate—the sun-warmed wooden shelves, paper and ink for drawing—but there was Aza's floral perfume, too, and the sweet powdery scent of the children.

"Miss Elsabeth! Miss Elsabeth!" Prince Maxim and Princess Sofia dropped their toys and ran to her with exuberance. Elsabeth laughed, gathering the squirming pair close, her heart wrenching with joy and sorrow. How much she'd missed the little prince and princess.

Max snatched her hand. "Come and hear Mother!" His fingers were moist and sticky. Elsabeth smiled. Someone had already gotten into the plate of little iced cakes this early in the morning.

"Mama reading!" Sofia breathed, her golden-green eyes wide and full of wonder. *Tao's eyes.* "Look!"

Dressed in black, and as pale as the marble floor, Aza sat in her favorite chair, a book open on her lap, or rather what was left of her lap. Her stomach had grown even larger in one short week. Only a couple of months remained before the babe arrived.

The two children took their places on each side of her.

Elsabeth sat on the couch opposite the trio.

The queen did not take her steady, questioning gaze

off Elsabeth. "The children don't know," Aza murmured to her with a warning glance. "They think their
uncle went away." Her regard sharpened. "Maybe, he
did."

Elsabeth remained neutral. "Maybe so."

Aza nodded, her eyes threatening to fill with tears
of relief. Then she inhaled, seeming to perk up. "He
always thinks of me. He'd want to know that I'm holding up. And, how much less crowded it is around here
now that all those soldiers have started moving west.
They are, Elsabeth. With their officers, the fine men
who once served with my brother. They're building a
city of tents, taking women with them, too. Soon there
will be no soldiers in the city at all."

Tao's officers were alive. The army was intact. Elsabeth sent her silent thanks for the information.

"Mama." Sofia poked the book cover with her little
finger. "Read."

Aza returned her attention to the book. "I wasn't
sure when you would be able to return to teach the
children, Miss Elsabeth, so I thought I'd best brush
up on my reading."

Shyly, the queen lifted the children's storybook in
her lap. *"The Starry Ark,"* she said, pausing to wink
at Elsabeth. "I have memorized that much, at least."

Elsabeth nodded along with Aza's halting phonetic
pronunciations, smiling when the children pitched in

to shout out the words that they'd already memorized from Elsabeth's prior readings.

The classroom door swung open with a crash. Sofia's tiny body visibly stiffened with fear as her father lurched into the room. King Xim was frozen at first, his handsome face pulled back in a mask of unpleasant shock. Elsabeth shot to her feet, aware at how casual and far too cozy the scene would look. "Your Highness," she said, curtsying.

His outraged glare swung from her to Aza. "How did this get in here?" He marched forward and snatched the book from Aza's fingers. "It's a book, Aza. A damned book!"

For a horrified moment, Elsabeth feared he might strike his wife with it, but the queen's gaze was steady, unafraid, and he changed his mind, grabbing Elsabeth's arm instead.

"No," Aza bit out through clenched teeth.

Xim's fingers dug into Elsabeth's upper arm. "You brought this curse here, Kurel! The books. Poisoning my family—my children—with your sorcery, year after year. This is the end of it. The end!"

"I took the book out, Xim." Aza pleaded, clutching her stomach as if in pain. "I'm to blame. I was reading it. Not Elsabeth."

Xim's fury—and his grip on Elsabeth's arm—ratcheted up another notch. "You took the book out of where? Are you keeping books in here? In the presence of my children? In my palace?" With a crashing of thrown toys, the king swiped the top of a trunk clear and lifted the lid, looking for more books. One lid after another, he slammed his way through the children's belongings, forcing Elsabeth to walk along with him.

"Where are they, Kurel?" he seethed. "Where have you stashed them?"

"There are no other books, Xim. I swear to you." Aza's ability to remain calm was challenged, yet she kept her self-control. Jerked along in the king's painful grip, Elsabeth fought to maintain the same commendable restraint.

"From now on Kurels are forbidden in this nursery!" Xim bellowed at her. "None will be allowed near my children. And none will be allowed near you!"

The children were crying. Elsabeth only now realized the volume of the chaos in the classroom, so loud was her pulse.

Xim turned to leave, propelling Elsabeth ahead of him. *Will he kill me?* Not if she could help it, but without protest she allowed the monarch to push her toward the open door. Whatever was to happen to her on the other side of it, she'd not let the children see the violence.

TAO BROODED LIKE A HOODED hunting falcon after Elsabeth departed for the palace. He felt more helpless now than he had when he'd depended on his crutches to walk. What kind of world had he entered where his woman went off to do battle, and he remained safely behind?

His woman?

"Furs," he spat. Elsabeth was no more his than the throne upon which she wanted to install him, but that wasn't the point. She was out gathering intelligence and he was stuck at home.

He couldn't simply sit around. He had to do something, be productive. The entire blasted day loomed ahead of him like an impassable canyon. *Cuh-choo-coo. Cuh-choo.* The cooing of the pigeons drew his attention back to a periodic, muffled banging noise. That hatch needed fixing.

Tao retrieved his boots, a cap and the money pouch. It was bad enough he'd put himself at Elsabeth's mercy. Now he had to use her money. His funds were far from his grasp for now, but he'd pay back Elsabeth and all the Kurel for their aid.

At the clinic next door, he found Chun. The man greeted him with surprise. An apparatus called a stethoscope hung around his neck.

"Direct me to a shop where I can procure wood, a dowel and a handful of nails," Tao said.

"Are you remodeling Elsabeth's house?"

"Only repairing her aviary. It has long been broken." Surely the medicine man could use his hands for something besides administering potions.

Rather than looking chagrined, Chun pointed in the direction of the south wall. "South Wall Market. Look for the sign for Eisengard's Hardware." After a brief pause, the doctor added, "It's written in red letters on a white background. You'll see it."

Tao fought a sense of shame. Irritating, this sense of being a lesser man for his inability to decipher their marks. *Book readers*. Men who could scribble but didn't offer to repair a woman's house.

With his best imitation of a dour Kurel demeanor, hunching over to pretend frailty—a slight and genuine limp adding to the effect—he tugged the cap low over his eyes and set out. The air was crisp and the sunshine fine. Having lived the majority of his life outside until this past week, he felt as if he were emerging like a pale grub from the ground after hibernation. The houses were taller than they were wide, reaching so far above that they blocked the suns in some places and threw everything into shadow. He likened the ghetto's busy streets to dark, noisy canyons filled with sights and smells foreign to him. A different world, Tao couldn't help thinking. A world he'd never known existed and yet it had been within the confines of his home city the entire time.

But he was very aware of whom he passed and who might have noticed him. The danger of a Kurel turning him in to the Tassagon authorities without consulting the elders first was almost nonexistent, but he'd not risk the chance of attracting the notice of a Kurel who might hate Tassagon soldiers enough to defy the elders.

As Elsabeth had.

Few gave him a second glance as he walked along. He took it to mean he looked like any other Kurel. Except that barely a week ago he'd commanded the planet's largest army, a vast legion that was feared throughout the Hinterlands. Barely a week ago he also would have refused any of the medications that he now credited with speeding his healing. And, barely a week ago he'd not have believed a Kurel girl would have filled his head with thoughts of making love to her, or that he'd be planning to spend his afternoon fixing her birdcage rather than perfecting his aim at the firing range.

Later she would be pleased, though, with his handiwork.

In the shadow of the towering southern fortress of the city was a busy market. So this was where the Kurel shopped—and this was why Tassagons could see a glow coming from this area into the wee hours. The strange, globular glasses that contained that light by night were dormant now, hanging from cords or mounted on poles. Of all the ominous possibilities behind that strange glow, shopping had never been suggested by any Tassagon he knew.

Unlike any market he'd visited before, the stores

were clean and tidy, and gave little hint as to the products sold inside them. Signs were propped on easels or mounted on the storefronts, apparently to be associated with the purpose of each shop, but the markings were of no use to him. Some marks he recognized as depictions of figures, but the rest might as well be the pigeon tracks in the grit in Elsabeth's aviary.

Eisengard's Hardware. He saw nothing to hint at such a name. Red letters, Chun had said. That narrowed it down. Some. If he were to step inside each door to confirm the name of the business, he'd be seen as a fool. *You are—to the Kurel. A savage brute.*

A kernel of frustration in his gut heated into anger as he prowled the storefronts, peering inside. Looks of suspicion were beginning to come his way. If he asked directions, he'd all but advertise he was a stranger. How long before someone observant remembered him from the homecoming march through the city?

He'd find the store on his own. That one sold various sundries. Another seemed to be filled with shoes. Why couldn't hawkers be screaming the nature of the wares out front like in Tassagon markets? It was loud, but effective. He stopped by a shop with brooms and brushes for sale out front. The sign above his head was lettered in red. He knew not what the marks depicted, *LINGERIE,* but judging by the merchandise out front, it was likely the hardware store.

He pushed open the door. A tiny bell tinkled merrily,

announcing his arrival, as if he'd been missed. A powerful concentration of perfume in the air hit him like a floral wall. He heard female giggles and then a shriek. A few blinks later, when his eyes had adjusted to the dim interior, he saw an assortment of amused and scandalized female faces, their hands over their mouths and, through a jungle of lace and silk undergarments, a woman fleeing with her dress half undone.

"Apologies, apologies," he mumbled. "I reached this destination in error."

He stormed out, scowling. *Great Uhrth.* He made an immediate escape, striding away from the market. Kurel cleared out of his path, but he barely noticed as he stormed through the narrow streets. His first solo attempt to accomplish a task using Kurel ways had turned into a humiliating rout, with gossiping women's tongues set atwitter.

Back at Elsabeth's house, reached easily when he had only to walk through straight streets that intersected in an orderly fashion, he shoved open the door, consumed by his failure to complete such a simple task. The smell of food stopped him short, that nostril-searing spice filling the room. Puzzled, he also detected the fainter, familiar sweet scent he associated with Elsabeth.

She came rushing in from the clinic next door, a shawl drawn hastily around her, her hair coming out of its bun. At once, his errors in the marketplace were forgotten in a rush of relief.

"Tao! I was going out to look for you."

"I was at the market." They stopped short of each other, their hands grasping at air. He'd nearly dragged her into his arms. Why? Because he'd been so concerned about her safety? Or because she looked so good standing there, her eyes so earnest, pretty face upturned, her lips so…

"Fired," she said. "I lost my job."

CHAPTER EIGHTEEN

"THAT COWARDLY, LYING bastard left fingerprints on your arm."

Tao's tone was as deadly as his glare, his warm hand wrapped around her wrist. Elsabeth felt his other hand sliding up her arm, the pad of his thumb callused as he moved it over the bruises, while she told him the events that had led to her being barred from the palace. The sound of the children crying haunted her, a wrenching farewell as Xim had shoved her out the nursery and toward a passing palace guard, commanding him: "See that this sorceress is put off palace grounds," before he'd turned back to the classroom.

Sparing her. The bruises Tao found unacceptable were nothing to her, not when the king could have easily commanded: "See that this sorceress is executed for violating the Forbiddance."

Elsabeth wondered why she'd been allowed to live, really. "I think there's part of Xim that doesn't want to alienate Aza completely. He still loves his wife."

Tao made a derisive growl in his throat. "If he does, he's certainly challenged in how he shows it."

"Maybe so, but his love for her is a weakness. Weaknesses can be exploited."

Tao tipped his head down to better see her, his regard admiring. "You would have made a fine battlefield commander."

"Not a general?"

His hands lingered on her, his touch warm, changing from the caring touch of first aid to…something entirely different. In that moment of stillness, the atmosphere became charged. She could feel the heat of his body across the narrow space between them, and yet neither pulled away. "If I promoted you to general, you would have been sent far from me," he said. "And I'd have wanted you to remain near."

What was he saying? Her pulse quickened, and she suddenly found herself imagining what it would feel like to have more than his hands on her. His mouth. His whole body, heavy and strong. What would it feel like to have Tao as a lover?

Tao let his hands slip away. "Forgive me. I can't visualize you in the Hinterlands. With the Gorr about."

She pulled down her sleeve, turning sideways so he wouldn't see how close she'd come to quenching her curiosity about that kiss. "I'm more worried about Xim than I am about the Gorr. I can't see Aza or the children. I can't see Markam. What am I supposed to do now? Rely on Navi for scraps of information?" She spread her hands. "All this because of books, because Aza was reading."

"A story for children, you said."

"Shocking, isn't it? What are the Tassagons so afraid of? Why is knowledge so wicked?"

"It's a fight that's been perpetuated out of fear and ignorance for centuries—your mistrust of war and warriors, and ours of science and books. We've all been fools."

"Not all. Not Aza. Markam reads, as do you."

He drummed his fingers against his chest. "Not I," he said quietly.

"I thought you knew how…"

"What I told you about obtaining a book in the Hinterlands was true. What I led you to believe, that I truly had read the book, was not." He stood and paced away from her. "I couldn't decipher the marks. I sat and I struggled, but I couldn't for the life of me fathom why anyone would waste their time when there weren't even pictures. Then coming here—" his voice lost its edge "—being with you, a learned woman, a beautiful woman, it shamed me to admit I didn't understand books when your entire society revolves around them."

Beautiful?

"Here. The proof of it." He pulled out her money pouch from his trousers pocket. It landed on the table with a chink of coins. "I went to the market while you were gone. I wanted to purchase building supplies to fix your aviary. I could not find the right store, because I could not read." He stalked away to the window, one hand flat on the wall as he peered toward the southern wall. "I seem…like an ignorant brute."

"Which you are not." It was hard to believe she'd once thought differently. "I don't look down on you for being illiterate. You simply were never taught. To expect you to read would be like expecting me to know the ways of war."

But consternation tightened his handsome features. "When the elders told me I'd have to live as a Kurel, I agreed only to appease them, and you. I agreed so that I could survive and I could serve—not because I had the desire to learn your ways." He dropped his hand and laughed without humor. "As an honorary Kurel, let me be as frank as one—foremost in my mind was staying out of the dungeon. But now I want to learn. Teach me, Elsabeth. Teach me how to read."

He strode to her main bookshelf and, after only a moment of deliberation, pulled a thick book off it. The cover was dark glossy blue with gold embossed lettering. With respect, he carried it to the couch and sat, patting the cushion next to him. "Come, Elsabeth."

The general looked as eager to tackle the feat of learning to read as she was delighted to be the one to unlock the doors of literacy for him. She chose a storybook from a selection she kept for the palace and joined him. His arm brushed hers as he drew it back to allow her room to fit next to him. His thigh was wedged firmly against hers. He'd sat so close to her she was practically in his lap.

Then she remembered the choice of proximity had been hers. But Tao seemed hardly to notice. He was no doubt used to women snuggling close.

He smoothed his hand over the book in his lap, almost reverently. "Today you will reveal the secret of these pages."

"No secret. Think of the letters as symbols, each representing a certain sound. For the most part. There are many, many exceptions to the rules in our written language. Of course, we won't worry about them now. I don't want you to feel frustrated before we even begin."

"I can well handle frustration, Elsabeth. Of all kinds."

His mouth curved in that private smile of his that always made her wonder at his thoughts. She was suddenly even more aware of his warm body pressed to hers. He tapped two fingers against the cover. "I have chosen this book to begin."

"Watson's Unabridged Guide to Exo-Horticulture?" At his look of alarm, she smiled. "The cultivation of plants. Tedious and boring." More, the text was too tiny and the words far too complex for his first attempt to

phonetically translate letters to speech. "Let's try this one instead." She replaced the blue volume in his lap with the storybook. The brownish cover was so worn it was rubbed bare at the corners. Tao looked skeptical, and even a little disappointed by the pages, yellowed from generations of use, an old reproduction of the original, carried across the stars from Uhrth.

"You can't judge a book by its cover," she assured him. "It's a Kurel saying. What's on the inside can't always be determined by what you see on the outside."

His green eyes flickered with mischief. "Like when you first saw this Tassagon warrior?"

"Yes." She lifted her face to his. "And like when you first saw this Kurel tutor."

"You mean the haughty, humorless ghetto dweller who was no less disgusted with my army than she was the manure in the streets?"

She frowned up at him. "Like when I first saw a battle-ax-wielding warmonger with an ego bigger than this entire kingdom."

"Ouch." His hand went to his heart. "The lady inflicts a mortal wound." His brow went up. "Warmonger, I can see. But an ego bigger than the kingdom—you really thought that?"

His expression was so boyish and endearing it made her want to kiss all the hints of doubt from his face.

And then kiss him everywhere else. *Mercy.* She hugged the brown book close. "Haughty and humorless?"

"I judged the book by its cover, clearly." He searched her face. "How wrong I was."

"And I," she admitted.

Emotion played over his face, raw and honest, and she wondered if he saw the same in hers. His mouth was somehow closer now. Or, was it hers that had moved to within inches of his? Close enough to feel his warm breath, tickling her chin.

He reached for her. For a panicked, thrilling moment, she thought he'd draw her into an embrace. She'd have gone willingly, but instead he gently yet firmly removed the storybook from her arms. "No more using books as shields. No more need to be on guard around me."

"Not even a little on guard?" she asked as disappointment swelled.

His gaze sharpened. He was trying hard to read her intent. After all, he'd been quick to disagree with Kurel descriptions of Uhr-warriors' mindless need for sexual conquest, and had overheard Marina's stark warning—and Elsabeth's reaction to it. Knowing the expectations she'd have of him, he'd be reluctant to steal a kiss, unless he knew for certain he'd be welcome.

How dare he be so…so eager to learn her culture, so hell-bent on saving his sister, so disarmingly humble—

So damned attractive! With her heart pounding, her hands shaking, folded in her lap, she stretched up the last few inches and brushed her lips across his. A taste. His scent filled her nostrils, spicy and exotic. His lips were warm, softer in feel than she'd imagined. Yielding yet firm.

It was the craziest thing she'd ever done, kissing a Tassagon warrior. Kissing a man. Yet, somehow it didn't surprise her that she had. She'd been fighting the bonds holding her in place for so long.

Then, slowly, she moved back far enough to see the bemused expression he wore on his face. She'd surprised him. His shock lasted only a heartbeat or two, replaced quickly with a look of satisfaction that bordered on smug. "That was very nice," he said. "And far too brief."

Now that she'd taken such a liberty, she blushed as reality set in. She could feel the heat rising in her neck and cheeks. She wasn't sure if she wanted to die of embarrassment, or bashfulness, or both. "I don't claim any skills in kissing."

Tao made a soft sound of protest and reached for her hair. "Ah, sweetheart. I meant brief not as a criticism but as a complaint."

Sweetheart. The affection in his tone melted her.

He took a few long strands between his fingers, sliding them down to the ends. Her body reacted instantly, awash in tingles. A thought intruded. Tao was a man accustomed to dancers and camp followers meeting his sexual whims. Was this gentle caress what it seemed? Or was he only inspecting the merchandise before choosing a bed partner, as he must have done many times before? She didn't know.

She wasn't supposed to care. Not at this critical point in her plans. She merely wanted to take a few steps down that road Marina had warned her about. *A road of my own choosing.*

"Perhaps, if I teach you to read, you can teach me how to kiss." Somehow, she'd managed an amazingly light, casual tone.

"Kissing lessons in exchange for reading lessons? Hmm. You are a master trader." He cradled her face in his hands, oh-so-lightly, oh-so-completely, as if he couldn't choose between studying her upturned face and hauling her close for another kiss. "I confess I've been curious for far too long about what you feel like. And to see if you taste as good as I suspect."

"Do I?" she whispered.

"Let me confirm." His thumb stroked her cheekbone, warm and callused. Then, playful, tender, he bent down and lazily tasted his way from one corner of her mouth to the other, the chaste kiss leaving her aching for more. *More what?* More everything. An entire gamut of intimate adventures she'd too long delayed experiencing.

"Yes…quite good," he said as he kissed his way along.

"Better than sumsala?" she mumbled against his mouth.

"No comparison. Hotter. But without the sting."

As she started to laugh, he buried his fingers in her hair, and her mouth opened farther under the gentle pressure of his lips, his tongue searching out hers. A shudder coursed through his body as he pressed her close, one big hand cupping the back of her head. The sensation of his caresses coupled with the stroking of his tongue made her so dizzy and breathless it was all she could do to hold on, his hard muscles shifting under the fabric of his shirt.

Finally, he broke off the kiss, pausing to soothe her tingling lips with gentle, tasting nibbles. "Lesson one," he said, moving his lips to her cheek, letting her feel the scrape of his beard.

Her pulse throbbed in every part of her body. "I have a lot to learn," she whispered.

He touched his lips to hers. "I have a lot to teach."

I imagine you do. She blushed all over again, drawing her hands back into her lap as she sat up. "Now it's your turn."

CHAPTER NINETEEN

ELSABETH DIDN'T WANT to end the kissing, but she'd made a promise. *Ben's Lost Dog.* She lifted the cover of the old brown book, a children's school primer.

"The marks are enormous."

"The letters," she corrected.

"Yes. Letters. And the story…" He flipped through the pages. "It seems to be of a dog. And children."

Patiently, Elsabeth explained, "The simpler the words, the easier it will be to learn."

"Easy. Bah. I have never sought out the easy path. I won't start now."

"When you first learned to fight, was it with a full-size sword?"

"Uhrth, no. A full sword would have weighed more than we boys did."

Days ago when he was first healing, he'd told her of how he was taken from home at twelve to train, his childhood over. Yet, he'd gone into Uhr training gladly, even excitedly, off to live the adventures she'd experienced only in her imagination. "You can't begin literacy training with a full-size textbook, either."

"But a lost dog?" he complained.

"We'll move on to something better. I promise."

"The same can be said about our kissing," he said, making her shiver inside. He relented with a quiet laugh and tapped the page with two fingers. "All right, Kurel girl. I stand ready to learn."

The next hour proved trying for Tao. But he was intelligent and determined to get it right, although sooner than was likely feasible. "It's impossible to master reading in a day," she said.

He pushed off the couch, stalking to the window, moving aside the curtains to peer into the street as he so often did, as if never fully relaxed. As if always half expecting an enemy attack. "I'm used to doing most things well, Elsabeth. Not that I plan on giving up yet." He flicked her a glance. "Or ever."

"There will come a moment when the symbols will become words, and indistinguishable from the thoughts in your head. I promise you, you'll be able to read without thinking about it. Then you'll see, Tao. You'll see what you've been missing."

He released the curtain. "Like when you kissed me and saw what you were missing." His grin was smug, rakish.

She almost protested, but he was right. The plan had been to introduce Tao to her world, not the other way around, but she was learning about his life. About him. She'd tasted what she'd never imagined.

And wanted more.

"There's plenty of adventure to be had in books, too. Growing up, I'd lose myself in books and pretend the adventures in them were mine." She waved a hand around the little house. "I guess I always believed there was more than this, these four walls, this life."

"There is more," he said.

"Because you've seen it. You've been there. Outside."

"There's no reason you can't go, too. Now that we're at peace."

Her blood surged with longing. "Just once, I want to know what Tassagonia looks like from the outside." She sighed. "As a girl, I'd climb up the tallest windmill to look out beyond the walls, and dream."

"So you ventured into the palace, and got yourself a far better view from the palace hill."

"I stopped looking. My parents' murders turned my dreams back inside these walls—the ghetto walls—to Xim and what he'd done, and how I'd stop the violence by stopping him."

"Those aren't dreams. That's a vow of retribution. You'll grow hard without dreams." The lines in his face that hinted at the harshness of his years in the Hinterlands, slaying Gorr, were back. Yet, the memory of his achingly tender kisses remained.

"Why are you not hardened by what you experienced? The slaughter. The Gorr. How did you manage to remain so...human?" When others like Uhr-Beck were anything but.

His expression mellowed, yet there was determination there, too. "I've got dreams of my own."

What did this warrior dream of? She was dying to know. Not love, she already knew that. A life with a cooperative wife, she supposed. A wife from his class, his people.

A woman not at all like her.

LATER THAT AFTERNOON, Chun summoned Tao to the clinic. Tao sat on the examining table in his undershorts. "How do I look, healer?"

"Good. Very good. The sutures are ready to come out. You'll feel sore afterward."

"Pash," Tao scoffed, using the word he often heard the Kurel say when they dismissed something. "I've been so immersed in learning Kurel ways, I've all but forgotten about these bites."

The physician's careful extraction didn't require Tao's attention. He sought out Elsabeth's gaze and winked, just to see her squirm. He remembered her taking charge and kissing him first, something he'd never expected she'd do. Pleasure had battled with bashfulness in those big blue eyes, and surprise.

She turned slightly away from him, feigning great

interest in the physician's work. Did she think she'd escape before he left her hungry for more? She might think she seemed all business when teaching him her ways, but he knew he could get under her skin and fluster her. He liked it.

Hell, she'd gotten under his skin, too. He couldn't stop thinking about the kissing lessons, couldn't stop imagining every other possible place his mouth could explore on that sweet little body of hers. He'd burn all night, no doubt, thinking of it, cursing the fact she was asleep upstairs, and he was all alone in his bed.

He'd been living with her less than two weeks, but every day she revealed a little more of who she really was—a woman of honor and conviction with a sensitive spirit and a strong, brave heart. It was clear she hadn't wanted the job of introducing him to the ways of the Kurel, but even she couldn't deny that they were both starting to enjoy each other's company. Yes, very much so. But with Aza's life and Tassagonia's future hanging so precariously in the balance, he couldn't afford to stay away from the palace for long.

Tink. Tink. Tink. The sound of little bits of metal clanged into a bowl, one by one, until all the so-called sutures were out. Tao dragged a hand over the fresh scars, examining the new additions to the physical evidence of his violent history. They were impressively flat with practically no puckering, unlike many of the others on his body. "Well done, healer."

"All in a day's work, general."

"Such techniques would be helpful to my people. To keep them to yourselves doesn't seem right."

Chun glanced up at him in surprise. "We Kurel have never denied medical treatment to a Tassagon."

"Then why haven't we seen such treatment in the capital? I know what the laws of Forbiddance say, but these sutures aren't sorcery. They're little more than metal fasteners. The technique might have saved my men from disfiguring scars, especially the kind that prevent the proper use of a limb. My men could have returned to the front to fight again. Especially with your potion—penicillin. We Tassagons have been too quick to shun the possible uses of your medical techniques. It can be used—sparingly—and for the greater good. Such as allowing soldiers to live and fight longer."

An idea that made Elsabeth cringe, as he should have known it would. "It's wrong to use technology for the purposes of war," she said. "Sinful."

"Is it? If it curtails war, or prevents it altogether? Is its use sinful then? If technology is the glove as you said, doesn't it matter what the intent is of the hand inside? Of course it does. Like my crutches, for instance. I had the choice to use them to walk again. Or, I could have used them to smash every cup of tea you brought to me."

Elsabeth didn't sigh or shake her head or give him

one of those patronizing looks that meant he knew not of what he spoke. She merely bit her full lower lip a little, worrying it as she considered what he said, which told him she was less sure than before that all military use of technology was wrong. "Chun," she said. "He needs to see."

A glance passed between the physician and Elsabeth, then Chun measured Tao with a thoughtful stare, finally nodding. "All right."

Tao frowned at this apparent new conspiracy. What was going on between the two, and how was he involved?

Then Elsabeth turned to him. "Today Chun treats his outpatients. I want you to come with us."

THEY BOARDED A CART hitched to a sturdy old workhorse with blinders on. Tao thought of Chiron, and hoped his warhorse was being cared for, growing fat in a palace barn. Then he thought of Aza in the palace, and her proximity to Xim and Uhr-Beck, and his mood turned foul.

There is nothing you can do about that today, or even likely the next. Tao willed himself to focus on the present, on learning to live amongst the Kurel, where their sanctuary would keep him alive until he could take back his reputation—and wrest control of his army back from Xim's henchmen.

Tao tugged a cap over his face and helped Elsabeth

climb up to the driver's bench. Chun snapped the reins and started out in the direction of the market. Along the way Elsabeth pointed out one neighborhood or another, and the peculiarities of each as they traveled along narrow, twisting streets barely wide enough for a cart, let alone all the people squeezing through the inches of remaining space. He'd never seen her so animated, her cheeks pink in the sunshine. Her dress was green as new grass, and it contrasted vividly with her fiery hair as she happily told him about life in the ghetto. The Kurel were not really conjurers, but this woman had cast her own spell on him, nevertheless. He'd certainly fallen for her charms, unable to stop savoring the sight of her.

They passed the bustling marketplace, and he hunched a little lower in the seat. "I never told you of my error while trying to find the items necessary to fix your aviary. I stumbled into a shop that was as different from a hardware store as one could get. A place I doubt any man had ever trespassed before." His tone was wry. "Lacy, frilly things hung everywhere. Female unmentionables."

"You went into the lingerie shop? Oh, Tao."

Chun was dignified enough to say nothing.

"I believe so. They had a broom outside the front door. I made an assumption. An incorrect assumption."

"I can see why you came home with your tail between your legs." Her sympathetic tone was belied by an escaped giggle.

"Hardly. More like burning curiosity." Did all Kurel women wear such items? Even without looking at her, he knew she'd guessed his question, and it caused her to blush. He smiled. "I have much still to learn regarding Kurel ways."

But the question was left hanging. He supposed that further exploration would be necessary to gain his answer.

Chun navigated toward the orchards and the merchant road, where the buildings of the ghetto petered out. By a big red barn, he parked the cart under the shade of a tree.

Inside the barn the scent of hay was thick and tickled his nose. A stale scent of manure told him livestock had been kept there, but not for a while. Chun busied himself by setting up a table and some chairs, throwing down a white tablecloth and then arranging medical tools and jars of many sizes on it.

Elsabeth took Tao up to a clean, fragrant hayloft, where shafts of sunlight pierced the plank roof. She hoisted her skirt high to crunch through the hay, offering glimpses of a white petticoat and bare legs before she threw down the blanket she'd carried rolled under her arm and spread it out. "We'll have the best view from up here."

He settled next to her and pulled a piece of straw

from her hair. "The best view, indeed." He began to consider the best plan of attack that would culminate in kissing her.

"Here they come," she whispered, pointing.

He peered out at the fields and orchards. Dust rose like smoke as several carts bounced along the merchant road toward the barn. Farther out, a covered wagon approached. Behind it, horses, some with single riders, others with two.

"Tassagons," he said. "This is what you told me about."

She nodded. "Kurel medicine might be illegal, and it is certainly feared, but in secret and when there are no other options, it's coveted." She settled onto the blanket. "It looks like Chun will be busy for a long time today."

That would aid him in his plans. "Then perhaps you'll tell me a story."

She began to unlace a shoe, distracting him with glimpses of her ankle again. "You can't get enough of dogs and children, hmm?" She removed her shoe completely, shaking out a straw that must have been annoying her. He'd been entertained by dancers with nothing of their bodies left to his imagination; he'd seen females in every state of undress. But rarely had he ever been as intrigued and tempted than by the sight of that one bare foot and its five little toes.

Too soon, the shoe was back on. He leaned back

on his elbows and said, "You said your mother was birthed in Kurel Town, but the woman couldn't be saved."

Elsabeth laced her shoe. "My Tassagon grandmother came here as many of your people do, desperate for last-chance remedies for dying loved ones—or themselves. Willing to risk anything, even a sorcerer's curse, or more realistically, arrest for violating the Forbiddance. All for the chance to live. Or in my grandmother's case, for her baby to live."

"Tell me."

"My grandmother was in labor and bleeding. Someone dropped her off at the ghetto gates from a cart, but fled before anyone could see who it was, or learn my grandmother's name. She couldn't say who she was, or she wouldn't say. We'll never know. Her only request was to save the baby. She didn't care what happened to her." She twirled a piece of hay between her fingers. "The physician lost a patient that day, but he gained a daughter. Years later, my mother's adopted father mentored a young medical student. It was how my parents met, and fell in love."

Tao listened, his back propped against the wall of the barn, his arms propped on his bent knees. "This charity, it's been going on for generations, then."

"Yes. But my father took it a step further. He became the first to offer aid out here in the orchards, and on a set schedule, so the Tassagons could come to rely on the care. This is his legacy, and my mother's, too. Chun carries it on now."

"Beth, your father was an incredibly selfless man. This could have become a lucrative black market, but he gave it all away."

"He never once charged a Tassagon for seeking out his care." Her brows drew together, her expression grew colder. "They repaid him by taking his life."

"Not honorable men like my officers, nor I. Not men like Markam, and all those who came to the orchards and never gave away the secret. Xim and Beck, and the ignorant, cowardly men under their command, are to blame. Surely you see that now."

For a moment she simply searched his face, silent, thoughtful and with classic Kurel reserve—and he despaired of her ever letting go of her bitterness long enough to differentiate between the good and bad soldiers of the kingdom. Then she reached for him, coming up on her knees, her warm finger tracing the outline of his jaw. "I do see it, Tao. Every time I see you."

Without waiting for permission, he drew her into his lap, then slanted his mouth to hers and kissed her. Lesson number two.

WITH DISTASTE, KING XIM studied the pile of charred bones the priest had presented. "You are certain, then."

"Yes. I swear before all the angels of Uhrth that the cracks read true. These are not the general's bones."

Xim slammed a hand flat on the table. The bones bounced. Even after they stilled, in the flickering torchlight they seemed to be dancing. Mocking him. It was all he could do not to sweep them off the table and onto the floor. "What does it mean, then? He's alive?"

"It means only that these aren't his bones."

Roaring in frustration, Xim paced away from the priest, wrapping a cape made of forest-kitt fur around his shoulders. A chill had settled into the old fortress and would not abate until the long cold season was over, many months from now. By then, Aza would have given birth to another child, proof of his continued virility and power. The spring thaw would symbolize a new beginning for his reign, and his plans to send the army into Rider territory would begin.

Spring was too far off. He needed answers now.

"You will say nothing about this, shaman." *Or, I'll have you killed,* was his next thought. But he didn't dare speak the sinful deed, lest a curse fall upon him. It was bad enough having to deflect the Kurel's wicked spells.

Xim peered out between the columns of the temple at the ghetto far below. It was after dark. All the Kurel were behind their walls, where a soft, eerie glow emanated—and not due to the moonlight. It was the glow of wizardry. Wickedness. Only the spires of the slowly rotating windmills and a few of the taller buildings peeked above the walls. The memory of his suffering, of being wracked with a nearly fatal fever, haunted him. Frightened him.

Aza had wanted him to accept treatment from the visiting Kurel healer. Chun was his name. But he didn't like the way the man had looked at him, as if Xim were weak, a trembling, sweating object of pity. They'd never looked at his father that way. No one had, not the Kurel, and not Tao. Orion had everyone's respect. *Why don't I?*

Xim's upper lip curled. He'd refused to be touched by that Kurel and had called for a Tassagon healer. For all he knew, the Kurel had created a spell to make him sicken and die in the first place.

Now, he thought of Markam's warning to Beck about the conscquences of angering the Kurel and shivered. He wanted the sorcerers out of the capital. Resentment burned that they frightened him too much to exile them. But if they were found harboring a fugitive in direct violation of royal decree, he'd have the excuse he needed to rid Tassagonia of the parasites.

"Tassagonia for Tassagons," Beck always said. Yes, it was how it was supposed to be, what the angels of Uhrth intended when they drove the Kurel and the Riders from the Old Colony. Xim would bring back the intended purity of his people, the only real humans and true descendants of the angels of Uhrth, and he'd be viewed as a hero for doing so. It would define his reign and secure his place in history.

In that moment, he chose to conquer his fears and doubts. Never had he felt so proud and so strong for making a decision all on his own. "Bring me a messenger!" he bellowed.

One of the guards standing outside the temple door hurried inside. "I am here, Your Highness."

"Summon Colonel Uhr-Beck to the palace."

The man snapped his heels together then ran off. Beck was away in the countryside inspecting the army, seeing what was needed to train them to march on the Riders come spring. But Xim needed him here. Now. The colonel always made everything so much easier. Markam's presence soothed him as well, but Beck offered more clarity, focusing on the simple rather than the complex, giving him confidence.

As soon as he had both his colonels here, he'd launch a search for General Uhr-Tao—amongst the Kurel. With any luck at all, he'd find evidence of their betrayal and use it to justify his plans. He'd see that all of those inhuman sorcerers were sent packing back to the Barrier Peaks, where they belonged.

CHAPTER TWENTY

A SEARCH OF THE GHETTO was imminent. Crushed in Tao's fist was the red note carried home by not one but two pigeons. A note with a written warning Elsabeth had translated for him: BONES READ. NOT GT's. K-TOWN SEARCH IMMINENT.

"Of course they weren't yours," Elsabeth said. "It was a lucky guess, nothing more than a priest's hunch. No science, no basis in fact or truth."

"You dismiss our ways as easily as I once dismissed yours," he scolded. "Our best priests can be uncannily right." He grabbed his amulet. "One of our combat shamans blessed this talisman. I believe it saved me, more than once."

She turned her hand palm up, acceding his position. This was no time to argue religion versus science. Whatever their people's beliefs, the result had led to the first organized hunt for him in Kurel Town since his escape. Tao had no intention of being anywhere within the ghetto walls when the guards arrived. His presence brought unacceptable risk for the Kurel who lived here.

There was precious little time. "I'll need a rucksack. Some food, water." Mentally, he listed the other gear he'd bring. It was barely light but growing brighter swiftly. *If this was the Hinterlands and a threat to safety this grave loomed, even my lowest-ranking sergeant would have had his squad packed and gone an hour ago.*

Elsabeth pumped water into a bladder, wiped it dry and wrapped in it a cloth, then found a rucksack on an upper shelf to load with supplies. She seemed to have an uncanny instinct for what to pack, choosing boiled-wool blankets, rope, cord and matches without him having to direct her. "You pack like an experienced trekker."

"I just remember everything I've read. I love survival guides." Watching him choose his coat off a hook, leaving hers behind, she sobered. "I'm going with you, Tao. Outside the walls." Before he could form a protest, she argued, "I'm the only Kurel banned on sight from the palace—by order of the king himself. That makes me a convenient target for Beck's men. I'd be easy to arrest, because I've already proven myself a troublemaker."

"The elders will hide you."

"Pash. They can hide you, too, if that's your argument. Hiding is a last resort. More, it brings the risk of being found, which increases the chances of violence. I can't—*I won't* be the cause of that." Strands of hair fell over her shoulders and she shoved items in the rucksack. "Besides, I promised Aza and Markam I'd keep you safe."

"Me safe?" His laugh was a quick, disbelieving bark. "What about you?"

"I'll be safer in your company than anywhere else." She said it with such conviction, it demolished all question of whether she trusted him. "You know where we can hide, and how to live off the land. It's not like the Hinterlands. Shepherds go out in the countryside every day to tend the flocks. We'll only be gone for a day."

"Two," he said. "And one night. We'll need at least that." *We*. By the arks, he hadn't uttered any agreement yet and already he was speaking as if she were coming along. In truth, he wanted her with him. He felt more in control of events outside these walls than inside—and he'd focus more easily with her in his sight, rather than out of reach with him left wondering about her welfare. "That's two days in the wilds, Elsabeth. You've lived a sheltered life. Do you have an understanding of what you're asking to do?"

She stuck a hand on her hip. "My sheltered life ended three years ago, the day I found my parents shot and killed. As for understanding what it is to escape the city, let me just say I've been preparing for this since I was a girl." She thrust the rucksack at him.

"By reading books," he scoffed, taking the bag.

"Yes." That stubborn little chin, the erect spine, those fierce eyes, all told him there would be no dissuading her. But then, her reasons for wanting to accompany him were sound. The more threatened Xim grew, the more unpredictable he became. Markam would be watching, ready to step in, but no one really knew what would happen when they came and searched.

"All right. We'll both go."

At least she gave him the respect of not cheering her victory. He finished packing, then asked her to inventory the gear. "Cook pot," he said.

Elsabeth rummaged through the rucksack. "Check."

"Ball of string."

"Check."

"Slingshot."

She hesitated. "This?" She held up a forked stick tired with leather and string. "Where did you find it?"

"I made it. When you've gone off to do your chores, I've been working on mine. There are pitifully few weapons in K-Town. Navi's proved himself quite helpful in procuring what little there is, but where I can, I fill in the blanks. My arsenal…" He went to his bed, pulled out a box from under it, where he retrieved two fine blades, thrusting one in a sheath on his belt before wrapping the other in a piece of leather and handing it to her. "Yours."

"Mine?" Her brows shot up, her regard of the carving knife now doubtful upon hearing it described as a weapon.

"Yes. Once we're under way, you'll wear it at all times." One place where the Kurel's ridiculous aversion to weaponry didn't belong was out in the wild. He'd make sure of that.

THE ELDERS ARRIVED AS they were ready to board a cart driven by Chun and Navi. Tao cursed the delay. It was almost full light. Farouk leaned on his cane with one gnarled first. "You're leaving," he accused.

With as much patience as Tao could muster, he briefed the elder on his decision and the reasoning behind it. "When we granted you sanctuary, we did so accepting of the risks," Farouk said, as if offended.

"I know this, and I'm grateful, but I believe my presence during the search may raise that risk to an unacceptable level." As if to punctuate the statement, the sound of children laughing down the street drifted to them. "The king will punish all of you if I'm found here. It's best I wait out the search outside the walls."

"Outside," Gwendolyn repeated, obviously horrified at the concept.

"Your act is one of honor, General. Selfless honor.

We won't forget this," Farouk said. A compliment from a Kurel. An elder, no less. Imagine that. "We can't hold you here if you choose to go, General. But the girl, Ferdinand's daughter…do you believe you can keep our Elsabeth safe?"

Tao took in the concerned faces of all the Kurel. Having gotten to know them, he saw true emotion behind their wall of reserve. It had always been there. He'd simply needed to look harder. That revelation was no less surprising than their apparent willingness to allow Elsabeth to leave with him. "I do," he said. "And I will."

Elsabeth swept her shawl around her shoulders. "Then no more talking about it. They'll be here very soon."

Gwendolyn wouldn't allow Elsabeth to leave without a hug. Marina stood near, contributing to whatever warnings the old woman was likely issuing. Undoubtedly to "beware the Uhr's desires." They'd be relieved to know he hadn't yet touched her in an intimate fashion.

But if they knew how difficult that had been, all their worst imaginings would be confirmed.

He cleared his throat. Elsabeth broke free of the women. Her eyes were moist. For the briefest of moments, she met his gaze, and what he saw there was not what he expected—not sadness or fear, but defiance and, incredibly, exhilaration. He should have known she'd be excited, yet his experience with other females had shown time and time again that they didn't crave risk and adventure to the degree Elsabeth did.

Then, with Kurel calm masking her true emotions, she boarded the cart. Following, Tao made the sign of Uhrth over his heart and hoped he wouldn't rue the day he'd suggested she'd be better off getting out to experience what the world had to offer than burying her nose in paper.

A SHORT WHILE LATER, they were climbing down from the cart. Tao hoisted the rucksack over his shoulder, took Elsabeth's warm hands in his and helped her down.

"See you in a couple of days," Navi said, nodding. A look of longing hinted at his desire to come along. But with the boy's propensity to finding trouble—and man-eating carnivores—Tao would have no part of it.

Chun handed Elsabeth a pouch. "Medical kit." His mouth compressed. "Just in case." For a typical Kurel, it was a powerful display of emotion.

Soon he and Elsabeth were under way, leaving her friends—and everything else she'd known—behind.

He knew every inch of the fortress walls surrounding Tassagonia. It was required of every Uhr. A short distance away was a leafy hardwood grove, and on the other side of the trees, the impassable northern wall loomed high. Impassable to those who didn't know the secrets he did.

In this deserted area, the wall was crumbling in spots, in as much need of repair as this kingdom. But then the wall had always served more as a reassurance than as an actual protection against the Gorr invaders. No attack had ever been launched on Tassagonia itself. Tao forced away the thought of Furs inside the capital. He'd spent his career ensuring it would never happen.

Kicking away stones and brush, he uncovered an iron ladder, each rung set between the stones and mortared in place. "A spy deck," he explained, pointing to a ledge above them open to the outside. "They were put in long ago to increase visibility on certain sections of the walls."

They climbed the ladder up to the spy deck, ducked through it, and walked out onto the narrow ledge. Elsabeth gasped in wonder at the view, the soaring wall to each side, the Plains falling away below them and onward to the Barrier Peaks. Behind them, the smoke of morning cook fires rose into the fair sky; ahead were free-grazing horses and cattle, growing fat and content on early autumn grass, and on rare occasions, the lone shepherd unafraid of risking the danger of life outside the protection of the city, and then nothing but empty lands for countless miles, an entire world abandoned in fear after nearly all its inhabitants had been destroyed.

Fear had for too long ruled these lands. It was never as clear to him as it was now. Fear between the human tribes, fear begun long ago in the First Colony and perpetuated down through the ages. Fear that he'd make damn well sure ended with King Xim.

"The view…it's breathtaking," Elsabeth said, hushed.

"You've seen a fine view like this from the palace hill."

"But not from here—from outside." Her eyes shone with gratitude and wonder. He'd like to see a little more caution in those eyes, even a smidgen of fear; nevertheless his chest swelled with her joy.

"You'll be far more outside than this." A chain ladder was coiled against the wall. "We'll climb down using this." He unrolled the chains as he dragged the ladder to the edge and lowered it a little at a time, testing its hold. The rust-encrusted links hadn't been disturbed for years. "Wait until I reach the bottom, then follow when I say so."

They rendezvoused below. Taking her hand, he led her as they raced into a grove of shade trees, Elsabeth holding her simple brown traveling skirt clear of the grass with her other hand. As she caught her breath in the shelter of the trees, Tao grabbed a loop of rope from the rucksack. "Wait here. I'll find us a horse."

Elsabeth peered through the branches to watch Tao stalk a herd of grazing horses. He moved like a predator, easy, slow, picking his target from the edge of the herd—a beautiful buttermilk buckskin mare with a long, flowing black mane and a full blaze running down the center of her face.

Only a few horses lifted their heads at his approach. A lifelong horseman, Tao was able to move amongst them without causing alarm. She understood their calm; he had the same effect on her. By the time Tao looped a figure-eight rope bridle around the buckskin mare, the horse was as besotted with the general as Elsabeth had been after their first kiss. With some hand waving and hat waving, Tao chased off a few curious followers, then jumped on the horse and rode her back to the trees.

"Now you'll be wanted for stealing a horse," Elsabeth said, stroking a hand down the horse's silken muzzle.

"Borrowing," he corrected as he dismounted to stand next to her. "That's no crime. Now, hike up your skirt."

It pleased Tao that she didn't require more than a moment or two of thought before lifting her skirt to her knees, exposing her white, frill-trimmed petticoat and those long bare legs—what had become in a matter of weeks one of his favorite sights under the suns.

He lifted her up and dropped her onto the back of

the horse. She laughed, half in delight, half in shock. "I've never ridden bareback."

"Never been outside the walls. Never ridden bareback. What else will you have done for the first time by day's end?"

He noticed that she'd gone silent. She was sitting on the mare, clutching the rope, her gaze alarmed but speculative. *Did she really think I'd meant making love to her?* Great Uhrth. Did the Kurel idea of the savage Uhr have no bounds?

He tried to pretend the mere thought of being with her didn't come with an interested heat in his loins, so he frowned as he hoisted the rucksack on his back. "Be still, girl," he soothed the mare, smoothing a hand down the side of its creamy neck. "You will like this, as well." He believed that in every beast was the yearning for a break from day-to-day drudgery, including a workhorse.

He used a fallen log to swing up and behind Elsabeth, taking the rope reins with her snug between his arms. "Let yourself relax," he murmured in her ear. "I won't let you fall."

Slowly, the tension went out of her. "Hold on with your thighs. Squeeze. Yes, like that. Follow the natural movement of the horse, don't fight it."

Her skirt had ridden up, revealing the soft skin of her thighs. That place right above her knees would be a perfect spot to kiss, he thought, sliding one arm more securely around her waist under the guise of keeping her safe. The fragrance of her hair was intoxicating. He thought of moving aside the curls to kiss her neck, but feared it might send both of them off the horse.

He felt himself reacting to her closeness, and shifted away a few inches out of respect. She'd set him ablaze, this woman had, but by Uhrth, he'd be an officer and gentleman until she was begging him otherwise.

Did Kurel beg?

In his dreams, yes.

At the top of a rise, he turned the horse around and stopped. Before them was the fortress with its four towers, each topped with banners of blue and white. "There it is. Our home, as it looks from beyond the walls."

"There are no words to describe it," she said softly.

"My point. No words, no pages, no books. Some things simply have to be experienced in person."

THEY STOPPED FOR THE day after traveling a comfortable distance away from the palace and its surrounding flocks, herds and their shepherds. They were atop a ridge with a view of the valley.

"We'll spend the night here," Tao announced.

She caught him gazing out from under the leafy cover of a stand of lop-lop trees to where the edge of the palace lands met the horizon. "My kingdom for a spyglass," he said as if to himself. His army was out there, she realized. The sprawling encampment was visible if she squinted hard enough. The discovery seemed to fill him with poignant relief and yearning, until his jaw hardened and he glanced away.

He's glad they're located where Markam said they'd be, but wishes he were with them.

And not Beck.

Elsabeth shook the dust from her skirt and stretched the stiffness from her legs as she marveled at the beauty of their surroundings. The hush was deep, even overwhelming. A distant raptor screeched, insects buzzed lazily, along with the sounds of grass tearing as the mare grazed and, most pleasantly, those of Tao efficiently making camp, but there was no city racket, no clanging chaos. "It's so quiet," she said.

Tao grinned at her as he measured and cut several long sticks. "What did you expect out here?"

"I...don't quite know." She grinned back. "None of the authors said anything about what the wilderness sounds like. Or, doesn't."

Nor did any mention the beauty of a well-built man working up a sweat in a white shirt, his sleeves rolled up, his skin golden in the late-day sunshine. His metal amulet caught the light, and his hair, grown longer since his escape, lifted in the breeze. She found a small boulder to sit on and hugged her knees close to watch him work. "What are you doing?"

"Seeking to end my hunger."

"I can get the food from the sack—"

"No, Elsabeth. I mean I've got a hankering for something fresh and hot." He flashed her a smile. "Hot—once we cook it over the fire."

She hoped her blush wasn't so obvious in the golden light of late afternoon. A day with him pressed against her back had her taking all his words the wrong way.

He took three long sticks and tested their suppleness before tying them together in several places. He fastened a single, long string to one end, and bent the sticks to drop one more loop over the opposite end.

Finally, he lifted the curved sticks, drawing the string taut as he sighted down his arm. "Good," he said. "Nice and tight. Now we have a finished bow. We need a few arrows. Help me find a few straight sticks, the straightest sticks that you can find out here. We need strong wood, because if the wood's too light, it's just going to fly away with little force."

He used his blade to carve sharp points on the sticks. Then, setting each arrow on a boulder, he fashioned a small wedge at the other end of each arrow, which he told her he'd use to seat the string. She watched with wonder, and admiration, along with a warm, contented and almost primitive sense of being protected. All his years of living in the Hinterlands were evident in the casual way he went about ensuring they were fed and comfortable for the night. None of what he'd learned had come from books. In the past, she'd have dismissed him as an illiterate savage, but his survival skills proved that opinion wrong. Centuries of wrong opinions had kept their peoples apart.

"There," he said. "It fits nicely. That's how you make a bow and arrow."

She heard a rustle in the grass. Tao spun around as a rabbit leaped across the field. In one smooth move, he fired the arrow and killed the hare. "Dinner," he said.

VIOLENCE IN K-TOWN. Markam urged his horse as fast as he dared through the crowded streets. "Move aside!" he bellowed. "Move aside or be run down."

In his urgency to reach the ghetto gates, he didn't doubt his capability to do just that.

Citizens fell away from him, allowing him through. "Hooligans," some protested, shaking their fists. Others pulled their children close, their angry, resentful glares following him. None knew the dual role he played, seeing him only for what he appeared: a guard dressed in blue and white, an instrument of a king they disliked more and more. Xim's arbitrary rules and the intimidating Home Guards tasked with enforcing them had tried the patience of all of Tassagonia, not just Kurel.

Xim ordering a search of the ghetto wasn't unexpected; Markam had stalled it for as long as he could.

But damn his dimwitted tool Beck for going in before the agreed-upon time, breaking the agreement they'd struck in the wee hours of the morning.

But when he reached the entrance to the ghetto, Beck was still on the outside, on Tassagon soil, his lean face sweating, his horse dancing nervously. His home guards milled around him. Not a Kurel was in sight, but a bow dangled from Beck's hand. Soldiers milled around the ghetto gates. His men—most of them still boys—were as pale as new snow, and as silent. Their expressions at Markam's arrival were more relieved than unwelcoming.

Markam pulled back hard on his mount. "There was to be no violence." *My strangling of you excepted.*

"I had to take care of a discipline problem." Beck flicked a gloved hand at a couple of men. "Get that body out of here."

It was then the soldiers moved apart far enough for Markam to see the soldier lying face down in the dirt, blood clotting in the dust. Two arrows were in his back.

Beck rasped, "Disobeyed a direct verbal order."

"Which was?"

"He refused to ride through the ghetto gates."

The rest of the guards listened in uneasy silence, clearly hoping they weren't the next ones ordered inside the ghetto, weighing mutiny over the threat of a sorcerer's curse.

A sense of hopelessness and remorse came over Markam. He himself had perpetuated the fear of the Kurel having the power to use disease as weapon. He'd put the fear of Uhrth into Beck in order to keep the man away from the ghetto. Now that decision had come back to haunt him.

Yet, a fighting force could not operate effectively if men refused orders, even when those orders frightened them.

Especially when the orders brought fear. He may never have served at the front in the war against the Gorr, but he'd shouldered the responsibility of keeping the palace and royal family safe. Fear grew each day as Markam saw more clearly that he might not survive to see his goal through.

"We can't execute soldiers one by one for the rest of the morning. We have to go in, Uhr-Beck," he said. "You and I. We can't ask them to do what we won't do ourselves."

The colonel coughed out a laugh. "Are you mad? Look at those deviants—those goddamn Kurel in there. Watching us. They don't even look human the way they stand there, no expression on their faces."

Their horses pranced, head to head, sensing the tension between their riders and in the guards around them. "A cursory check," Markam proposed. Then under his breath he added, "Just so we can say we accomplished it. Then Xim's happy, and the Kurel are happy."

Beck's narrowed eye pondered him first, then the streets on the other side of the ghetto gates. "They won't give us the fever?"

"Not if we don't provoke them."

Beck's jaw slid back and forth, as if he were grinding his teeth. "I hope we find him in there—Uhr-Tao. What I wouldn't do to get a hold of that bastard. Six years I've waited for the chance. I've got his army, but it'd taste a whole lot sweeter sprinkled with his blood." He kicked his mount. "Let's see if we can dig him up." He waved at Markam. "After you, Field-Colonel."

CHAPTER TWENTY-ONE

WITH THE RABBIT MARINATING in salt, spices, wild onions and various other herbs they'd picked, and hanging from a branch in a waterproof sack high enough above ground to keep it away from any hungry visitors, they walked to the stream to wash away the day's dust and grime.

Tao stood guard to let Elsabeth bathe first. As she lifted her skirt and ventured barefoot into the water, she let out a gasp. "It's cold!"

"If you need help keeping warm, I can always trade in advance for the next reading lesson."

"You're so considerate."

He heard the humor in her reply. "You know where to find me."

"Yes. Up there, covering your eyes." She pinned up her hair, then splashed water in his direction. "Go on. And no peeking."

He'd have answered that he wouldn't dream of peeking, but that would have been a bald-faced lie.

Chuckling, he turned around to give her privacy, one part of his awareness devoted to listening to his surroundings for possible danger, and the other trying to discern the difference between the various splashes, and just how she was using the cake of soap to sud her body. What he wouldn't have given to join her and help her get clean. To carry her, wet and eager, from the water to his bedroll and make passionate love to her—as he'd done over and over again in his mind since practically the first moment he'd seen her. He'd never waited so long for a woman he'd wanted so badly. He'd never waited at all.

You never hungered for a woman like this.

No. And he had the feeling his craving would grow even worse before the night was over.

TAO HAD ROASTED THE rabbit to mouthwatering perfection. There almost hadn't been enough for the two of them. "A little hungry?" he asked, amused, watching her while she ate—with her hands. Like a Tassagon. Utensils simply wouldn't have worked as well to tear apart the meat.

"I don't ever recall being this ravenous." She popped a finger into her mouth, sucking it clean, then did the same to the next, cleaning each one as delicately as she could manage.

Until she noticed Tao's keen regard. His lips had formed an appreciative yet almost feral smile that caused a now-familiar inner shiver. "It must be the outdoors," she tried to explain, "that makes a person so hungry."

"It can do that, yes."

It was suddenly awkward, being made aware of their attraction so acutely, and not knowing what to do about it, how to quench the heat, and her curiosity.

Their curiosity. Yes, he was interested in her, too—experienced Tassagon Uhr-warrior that he was. Tao seemed to have to force his attention away to throw another log on the fire. It was a very satisfying realization. Quite. She turned back to the fire, secure in her knowledge.

The glow of the scattered embers matched the ribbon of fire on the horizon as Little Lume disappeared. Sunset in the wilds entranced her. The entire sky was a color show—peach, then orange, crimson and finally a deep purple sprinkled with the first stars. The dusk stretched on and on, holding off the night, her first ever to be spent sleeping out under the stars.

Tao disposed of the remains of the meal, tossing the cleaned bones from the rabbit into the flames. It made her think of the bones the palace shaman had used to incite Xim into ordering a search of the ghetto. "I wish we knew what was happening at home," she lamented.

"I have confidence Markam will make sure the search is conducted properly. He's protecting your people. And mine." The firelight flickered in his suddenly somber eyes, and she knew he was thinking of Aza.

"Markam will watch over her," she said.

"I hope not too closely. Not under Xim's jealous eye."

Her head jerked up. "So it's true. Markam's in love with her."

"That was as much of a guess as the shaman's with the moat bones. Markam didn't say. I only suspect it. Has Aza told you anything?"

Elsabeth shook her head. "No, but I see it in her eyes sometimes. The feelings. But she's careful to hide them, even from me."

"Good." He added another log to the fire. "Aza is married to Xim, and she cannot, and must not, take up with another man. It is her duty to be his queen."

"You'd be proud of her," Elsabeth whispered. "I don't think she's neglected her duties, even for love. Both of you were taught that marriage is a duty above all else. A deliberate effort. For Aza, unfortunately, that's proven true."

Tao poked a stick in the coals. "You disapprove. Minstrels sing of true love. A page right out of one of your storybooks, Elsabeth. A notion with little applicability to real life."

She sat up straighter, her hands flat on the log by

her hips, to keep from flying up to shake some sense into the man.

Or kiss some into him.

"I believe differently," she said.

"That is one of the most charming things about you. Your naïveté."

"I'm not naive!"

"Innocent, then."

She opened her mouth to argue the point, but couldn't. "I'm less innocent every day I spend with you, Tassagon."

He was laughing now. "As if that idea of kissing lessons was mine."

"I didn't see much protest on your part," she pointed out. "Do you want to know what my aunt and Marina told me about you when we left this morning?"

"I have a good idea…"

"They said to keep you close."

"Ah, but with my hands and feet tied, I bet. The only safe Uhr-warrior is a hog-tied Uhr-warrior. Am I correct?"

She laughed at his ridicule. "Actually, they were worried about you. Worried I'd pulled you into my rebellion. That my vow of revenge against Xim could end up killing you."

His smile faded into a frown of insult. "Those two elderly ladies were fretting about me? Do they not feel I can take care of myself, as well as you?"

"They think very highly of you. It's why they don't want to see you being too quick to give your life to protect me, and also them, when we very much need you alive."

He sat back on his log, pondering what she'd told him. "Well. How about that." Briefly, a second or two, he seemed pleased. Then his lips compressed with faint worry, as if her description of the elders' concerns had translated into a challenge to look out for her. He checked that his blade and the bow were within hand's reach. "Get some sleep, Elsabeth. I'll stay up on watch."

Her ears strained to hear any possible danger as she peered into the deepening dusk. "Do you expect trouble?"

"Only if I think of you overly much," he admitted, lower.

"Is that such a bad thing?" She leaned forward on her log, inspired by her daring.

"You gave your word to the elders, and I gave mine—to keep you safe."

Safe from the dangers of the countryside, or from him?

Turning a shoulder to her, he settled onto his blanket, reaching for the blade to whittle a sharper point on an arrow. He'd made it clear no answers would be forthcoming. Reluctantly, she lay down on her back on her own blanket near the fire. Sleep would be a long time coming unless she gave up thinking of excuses to join Tao on his covers.

A scrape of boots on dirt and the sound of the mare blowing jarred her alert.

She sat up, her heart thumping. Tao brought a finger to his lips, and she nodded to let him know she'd gotten the message. He motioned for her to stay where she was. A glint of something in his hand. His blade.

Danger. Who was here? Her mouth went dry. She'd been treating the trek like a fairy-tale adventure, when in reality they were in the wilds with no protection.

No, she had protection. This warrior.

And his backup was her.

Her fingers crept over the dirt to the blade he'd insisted she keep at all times. As Tao stepped silently toward the edge of the ridge, she combed it into her hand.

He stood in silhouette against a huge rising moon that cast the entire valley in silvery-blue light like a winter's dawn. He was so still he looked like a magnificent statue.

She rose to her knees on the blanket, the unwrapped blade in her sweaty hand.

Tao beckoned, whispering. "Elsabeth, come here."

Barefoot, she joined him. He pointed. "Look there. By the streambed."

She peered into the moonlit landscape. "I don't see anything," she whispered back.

"See where the outcropping of rocks sits in the curve of the stream?"

She searched until three shadows she'd overlooked moved. The shadows coalesced into three riders on lean, gangly horses that looked bred more for speed than life behind a plow or wagon. Alarm flared like a burst of lightning. "Who are they?"

"Riders."

"Riders of the Plains?" The third human tribe.

"Yes. There's a woman with them. See her?"

All three wore similar outfits with leather riding pants decorated with fringed seams and vests with painted designs. But sure enough, one of the riders was female, long legged with flowing white-blond hair, sitting as confidently as the males. The Riders noticed them then, as if their instincts told them they were being watched.

Tao brought his hand to his mouth and made a loud, warbling call. Her heartbeat accelerated as the same forlorn, warbling call came back to them after a definite delay. There was no doubt in her mind the trio of Riders were shocked to encounter them out here. Tao brought his fingers to his mouth and repeated the sound exactly, one more time.

The apparent leader of the group wheeled his horse around, galloping up the ridge to meet them, his bow drawn, his open vest flapping, the muscles of his sculpted torso decorated with paint or tattoos that looked black in the moonlight.

Elsabeth would have squeaked and cowered behind Tao if the need to stand with her man hadn't been so strong.

Her man? Yes. She sensed if she didn't give the appearance of a warrior's woman now, the chance would be lost.

The leader dismounted, his bow lowered but still fearsome as his lanky legs carried him closer. A shell bracelet encircled one wrist, a choker of more shells and glass beads was snug at the base of his throat. His hair was brown like Tao's but long, spilling around his shoulders. His eyes were blue like hers.

Tao's hand landed on her back, a firm, almost possessive touch. A sweep of his thumb told her he stood with her, and asked that she stand with him.

"Tao," the rider said, the even teeth of his grin capturing the moonlight as he came forward, his hand extended. "Too long."

"Too long, Pax."

The men gripped each other in a brief but fierce embrace, moving back to smile some more. "You've gone Kurel?" Pax queried, running a curious but admiring stare up and down Elsabeth, head to toe. "She has hair like fire. I assume she has the personality to match."

Elsabeth clamped her mouth closed lest she say

something to overturn this unheard-of encounter between the three tribes of humanity.

"Elsabeth, this is Pax, leader of the Blue Hills band. A brave warrior, and friend."

Friends…with a Rider?

Reading her surprise, Pax said, "This is what happens when two parties, one of hunters and one of warriors, wait out an unexpected blizzard in the same cave."

"A long three days," Tao remembered.

"Made much warmer with the jugs of Blue Hills spirits." As Tao laughed, Pax sniffed the air. "It smells like rabbit."

"We had only one," Tao apologized.

"We have six." He turned and called to the other two riders. "Let us party by the light of the moon."

CHAPTER TWENTY-TWO

THEY FEASTED FOR THE second time that night high on the ridge overlooking the Tassagonian fortress, members of three tribes sitting together as one.

Tao relayed the story of his homecoming and arrest, his quest to separate power-hungry Uhr-Beck from King Xim, and his hope to restore some semblance of sanity to the realm. More information was exchanged about the Gorr—they were still in retreat—and the Sea Scourge—still raiding any traders who dared trespass the high seas, as well as those foolish enough to build settlements too close to the shore.

"The Scourge still taking human females?" Tao asked.

"Yes." Cambria had spoken, the blonde woman. She was bronzed and strong, her garments snugly fitted to her curves as well as her muscles. A warrior in her own right, Elsabeth thought, openly respected by the two males.

"A cousin of a cousin was kidnapped," the horsewoman continued. "Years ago. She found her way home last spring, a widow mourning her mate."

"She was force-mated with a Sea Scourge pirate?" Elsabeth asked, appalled for the poor woman.

Cambria tore the last of the meat from a leg bone before throwing it into the blazing fire. "Not forced. She found love."

"There have been stories of such matches with the Sea Scourge," Tao said to Elsabeth. "Rare, but they do exist. We know little of the pirates."

Pax's mouth tipped into a conspiratorial smile. "You knew of Commander Yarr."

"Furs," Tao spat. "I sure as hell did. That scoundrel Yarr." He turned toward Elsabeth to explain, to include her in the men's exchange. "Yarr is the Scourge captain of their largest fleet. Part Gorr, part human, like all Scourge are, but he was too resilient, too arrogant, too clever a tactician to ignore. Any units I positioned close to the sea, he plundered. If not for my hands being tied fighting the Gorr, I'd have sent my entire legion after him to teach the no-good thief a lesson."

"He'd have loved the attention, Tao, proof that he got your goat. And he still would have gotten away," Pax said.

"Likely so."

The Riders and Tao shared a hearty laugh. Elsabeth felt a little more like a Kurel amongst warriors then, not quite belonging, even though Tao's fingers lightly touched her back or her arm from time to time, reminding her they were a team.

If not a couple.

The third rider, Kato, winced a bit as his laughter subsided. Young and almost as attractive as Pax, with tattooed swirls over each pectoral, he sat with a protective hand covering his right side. "May I see?" she asked.

The Rider frowned in surprise. "It's fine."

"That's what you all say. You're injured. That's clear. Have you treated the wound?"

Kato exchanged an evasive glance with the other two.

"The Kurel are master healers," Tao reminded them.

"I'm not," Elsabeth assured them. "But my father was. He taught me a little. I can manage field medicine." She coaxed Kato to lift his hand and then the hem of his sturdy leather vest.

A purple-and-red bruise marred the right side of his torso. The welt was oozing pus. "Mercy. It's infected." She crouched next to him and felt his forehead. "You have a slight fever. You'll want to take care of this, or you'll soon be too sick to ride."

She met the Rider's gaze. A slight smile had curved his lips as he looked up at her, a flirting sparkle in his dark eyes. He inhaled through his nose, as if savoring her scent. "I'll need some tender care."

Behind her, she heard Tao standing up, the crunch of his boots as he walked closer and dropped the kit Chun had given them next to her right side. She could only imagine his expression, for the Rider was suddenly not meeting her eyes, his face as neutral as a Kurel's. She ignored all of them as she began to work, cleaning the wound, then handing Kato a small vial of pills. "Take one now, then each morning with breakfast."

"Thank you," he said.

Pax nodded with approval. "Your woman is a fine healer, Tao."

Tao didn't correct his friend's assumption that they were a couple, saying only, "She is a woman of many talents."

Pax rose to his feet, and the others followed suit. "We have to press onward tonight, my friend. We have many clicks to cover before our journey ends."

"Why did you come here, Pax?"

"Why do you think? To see how many horses you Tassagons have."

"You didn't take any with you this time," Tao said dryly.

"Not this time." Pax smiled but his eyes were somehow harder. "But with winter coming, it's good to know the state of the herds of our neighbors."

Elsabeth had learned long ago that the original sire of all the horse-breeding stock on the planet had come from the Riders. They were the ancestors of the Old Colony's ranchers and farmers who refused to align with either Tassagon or Kurel. They followed the ways of the warrior, like the Tassagons, and didn't fear science, like the Kurel. Their own unique, fierce independence set them apart from both of the other tribes.

Tao placed his hand on the Rider leader's shoulder. "I will leave you with a warning, my friend, and not about the horses. Xim, the Tassagon king, has dreams of sending in the army, my army, to take over your lands."

"What is this?" Pax was suddenly livid, his face turning hard. The moonlight caught the swirl of his tattoos and made them glow.

"When he's taken the Riders, he'll go after the Kurel of the Barrier Peaks after that. His goal is to rule over all humans."

"He will never…"

"Do not underestimate the man," Tao warned. "I did, and look where I am—on the run, hiding out in the wilds while he hunts for me." He pressed his fist to his chest in a gesture of solidarity. "Pax, I'm telling you this for one reason only. If the Tassagonian army marches against you, know that it's not commanded by me, nor even marching with the will of all Tassagons, but by the order of one man with misplaced ambition."

"I am grateful for the warning, my friend. I'll bring

the knowledge back to my people. We'll be ready, come spring."

"By then I hope we no longer have to worry about Xim," Elsabeth seethed. The open exchange of information this evening required no less than complete honesty from her. "He'll be off the throne for good."

Pax's brows lifted at her ferocity.

"Preferably, neutralized," Tao qualified, stroking his hand down her arm in a move meant to be either soothing or restraining. "After we've removed Uhr-Beck as an influence."

Xim deserved worse than that. He deserved what he'd handed out to her parents—an untimely death in the streets like a dog. She pressed her fists against her sides to keep from further debate, understanding the message in Tao's touch. Now wasn't the time.

"Fiery, yes," Pax murmured, observing her banked hostility. "Kurel have changed since I last encountered any. Requiring a Tassagon to pull them back from the brink of war."

"Elsabeth isn't a typical Kurel," Tao muttered.

"I don't want a war. My fight is against only one man," she argued. "Xim. My people have suffered enough."

"Elsabeth is quietly leading a secret rebellion— ghetto-dwelling Kurel against Xim's reign," Tao explained. "But the more the king acts out against them, the more Kurel will turn to ways of open violence to solve the problem. If it's the last thing I do on this world, I'll keep war from starting."

If humans turn on each other, darkness will consume us and we will be lost to Uhrth forever. Tao was the light. Impulsively, she found his hand, squeezing it. He slipped warm calloused fingers between hers.

Pax addressed Elsabeth. "If I were to choose any ally in all the lands, it would be Tao. He's legendary amongst the Riders. And amongst the Gorr. They more than fear him, they respect him. He drove them into hiding—and then some, until they were running with only the fur on their backs as protection. In all of history, he's been the only one to do it. You are fortunate to have this man as your friend."

"I know I am," Elsabeth said firmly. The Riders' deep respect for Tao touched her. They proved that she and Markam had been right about the general. As long as he lived, so did the hope of peace. He might be too humble to seek credit, but he was in fact a great man. A legend in the flesh.

"But, before I leave, you need a real bow, my friend." Pax handed Tao his weapon and some arrows, explaining the gift with a pitying look at Tao's homemade version.

"And spirits, too." Cambria placed a small, sweating jug in Elsabeth's hands. "It will chase away the cold."

The Riders mounted their horses with as much ease

and grace as she'd ever witnessed, setting out across the moonlight-soaked plains. Even the buttermilk mare lifted her head to watch them until they were no more.

Elsabeth became aware of the jug in her hands. "These spirits of theirs chase away the cold? It's a mild night, but not too mild for a taste, I think."

"It will indeed keep a man warm."

"And a woman, too," she insisted, thinking of Cambria and how she rode with the men of her tribe as an equal.

"Right, you are. Blue Hills spirits—the great equalizer. No one walks away from a night spent drinking this wicked stuff, man or woman." Tao took the jug and uncorked it, holding it close for her to take a sniff. The fumes made her cough and immediately set her eyes to watering.

Tao's grin glowed in the moonlight. Clearly, her reaction amused him. "It doesn't seem so bad," she lied.

"We will see." He sat on the log by the fire, patting the spot next to him for her to join him. "Until I tasted your Kurel cooking, these spirits were the only thing capable of reducing me to tears." He poured a very small amount in each of their water cups. He tapped his cup against hers then threw the contents of his into his mouth, exhaling in a wheeze. "Just right," he said, a teasing reminder of the time he'd first sampled her spiced stew. "Go on. See if you don't agree."

"We Kurel are immune to fiery food and drink."

"But not Blue Hills spirits."

"Pash." She took another sniff of the clear liquid swirling on the bottom of the cup, and blinked away the sting. "Our babies could sip this."

"It seems to me from the amount of time you've spent talking and not drinking, that you're afraid to. Typical Kurel reaction." Folding his arms, he lifted his brows, his amused expression a study in condescension.

She'd show this smug Tassagon—and those Riders. She wouldn't let the Kurel people down. She braced herself, then poured the liquid down her throat. It burned her tongue and then her nose, from the inside out. Blinking away tears, she composed herself, careful not to show any emotion. "Not bad," she said, taking their cups and placing them on the ground. "But sumsala burns more—"

Vertigo hit as she sat up, her head whirling before it righted itself. She swung her arm out to grab hold of Tao. He looped an arm around her, laughing at her dismay, his eyes shining.

"Mercy," she rasped. "That's strong."

"Now, imagine my men and I trapped in a cave with Pax and his band of hunters, waiting out that snowstorm, sipping spirits to stay warm. Those Riders, they can make a party out of the most severe conditions." He chuckled, steadying her with his hand pressed firmly to her back, his thumb rotating a scant inch above the swell of her bottom. It felt quite nice, that. She also liked the way the spirits had left her feeling so light. Lighter than air.

"Riders." She sighed. "I never imagined I'd see them in the flesh. I never imagined any of this. I dreamed of it, though."

"This is what happens when you pull your nose out from books. You *live*."

"For an Uhr, maybe. For a Kurel woman, living means a life spent inside the ghetto walls." Tao's fingers continued to move at the base of her spine. Every time they did, she shivered. "Sometimes I wish I never aspired for more."

One of the logs broke apart, spilling red-hot coals. Embers soared into the air. She tipped back her head, following them until they winked out high above her head, and then she threw her gaze even farther, to the stars and beyond, past heaven where all the souls lived to Uhrth itself and the mysterious origins of the founders of this world. Who were they really, and why had they chosen to colonize this world? *Did they forsake us, or did we simply become lost?* "I'd board an ark," she confessed. "I would. I'd sail away across that sea."

"You'd die willingly and without reason?" The concept seemed to stagger him. "Sorry, but that will never happen. If I have to stay by you every minute of every day and night to keep you from taking your life, I will."

A familiar inner shiver warmed her at the thought of him being with her around the clock. A few ways he could keep her heart beating came to mind. "No. Not that. Of course not. I mean an ark—a real ark. They really existed."

His sniff was one of faint exasperation. "And you think we Tassagons are silly, believing in the reading of bones."

She lowered her voice although there was no one else there to hear. "Gwendolyn says there are arks stored in the caves deep below the Barrier Peaks. She's never seen any, but her grandmother did. There are arks in the caves, and more. Things from the Old Colony. Hidden ever since."

With his amulet glittering in the moonlight, Tao took in the information with part disbelief, part calculating interest, as if she were describing the number of weapons in an unexpected cache. A pang of doubt reminded her that he was indeed still a Tassagon and she a Kurel, that their tribes were enemies at worst, wary neighbors at best. It wasn't her place to divulge such sensitive secrets.

No. She trusted him, or she wouldn't be with him

now, alone on a ridge in the wilds, watching the moon climb higher in a star-filled sky.

He could have asked her about the items stored in those caves, and about what use avowed pacifists would have for them. Instead he asked, "You said you wish you never aspired for more than the life you were born to. Why?"

"Sometimes it's better not to know there's more. You can't hunger for what you never knew you wanted." She waved a hand at the valley, stopping short of doing the same to him. Tao had been as much of an unexpected adventure as leaving the city. "But it's too late for that. Now I'll never be able to forget the things I want."

Tao threw one leg over the log to face her. "Like this Tassagon?"

"My, you do have an ego larger than the kingdom."

His quick, surprised laugh rang out in the hushed night. "Is that so?"

"Yes." She emphasized the remark with a sassy swing of her hair. "Just because I suggested kissing lessons doesn't mean I hunger for you."

"But you do." He lowered his head to brush his lips over hers. A slow and tender exploration.

Her tingles became a roaring blaze. "Earlier, you said it would be dangerous to think of me overly much tonight. This isn't helping."

With a shudder, he moved back, his gaze regretful.

"Stopping isn't easy to do, my sweet Elsabeth. Take advantage of my self-control and go to bed, if you know what's good for you."

He left her sitting on the log, burning for him, cursing the fact that she'd reminded him of their unspoken, mutual decision to not end up in the same bedroll. "I know what's good for me." She followed him to where he was spreading out his blanket to sleep, setting his blade and the bow and arrows within hand's reach. "You are. Tao, I want you. I want to be with you tonight."

"You've never been with a man before—" he turned to look at her "—have you?"

She shook her head. "I'd like to, though. You can teach me." She held her breath for a heartbeat, afraid her Kurel frankness was not the right language for seduction.

But Tao let out another quiet, almost defeated laugh that gave her hope she was chipping away at his defenses. He stood, his arms hanging at his sides. "Elsabeth, you have your Kurel values. I don't want to compromise them. I've…worked very, very hard not to these past weeks." His blunt admission and the heat in his gaze hinted at the cost of his struggle. "You heard what Marina said. I saw your shame at your Tassagon blood. Don't do something you'll regret later."

She stepped closer. "I'm beginning to think my Tassagon blood is one of the best things about me." Her fingers went to the top button on her blouse, releasing it with her thumbnail.

"Great Uhrth," he muttered as she undid the next one.

He snatched her hand. His palm was roughened and hotter than Kato's fevered brow. "I fear I'm beginning to believe your Tassagon blood is the best thing about you, too."

The pause was deep, breathless, as if everything in the universe had stopped, waiting to see if he'd accept the honest, yearning invitation in her eyes. *I want this, Tao. I want you.*

He nodded once. Then, with a very male, considering smile, he lifted her hand to his lips and pressed his mouth to the inside of her wrist. "But, I also admire your Kurel blood," he said, kissing her pulse then the heel of her thumb, his whiskers prickling her tender skin. "In fact, I like just about everything about you."

He sat down on the blanket and pulled her with him, onto his lap. "How you smell and how you taste…" He kissed her as he spoke, working his way along her jaw to her ear. "And how every time you lift your dress and oh-so-innocently give me a peek at your legs. I like that…" His hand swept along the length of her body and slipped under the hem of her skirt. "These gorgeous, long legs." His hot hand dipped under her knee, lifting her leg as he bent to playfully kiss her kneecap, then that traveling hand continued on, up under her thigh and higher, his thumb swiping over her hipbone.

He lowered her to her back, replacing that clever hand with his lips. Her head spun, her body throbbing. She'd thought the Rider's spirits had been disorienting, but it wasn't even close compared with Tao's mouth on her skin. He moved dangerously close to her privates, and she startled, but he was already in retreat, maybe remembering she wasn't like his dancers. All this was new to her. Exhilarating, but still new.

He came up on his knees and grabbed her hands, pulling her upright to sit. She buried her face in the warm hollow of his neck, her arms wrapped over his shoulders. "I want you naked," he murmured in her ear.

She trembled. Smiled. "Only if you're naked, too."

"Oh, I intend to be. After waiting so long for this—for you—you'd better believe I won't miss lying with you, skin against skin."

Skin to skin.

Finally.

He unbuttoned his shirt as she sat there, watching, her legs splayed on each side of his knees. Awkward in her nervousness, she helped him slide the shirt off his shoulders. Hers was not the practiced, erotic disrobing of a concubine. But if the heat in his eyes was to be believed, her tentative moves had aroused him all the same. Maybe even more so, she wanted to believe. She wanted to be more to him than those girls. She wanted him to remember this as she certainly would.

With his hands busy unbuckling his belt, she reached up and touched her finger to the very center of his chest, the hollow between his pectorals, and slid her finger downward, tracing a scar here and there until she'd reached his hands, now frozen in the act of unfastening his belt. Her touch seemed to have had the most amazing effect. Goose bumps had appeared on his body despite the warmth of the fire, his nipples contracting as if he'd dipped into a cold pond. Fascinating. "You're beautiful," she whispered. A beautiful man.

He chuckled, shaking his head but appearing mightily pleased. "That's the first time anyone's called me that."

She smiled back. "I'm glad I can be your first time for something."

Emotion played over his face, honest and raw. "You'll be a first for me in more ways than that, sweetheart. I have the feeling you'll continue to be." He yanked open his belt, shoving down his trousers and undershorts in one sweep. His manhood sprang free, capturing her entire focus even as he discarded his clothes without a care, a man clearly not shy about being naked.

Down he came, lowering his body to lie next to her.

Propping his head on his hand, he smiled. "You're wearing a lot of clothes, Elsabeth."

"I hope that's a complaint."

Two fingers walked to her blouse until they found the topmost of the still-fastened buttons. The delicate pearl would have no chance against that determined hand. Yet, he didn't do as she'd expected.

He began to move his flattened hand over her blouse, finding the swell of her breasts. With the fabric between his skin and hers, he caressed her, molding one breast until it ached for more. More what? The sharp feel of his skin, his mouth. She was suddenly aching to be suckled, a craving that had never filled her mind before.

As if he'd guessed, or he'd interpreted her arching back or little mewling cries as encouragement, he coaxed one hardened nipple into his mouth, suckling her through the fabric of her blouse and the camisole underneath, leaving a chill behind with dampness when he moved to her other breast to pay it equal attention. She didn't remember digging into his bare back with one hand, or practically tugging on his hair with her other, but he almost had to untangle himself to lift up over her on all fours.

On his hands and knees, he smiled down at her. "You still have too many clothes on."

She laughed. "All right then. I'll help remove them." She reached for the buttons, but he stopped her.

"I need no help." His green eyes glittered with desire and mischief. "Do you think I need help?"

"I'll withhold judgment until I see how much longer you stay naked and I remain completely dressed."

"Elsabeth, Elsabeth." He shook his head. "I thought you were a woman of patience." He uttered the teasing words as his hand found its way under her skirt again, traveling under her petticoat until it stopped, cupping her mound, where she'd grown damp and throbbing. This time, she didn't jolt at his touch.

His gaze turned knowing. "You must know your patience will be rewarded." His thumb, the very tip of the pad, found and circled over her exquisitely sensitive nub.

It left her breathless; there was no more air. His touch conjured a deep, delicious ache that swiftly built, her pulse drumming deep inside her, an urgent sensation that needed to be satisfied.

Soon.

Now. She arched into his hand and moaned.

Then his hand was gone, and he was sitting up over her, magnificent in the moonlight, a silvered warrior with an eager, boyish smile. She protested, trying to draw him back to her. "But I liked that. What you were doing."

"I know you did." He took each of her hands and placed them back on the blanket above her head. "I told you. Your patience will be rewarded."

What now? Preparing to make love had so far been a lovely, delicious surprise, nothing like what she'd thought. She'd read her share of romantic books, spoken openly with other, more experienced women, and had come to the expectation that her first experience would be sweet and over quickly. Enjoyable, yes, but gone too fast, like a slice of fruit pie in summer, devoured. But this…it was a long, sensual, feast, every moment drawn out and savored.

"This is getting in the way," Tao said and reached for the buttons of her blouse. As she smiled up at him, he undid the next button and slowly made his way down the row to the hem, as she lay there helpless to do anything but watch. When she did try, he'd shake his head with mock exasperation and place her hands back by her head.

With the utmost of care, he opened her blouse, then unlaced her camisole, her breath hitching as he exposed her to the cool air. He admired her with hungry eyes and leaned down to tug at the lacy strap of her undergarment with his teeth. "I do like Kurel unmentionables. Dainty. Far better looking on you than hanging in that shop."

"Is my patience to be rewarded?" she whispered.

"Oh, sweetheart." He laughed quietly. "Like you won't believe." He leaned down closer. "Mine, too," he promised and captured her mouth, the kiss hungry, their hands searching, stroking, her legs coming up to hold him close.

"Wait," he said after a long while, sounding as if he'd run a mile. "There's more work to be done."

"What? This is like work? I suppose, if you're making a *deliberate effort*."

He answered with a darkly amused glance. She'd not let him forget his ridiculous views on love and marriage. "If you're not going to be patient, Elsabeth…"

"I will." She went still, every inch of her straining for his touch, craving him. Despite the night air, perspiration had dampened her skin. And his, as well. He was engorged, fully erect, yet he was so…in control. How did he manage it? Then she remembered this was the same man who'd pulled himself out of a moat in the throes of agony. Self-control, self-discipline, was something he possessed in spades.

Acting as if he were enjoying every new inch of skin bared, he unfastened her skirt, throwing it off and away. Together they stripped off the remaining undergarments. Her reward, another kiss, his hands angling her head to kiss her long and well. Warm skin, his scent, the scrape of his whispers, the bulge of muscle moving under smooth skin—she savored him, every taste, every touch. Then he was caressing her again, between her legs, a purposeful but gentle circling.

The luscious pressure built, a quickening, and she knew this time he wouldn't stop. He prolonged the pleasure, ignoring her pleas for completion, for consummation, her moans and arching hips all the cues he seemed to need, until he gently thrust his fingers inside her and the building tension finally shattered, her body squeezing, pulsing.

He caught her soft cry with his mouth, soothing her, praising her. "I want you so badly, Elsabeth," he murmured in her ear, releasing more quivers inside her. "More than you can know."

She whispered back, "Then let me know."

He laughed as he lifted up over her, his shoulders bunched, his back tight and hard and moist with sweat. With his knee he coaxed her thighs apart. "We will go very, very slow."

"Not too slow…"

"Patience," he said, "will be rewarded."

His hard body trembled, muscles shifting as he bore his weight on his arms to enter her body, one exhilarating inch at a time, until he was fully inside her. A luscious, complete, indescribable fullness. She was shaking, inside and out.

"Mercy," she whispered.

"Are you all right?" His voice sounded strained. Thicker.

"By the arks, yes. I had no idea it was this good…"

"It gets better," he promised.

And it did. Her breath hitched as he began to move his hips, a deep, slow, rolling motion. He made love to her with banked passion, and the more he moved, the more she wanted him; with each measured stroke, her body responded.

"Ah, Beth," he said, tightly. "You were worth the wait."

He kissed her, long and hard, seeming to lose himself in her for a moment, becoming more passionate, fevered. Then his body shook as he tried to rein himself in, his muscles bunching in his effort to hold back.

But she didn't want him acting as if she was fragile. He was the epitome of self-control in all things. *Please, not with me, Tao.* "Don't stop," she whispered.

"You'll be sore."

She protested, but he kissed her into silence. "No," he said. "Next time, or the time after that."

Tao was determined to hold fast to that promise. Fists clenched atop the blanket, he fought to hold off the explosion he knew was coming. He didn't want to make her sore. Already his loins had begun to clench with the heavy, potent pleasure-pain he knew preceded release. He locked his jaw, wanting to give her what he'd never given any other, his whole self, not just his body and experience. Only with her did he crave such a bond that seemed to rise above the joy of physical sex somehow, turning it into something far more.

With each stroke, her body responded, clutching him, her inner muscles convulsing wetly. Then she cried out, a throaty plea. That he could give this sweet girl such satisfaction magnified his own, and what was left of his discipline went up in a blaze of pleasure.

He pushed up on rigid arms, his back arching, a low groan of pleasure slipping from his throat. One, two jerks of his hips and he pulled out, barely in time, and rolled away, onto his side.

He hauled her against him, his thigh resting heavily across hers. They lay quietly, no words to express the pleasure they'd discovered in each other's arms, and could only kiss and stroke and nuzzle, holding each other close until their spent bodies had stopped trembling.

After a while, Tao lifted up on an elbow, drawing the blanket over them. The fire had burned way down, but he wasn't of the mind to add more logs just yet. Elsabeth felt too damn good lying next to him, and looked too good, too, lush and naked, and satisfied. *His.* He was her first. She'd chosen him to be. No elders had required them to wed. No families had arranged a formal wedding night between man and virgin bride. No, Elsabeth had wanted him, simply him. His chest tightened, and an odd feeling of lightness swept through him.

Her cheeks were flushed pink, and her lips were puffy. Damp curls framed her face. He drew a finger down along her temple, coiling the tendrils of damp hair and letting them spring back to their corkscrew shape.

"What's that smile for?" she murmured. "It looks sweet, and silly."

"Silly?" He gave his head a shake. "Maybe so. I was remembering the day you cooked breakfast for me, that first morning in your house. I imagined you'd look just like this—naked, with your hair spread out, all your curls—after I made love to you."

Her eyes turned a soft, summer-day blue, the kind of afternoon where you could lose yourself in the expanse of the sky.

The kind of day he'd experienced too few times in his life, and usually at times when he couldn't afford to turn his attention to anything else but war.

Even now, knowing they were fairly protected up on the ridge, in the trees, he couldn't forget they were at risk. While there were no Gorr to worry about, other dangers existed.

But his bow was within reach, and so was his blade. He could savor this a little longer.

"It was good, Tao."

Her frankness touched him as well as amused him, but at least he would always know where he stood with her. "It was indeed good, sweet Kurel girl." He leaned over her to whisper in her ear. "I'll look forward to the next time. It will get better and better for you."

Her gaze turned questioning. "And for you, right?"

"It's already good."

A funny look came over her face, and she flipped

onto her stomach, resting her head on her folded arm. "You've been with so many women."

He choked out a laugh then saw she was serious. "Not that many. I mean, I've had my share, but others have partaken of far more bed partners than I."

She was drawing circles in the dirt with her fingertip. "Were they skillful? Did they know what to do to drive you crazy?"

"Drive me crazy? Elsabeth, what are you talking about?" He rolled her over, pinning her hands by the wrists. "I don't understand."

"I'm inexperienced."

"You are fantastic," he argued. "I'd change nothing about tonight."

"But those women…"

"Those women were nothing to me. Wait—yes, they were. All of them."

She strained up against his hold. "What?"

"Because of them, I learned how to give pleasure as a lover. Without a past, I wouldn't have had the skills I accumulated to share with you. To make it better for you."

She smiled up at him. "A very good answer, Tassagon."

He grinned, dropping down to kiss her on the forehead. "And it's the truth." He got up, padding around the campsite to stoke the fire, taking another look around for threats and adding Elsabeth's blanket to his. "You're sleeping with me."

"I'm so tired," she mumbled sleepily, cuddling close in the shelter of his arms as he lay on his back under the covers. She let out a shuddering yawn. "I never knew lovemaking was so utterly exhausting."

He drew her close. "See? Not everything can be learned from books."

"You're exactly right."

He couldn't believe it. She actually agreed with him. Or, more accurately, she was so tired the fight had gone out of her. He'd have to remember the technique for the future. Exhaust her in bed to ensure victory in a debate.

A few more moments went by, and he felt her fall asleep. He lay there, marveling at the moon and the stars, listening to the crackling fire and her quiet breaths. Up on that ridge overlooking the Plains with Elsabeth asleep in his arms, he was, without a doubt, the closest to heaven he'd ever been.

"IF TAO IS STILL ALIVE, I know how to find him."

Xim's hand was unsteady as he lowered his goblet of wine and tried to focus on Beck's face. Hours of drinking had so far failed to mute his frustration at coming away from the ghetto empty-handed.

At this late hour, his study was hollow, silent. Smoky torches had formed a roiling haze near the ceiling.

Markam was off somewhere, making his rounds of the palace sentries as usual. The man had no idea how to do anything other than military routines. But Beck had showed up despite the late hour to sit vigil with him, understanding his anger at the failed search. "How, Beck? Everything else we've tried has failed. Maybe the priest was wrong." Xim made the sign of Uhrth over his chest to counteract the blasphemous statement. "We've been wasting our time and Uhr-Tao is dead."

"Do you take that chance when he could be out there, plotting against you, building his power base? Sending spies to turn the army against you? His officers show no signs of mutiny, but they'd turn on you in a second if their general returned and took charge."

"Enough!" Xim slammed his hand down on the table. His goblet bounded. Wine splashed onto the wood like spilled blood. "If you know how to find Tao, tell me."

Beck tossed back the last of his goblet's contents and dragged an arm across his mouth. "My Liege, I actually have to show you." His eye shifted side to side. "I don't know who may be listening. Markam has no stomach for my harsh measures, but we both know that desperate times often call for such methods."

Xim waved a hand at the colonel. "Show me then."

Beck nodded. "In the morning."

"No. Now." He pushed upright. It set his brains to

spinning. He winced, growling. "If this turns out to be frivolous, Beck, some silly half-baked scheme, I swear I'll demote you and put you out to pasture for good. You and Markam both. My two top officers—useless fools!"

Beck's smile was slow. "I don't think you'll agree after you see what I've procured for you, My Liege."

Xim grumbled as he followed the colonel through the deserted hallways, then down the stairs to the lower level. Beck paused there to light a torch.

"Where are we going—to the dungeon?"

"The old wing, actually." Beck unlocked a heavy door, allowing Xim to walk through. "The stink of the pipes is so bad down here you can't hardly smell them."

"Smell what?" Xim sniffed. The sour smell of the pipes was underlain with an unpleasant odor of musk. "What is that, animals making their nests down here?"

"Gorr, My Liege. Four little Furs."

"Here? In the palace?" Xim jumped back, scouring the shadows for monsters. He didn't even know what they looked like. "What the hell are we doing with them locked up so close to me? They're deadly."

"But not invincible. They can be captured and caged like any other creature."

"Oh." Xim was shaking. His mouth had gone completely dry. His bladder felt ready to empty. "They can't get out?"

Beck's eye narrowed. "Do you think I'd risk your life in such a cavalier fashion? Any of our lives? Your family?"

Xim felt foolish for overreacting. But Gorr—here— he was afraid. To his further terror, he could hear shuffling from the cell down the dim hallway, and a scrape like claws on rock. The cloying, musky scent had grown sharper. "How did you get them?"

"I had reports of wild dogs attacking cattle. I sent out a patrol, and they found these four Furs. Spies, probably, thinking they could come in, have a look around, and get back to the Hinterlands without being noticed. Maybe they would have, but they were in pretty bad shape. Emaciated. Starving." Beck tossed his head in the direction of the disturbing noises "Don't you want to see? It's safe, as long as you don't look directly at them. And they can shut it off, the charming, if they want to. If they're not planning to attack."

"What is your plan?" Xim all but whispered, desperate to leave the dark, stinking dungeon.

"Release one of them. Send it out to hunt down Tao. If it's successful, if it brings back proof of the kill, we'll release its packmates. If not, well, we were going to kill them anyway." Beck raised his torch high. "Isn't that right, my pups? We have an agreement, don't we?

I release your captain, and if he returns successful, the rest can go free."

Suddenly, a horrible snarling filled the stone corridor, the sound of something hitting the bars of the cell he couldn't see. It speared Xim's heart with mortal terror. "How do you know it'll cooperate, if you let one out?"

Out of sight, a rumbling, monotone voice answered, "If I say I will do, human, I will do."

Xim jumped backward, slamming into the wall. "They speak!"

"The alphas can. We've shared this planet long enough for them to learn the language."

Xim swallowed hard, afraid to say anything now lest he be overheard. These creatures weren't mindless. It made them even more terrifying.

To his relief, Beck led him back to the stairs. "Will they cooperate? You heard it—yes." His mouth spread into a grin. "If there's anything I learned in my years in the Hinterlands fighting the Furs, it's how loyal they are. The pack is everything. They're bonded until death." The colonel pulled a wadded-up piece of cloth from his coat pocket. As he shook it open, Xim saw it was a sleeve torn from one of Uhr-Tao's uniform shirts. "From Uhr-Tao's trunk. A Gorr's sense of smell is infallible. They can scent prey from miles away. If General Tao is anywhere in the kingdom, our furry little friends will find him." Beck pressed his lips together for a moment, regretful. "They hate Tao, these Furs do. He killed countless thousands of their kind. If they find him, they'll shred him. He'll be dead just as you wanted, only you won't have the pleasure of seeing it accomplished. My Liege, all you have to do is say the word, and I'll send out the assassin."

Beck held the torch high. To Xim it seemed the warrior's eye could charm like a Gorr's, because as he stared at him, waiting for his answer, he couldn't summon the strength to look away.

ELSABETH WOKE TO THE gritty sound of Tao's boots on the dirt. She sat up, squinting in the dawn light, her hair in disarray as she hugged her blanket around her. He'd already rekindled the fire. It crackled under a small kettle.

"Is that tea?" she said hopefully.

"It will be. The water's not yet boiling." He crouched in front of her, smiling with his eyes, as if her appearance amused him. Unlike her, he wasn't at all disheveled. He was washed, brushed, dressed and ready for the day.

Just like a general.

An adorable, sexy general.

"Good morning, Sunshine," he said and leaned closer to kiss her smiling lips. Her body felt battered from yesterday's long ride and then the lovemaking, yet with that single kiss, passion flared. She'd gladly forget about her aches and pains to stay abed with Tao.

But the ghetto had been searched; they didn't yet know the results. They had to return home.

He ruffled her hair. "Get dressed. We move out after breakfast." He returned to the fire, and she saw he'd left her clothing by the blanket, a neat, square pile, folded and ready, along with a damp cloth and a cake of soap for freshening up. Laughing softly at his efficiency, she reached for her camisole and proceeded to dress.

CHAPTER TWENTY-THREE

"TELL ME ONE, TAO. Just one story before we sleep."

Tao chuckled at Elsabeth's request as he climbed into his bed behind the screen in her living room, dressed in pajama pants for modesty in the event of unexpected visitors. It was the end of another very long day, a reversal of the journey of the day before, culminating in an uneventful return to the ghetto through the spy deck, where they'd been met by Navi and the cart. "Only Markam and Beck came through the gates to search," the boy had told them. "You should have seen Beck, how scared he was. Especially when Elder Farouk demanded to know what they were doing here." Needless to say, the pair hadn't stayed long in K-Town. Tao hoped it meant the suspicion that he was hiding amongst the Kurel had now passed.

Still, there had been no communication from Markam. No flags of any color had arrived in the aviary. What did the silence mean? Tao was doing his damnedest to think of every possible ramification.

A whiff of Elsabeth's clean, lightly perfumed skin dragged him back from his thoughts. She'd walked up to the bed, her expression vexed. Her white nightgown was conservative and yet incredibly arousing—the white fabric reached to practically her neck, but it was charmingly, innocently and quite unintentionally, he was sure, almost transparent if the light hit right. As luck would have it, in that moment the light was hitting just right. He could see her slender form right through the garment, from the outline of her breasts to the curve of her waist and the sweet place between her thighs that made his loins ache in anticipation of making love to her again.

"Tao." She fell to the edge of the bed in a cloud of white cotton, her lips pursed. "It's like you're looking straight through me."

"Straight through your nightgown, actually." Before she had the chance to blush too crimson, he grabbed her wrist and pulled her down to him. "Lucky for both of us you always wore a robe before." He kissed the giggle from her lips then pulled her fully onto the narrow bed. "You asked for a story? I have mastered *Ben's Lost Dog*."

He'd remembered the sounds of the various letters she'd taught him before their trek. The remainder they'd practiced after dinner—at his request. It had given him all the knowledge he'd needed to read the simple, one-syllable words in that inane book for babes. He wanted to move on to more adult fare, and see if he could actually unlock the secret to enjoying reading, as she had. But in the immediate moment he'd found another, definitely adult, pastime he liked far more.

He smoothed a hand over her hip and thigh, reaching behind her knee to pull her leg over his, a better position to cup her perfectly rounded bottom. She was grinning, her eyes sparkling. "Tell me about your relic from the Sea of Glass." Her fingers skimmed along his shoulder and across his collarbone until they found his dangling amulet. "You never explained how it protects you. How do you know it's good luck?"

"Ah, an excellent question. However, not all my adventures were exciting in a good way. The very afternoon I tied it around my neck, I was standing on a ridgeline. My focus was carelessly on only the view through my spyglass. It was high summer in the Hinterlands, the suns were brutal. I felt a sudden burning below my collarbone. 'A bee sting?' I thought. I bent down to have a look and an arrow flew over my head so close I could feel the wind of it in my hair."

She tensed. "By the arks, Tao," she breathed.

"Yes, by the arks—almost literally. Had it not been for the amulet heating in the suns, I would have set sail for the heavens with Uhrth's angels. I'd have taken that arrow right between the eyes. It's protected me in countless other ways over the years."

She whispered, "No more of those stories tonight."

"No more, indeed." He rolled her on top of him, her hair spilling forward, forming a fragrant curtain around their faces. "We have a better tale to tell tonight," he said, and pulled her down to his mouth.

As soon as they began to kiss, he knew their exhaustion wouldn't hold them back from making love. Passion had rekindled too quickly. Together they reached for her billowing nightgown, flinging it to the floor, where his pants soon landed in a pile.

He kissed every inch of her, loving the way she hungered for him so openly, eagerly, none of her actions artful or practiced, her reason for being with him simple: she didn't want to be with anyone else. He knew it was so because he felt the same.

When he rolled her beneath him to complete the act, he was still gentle, but not as careful as the first time, moving against her in just the right way, until her gasp of delight and the shudders inside her body told him she'd peaked. She clung to him until his own pleasure left him shaking with exhaustion and wonder.

HOURS AFTER THEY'D dressed and gone back to bed, Tao woke in a sweat, his heart pounding, gripped by a sense of dread left behind from a nightmare he couldn't seem to remember, a dream so vivid he could smell the musky odor of Gorr. From up in the aviary came the sounds of cooing pigeons and the hatch banging in the wind. That's what had woken him. He needed to fix that damn door.

Elsabeth protested his restlessness with a sleepy murmur. He rolled onto his back, drawing her into the protection of his arms, and shut his eyes.

A whiff of a sickeningly familiar odor called him back from the edge of sleep. Alarm burst inside him. *Gorr.*

Elsabeth woke to the press of Tao's hand and the sound of her own smothered gasp.

Be silent. There was no mistaking his intent. There was enough moonlight from outside for her to discern his face. His eyes were dangerous, his face beaded with sweat.

Above their heads, a crash.

Tao's quick reflexes had them both off the bed and on the floor before she realized the crash had come from the roof.

Squawking pigeons and feathers fell from the opening to the eaves and the aviary. Tao's legs pumped in his effort to slide them backward on their rear ends to get distance between them and the bed, knocking over a table and footstool.

"Tao—"

"Gorr."

Terror came in a blinding rush of adrenaline. Gorr—*here?*

He shoved the legs of the footstool into her hands. "Take it. Use it as a shield." He yanked the crossbow off the wall above them. He'd barely gotten it loaded when something dark and heavy thudded onto the mattress, snarling.

It was in the room.

She sensed its power, a predatory menace. Her pulse throbbed in her throat. A sharp, gamy odor filled the air. Movement in the corner of her eye—a flash of fangs and a furred, muscular body like a forest dog but upright like a human. "Uhr-Tao," it said. "I smell you."

A pair of glowing eyes, slits of pale gold, flicked in their direction. Utter malevolence. This being sought only to harm, its stare bottomless, endless. She was falling into those eyes. So beautiful...

"Don't look at it!" Tao shoved her head to the side.

He lifted the crossbow and fired. In the small confines of the living area the arrow went wild and struck the wall. Tao had begun reloading the instant the arrow had left his weapon. Glass in a picture frame shattered as she heard the distinctive cocking of the crossbow mechanism. The creature leaped away agilely, snarling at Tao, or was it laughing? There was unexpected intelligence in that alien sound. Triumph. *Hatred.* It sprang again. Momentum carried its body toward her. She raised the stool, bracing for the impact.

Tao fired again. A moist *thwunk* told her the arrow had hit flesh. A shrieking caterwaul left her ears ringing.

The Gorr's momentum carried it toward them. It skidded over the floor, crashing into the footstool, almost wrenching it from her hands. Its claws scrabbled on the wood planks, a hairbreadth from her folded legs. Musk clogged her nostrils. She lifted the stool and slammed it down, hitting its squirming body.

It staggered away from her, then sprang across the room like a grassalope, leaving a black glistening trail. Blood.

The Gorr's breaths were wet, labored. Even in its agony, it hurled itself at the window with enough force to shatter the glass, leaping outside to the street.

"No!" Tao's shout was guttural, as if wrenched from someplace deep within. With his crossbow already reloaded, he shoved through the door in pursuit.

"Tao!" Her scream echoed in the empty room. Glass splinters pierced her hands and knees as she pushed upright, shards of it tinkling to the floor as she shoved her arms through the sleeves of her robe and followed Tao out the door.

The wounded Gorr was in the center of the street, howling, a terrible sound. Lights in windows up and down the street were turning on, heads appearing to see what had caused the commotion below.

"Don't look!" she cried to them. They'd be charmed

by the creature's eyes. What could it compel them to do, even in its dying moments? "Close your curtains!"

But no one took her warnings seriously, it seemed, just as she hadn't, after only hearing the tales of the power of a Gorr's stare.

Blood coated the Gorr's fangs as Tao advanced on him, the crossbow coming up, his face slanted away to prevent a direct meeting of the eyes. The Gorr extended his skinny arms to the sides as if in welcome. Tao took aim, and the Gorr filled its broken lungs to let out one last ear-splitting howl. Then it sprang at Tao.

An arrow pierced its neck, throwing the creature backward. Grim, Tao walked up to it and gave it a push with his toe to see if it was alive. The crossbow dangled from Tao's hand. He was naked from the waist up, smeared with sweat and blood. With his chest heaving, his eyes dark with the tension of battle, he looked part beast himself as he slowly turned to her.

We're alive. Her heart slammed against her ribs as she swayed on her feet. Then Tao was with her, his firm arm under hers. "You're bleeding," he said tightly, prying her rigid fingers from the leg of the footstool she'd forgotten she carried out with her.

"Just some broken glass…"

"Just?" Angrily, Tao flung the stool away then crushed her to his chest. "Beth, if it had killed you, I'd have gone back to war." His deep voice rumbled.

He spoke into her hair. "I'd have left this very day, and I'd not have stopped until I'd found every last one of them."

Her knees felt almost too weak to support her, but he'd half lifted her to her toes. "I'm sorry—I couldn't help it," she said, her voice a shaky whisper. "I couldn't look away."

"You'll know for next time."

"Next time?"

He cupped her face as he tipped his head to look into her eyes. "They always travel in packs."

CHAPTER TWENTY-FOUR

WORD OF THE GORR ATTACK raced through the ghetto like a torch touched to lamp oil. As the horizon silvered with the coming dawn, a bell clanged from the tallest windmill, issuing a warning.

"Keep calm." Tao was directing the crowd gathering outside Elsabeth's house. He'd grabbed the creature by its tail to drag it out of the street.

The Gorr had been a mature alpha, judging by its size and ability to speak the language. They were usually robust and muscular, but this one was practically fur and bones, half starved to death. He made the sign of Uhrth over his chest, brushing his fingertips over the amulet and bringing them briefly to his lips. It had not been his night to die, thank Uhrth, nor Elsabeth's. They owed the fact they were still alive to the Gorr's weakened condition—and also that loose hatch door, waking him in time. Now the question remained—was it a lone alpha? Rare, but possible due to the Gorr being in retreat. If there was a larger attack looming, there'd not be time to properly prepare anyway, but in the immediate moment, quelling panic was paramount. Else he'd not be able to teach these generations of pacifists how to set up a proper defense.

"Just a few cuts," Elsabeth said bravely as she emerged from the clinic, where Chun had treated her wounds. She'd changed out of her stained and torn nightgown into a plain, blue wool dress, her tangled hair twisted into a bun at the base of her neck. "The blood made it look worse. What about you?" She tried to pull his arm back to see his blood-spattered skin. He'd donned a coat over his bare chest, a hasty concession in deference to Kurel modesty. "Go see Chun," she said.

"I'm fine," he muttered, pulling free, the crossbow gripped tightly in one hand. He paused, seeing her dismayed expression. Didn't she know that when a general said he was fine, no one doubted his word? No one had fretted for him on the battlefield. "I really am," he assured her, gentler.

She was as pale as he'd ever seen her. "It killed two pigeons. Blood and feathers everywhere. The rest are uninjured, but agitated." She reminded him of a field captain reporting casualties—one who had suffered a great loss of troops.

She had no idea of how much life a battle could extinguish.

"Imagine that hundreds of Gorr had attacked in

the night, perhaps catching your regiment by surprise. Think of the lives lost, men you knew, friends, even family." He found her troubled gaze. "Is it so difficult to understand now why I went to war? And why hearing the Kurel call me a monster when these were the true monsters was so galling?" He gave the dead Gorr a shove with his boot. Those closest in the crowd took a collective step back. "Monsters I tried to keep from your doorstep," he added angrily. How did it get here—and with apparently single-minded purpose—to find him?

Nearly killing Elsabeth to get at him. The loss of her one life would have shattered him as the thousands of others had never completely done. Sliding his arm over her shoulders, he gathered her close. "I am sorry about the pigeons."

She shook her head. "No, you're right. They were birds. They could have been neighbors." She leaned into his embrace. "They could have been you."

He closed his eyes, murmured into her soft hair, "I didn't mean to lose my temper."

"You were worried."

More like terrified—of losing her. He also needed to let his anger go, and stop rubbing it in Elsabeth's face that she'd once thought he was a monster like the Gorr.

The elders arrived to view the scene. Farouk's distinctive hair bobbed like a ball of white fluff above the other heads. "Move aside. Let me through." He used his cane as a battering ram to push people aside until he had a clear view of the corpse.

The ancient viewed the dead monster, his gaze traveling from the Gorr's sharp, yellowed fangs to the furred limbs, the claws and whiplike tail, and the thick, callused pads on the feet that facilitated nimble travel without shoes.

As advanced as Farouk was in years and experience, he'd never laid eyes on a Gorr. It was obvious in the horrified amazement contorting his withered features.

He shifted his attention to Tao. "This is your area of expertise, not ours. Tell us what to do."

"Allow me to address the crowd."

"Do it."

Tao cupped his hands around his mouth, calling out, "We don't know if this Gorr is acting alone. There could be others. We can fend them off, if we're prepared. Arm yourselves. Have your neighbors do the same." He stopped himself. By the arks, these were Kurel. They had no weapons. "Big sticks to bat away claws and jaws," he told them instead. "Anything you can use as a shield—a table, a stool. Assign one member of each family to carry a torch, the oilier the better. The Furs don't like smoke. But for the love of Uhrth, be careful. We don't want to burn down Kurel Town. When that is done, meet in the town center with your weapons to be assigned your defense station locations." He squinted at the swiftly lightening sky. "When Little Lume is at one hand. No later."

The crowd dispersed. He'd told them frightening news, given them even more terrifying instructions, yet there was no screaming, no panicked pushing or shoving. If they felt fear, they controlled the symptoms well. He turned to Navi. "Repeat what I just said to as many others as you can."

The boy ran off to do his bidding.

"Why help us?" a woman asked, tugging a wide-eyed child behind her as she stepped nearer. A circle of curious Kurel gathered around to hear his answer.

He suspected this was the first time any of them were willing to speak to a warrior. "Because we're *humans,* and every last one of us counts—Tassagon, Rider and Kurel. We can't afford to lose a single one of *us* to *them.*"

From that point forward, Tao focused on preparing the Kurel to defend their enclave against the Furs. It wasn't as difficult as he'd predicted, not with Elsabeth by his side, setting the example for her people, and Navi acting as able messenger. The effect of the Gorr attack had been galvanizing. Tao knew the war had always felt very far away for the Kurel. No longer.

After gathering in the town center, everyone was sent to his and her stations. The streets filled with Kurel darting this way and that, torches smoking, to be carried to the edge of town on all sides. The scene seemed chaotic at first impression, but the seriousness of their faces showed their focus on their tasks. He assigned a trio of capable-looking men to observation duty at the top of the windmill. "Do you have spyglasses?"

"We have binoculars." One of the men, a self-described "engineer," showed Tao the odd, double spyglass, helping him focus the lenses to see through it.

"By the arks." Tao gaped through the dual sights. "It's magic." He caught himself and winced at the gaffe. It had been some time since he'd explained away Kurel science as magic or sorcery. "To use a figure of speech," he corrected, taking a pair for his use, slinging the strap over his neck. "Ring the bell if there's a sighting. One for north, two for east, three for south and four for west." Once he was confident the men understood his instructions, he ordered them up to the top, the tallest point in the ghetto—and in the entire capital, save the palace hill.

He cast a look in that direction. The fortress stood alone and lonely, overlooking the city. Was Aza all right? And where was Markam?

Elsabeth raced back from her task of readying the clinic with Chun, in case there were injuries. They knew there were insufficient resources for mass casualties, but they had to prepare as best they could.

He welcomed her with an arm slung over her shoulders to draw her close. He was no longer caring of who saw them as a couple. Nor did Elsabeth seem to be concerned. They were together now and that was that.

The bell pealed, three rings shattering the still morning air.

A familiar rush went through him, a call to extreme readiness, allowing absolute composure to take over. It was time for battle. "South," Tao said with urgency. "There are Gorr in the southern part of K-Town."

Elsabeth went pale. "That's the market."

Nodding, Tao took her by the shoulders, looked into her eyes. "I don't know how many Gorr yet. Get Chun, and the wagon. Load it with bandages and medicines. No delay."

What about you? She wanted to plead. *Where will you be?* But she knew the answer: he'd be with everyone else, the unlikely defenders of Kurel Town, guarding their home with everything they had.

He squeezed her shoulder. The Tao she'd come to know, the tender lover she was falling for—whom she *had* fallen for—was gone, stowed behind the fortified wall that was the legendary General Uhr-Tao. "Meet you there."

Turning to jog away, his bow at the ready, he reloaded with an arrow from a supply stored somewhere in his coat. The arrows looked homemade, like his slingshot. He seemed to have built an arsenal while she wasn't looking, preparing for a day she never knew would come. Maybe that was the real reason for armies—not for shows of power, the love of violence or the sheer arrogance of flexing muscle, but to ensure that the defenseless were protected.

No delay. She wheeled around and sped off to do as her general had ordered.

"YOU'RE GOING TO KILL someone."

Elsabeth drove the wagon through the streets like a madwoman, even as Chun warned her to slow down. "We're at war, Chun. People have to watch out for us, not the other way around."

She yanked hard on the reins, steering the horse around a trio running hard to catch up with those answering the bell's warning. She barely missed them, but they didn't appear to notice. Carrying clubs and a broom, they were running toward the market and the disturbing sounds of shouts and screams.

Gorr. There were monsters in the city. The Kurel's true enemy were the Gorr, not the Tassagons. She felt shame at the way her species had conducted themselves since the Gorr first invaded, fighting each other, not focusing on the real threat. Their attention had been on the difference with their fellow humans for far too long.

It was time to learn never to make that mistake again.

Ahead, Tao rode a nervous mare, apparently called into unexpected action like everyone else in the ghetto. That horse had probably never carried more than a placid farmer on its back. Now it bore Tassagonia's most decorated war hero into battle.

"Here is good," Chun said, and she stopped the wagon. The physician had called no less than a half dozen nurses and another doctor into action. But she couldn't make herself feel part of the group as Chun gave them instructions; her attention kept returning to Tao and his effort at setting up effective military defenses in a pacifist ghetto. Her skills lay more with the group of healers than they did the volunteer soldiers, but she felt useless waiting for someone to be wounded in order to act.

Tao's horse whinnied and reared up as he lifted a pair of binoculars to his eyes, his coat flapping behind him. He'd seen something.

What and how many, and were they headed his way?

He took off riding, and her whole world tunneled. She was back in the streets of three years ago on that desperate run to see if her parents had been killed by the guards. Inside her mind, she saw the grasping hands of her neighbors as they tried to stop her from reaching them, and she relived her choking horror when she had. Now Tao thought he could ride off and leave her here? She refused to stay behind when others, even some other women, had already answered the call to fight. No, she had to obey the primal instinct inside her that commanded her to defend and protect what she loved—her city, and her man.

"Take one." Hashimoto the blacksmith was handing out crude spears made of blades lashed to sticks.

Elsabeth jumped down from the driver's seat, slinging a medical supply bag over one shoulder and snatching one of the spears from the smith with her other hand. "Thank you, I will." She left Chun gaping after her as she ran into the crowd, following in Tao's wake.

TAO SMELLED IT ON THE wind. Musk. He pulled around the skittish mare and peered past a line of Kurel defenders bristling with sticks, rakes and clubs, whatever they could grab. "Be ready," he shouted. "Do not look them in the eye."

A crash—the crunching of wood and shattering glass—and two abandoned produce stands collapsed. Something was inside them. As several melons rolled over the dirt, the stench of Gorr sharpened. The musk was a warning, a battle cry. The creatures were poised to make their attack.

He was ready for them.

He aimed the crossbow, sweeping it from stall to

empty stall. Movement in the corner of his eye. Then another crash. Three dark shapes streaked out of the morning shadows, racing across the eerily empty marketplace.

Their gold eyes were honed in on him. He angled his gaze away, tracking the advance obliquely. Gorr—an immature alpha and two smaller betas. They, too, looked emaciated, but being all fangs and claws, they'd be no less dangerous for the lack of body mass.

"Fire!" Tao bellowed and let his arrow fly.

His arrow caught the alpha through the torso. He'd missed the heart, but the creature bled out within a few leaps, falling in a twitching ball of bloodied fur.

The howls released by the remaining two were as plaintive as they were ear piercing. Despite the bell in the windmill, that caterwauling was going to be heard throughout the capital.

Panicked without their alpha, the pair fled, heading in the direction of the ghetto gates. Tao rode hard after them.

The street leading up to the palace hill would soon be bustling with townspeople starting their day. He couldn't let the two Gorr enter the capital proper and wreak havoc. While the Kurel had been semiprepared, a Gorr attack would take the Tassagons completely off guard.

A grinding, grating rumble told Tao the bad news: Big Lume had barely peeked above the horizon and the entrance to Kurel Town was already being pulled open for the day. By the arks! Of all mornings to be opening the gates early. Hadn't the guards heard the howls?

Even if they had, they wouldn't know what they meant, likely assuming the howls were a sorcery of some kind. Gorr were familiar to soldiers and few others. "No!" he shouted to the guards in the gate shack. "Keep them closed!" But the men stared at him, stupidly, too baffled by the sight of a bare-chested Kurel on horseback, armed with a crossbow, chasing after two monsters from the Hinterlands.

A group of Kurel formed a hasty blockade bristling with clubs, homemade spears, rakes and hoes. Tao's chest swelled with pride at the courage of the spontaneous militia, and also alarm; they were civilians at the mercy of their inexperience.

Fangs snapping, the Furs clawed their way through the Kurel to reach the gates. Tao had feared he'd see many more fall to the Gorr, but those who'd taken a blow from a passing claw were being pulled out of the way by the others.

Home guards waited in the street on the Tassagon side, likely drawn close to the gates by the howling and chaos in K-Town. But they were unprepared for what was coming at them.

The larger of the two Furs took a guard down. Horrific snarling ended the man's scream abruptly.

"Move aside!" Tao warned the remaining, shocked guards. Like the Kurel, they'd never fought or even seen the Furs. He wanted them out of the way and the streets cleared for battle. "Stand back."

Automatically in the confusion, they responded to the military authority in his voice. Meanwhile, shouts of "Gorr" had sent screaming townspeople scurrying.

Tao kicked the mare and rode out the gates after the Furs. A tall, lanky Tassagon guard remained in the middle of the street, in the path of the loping Gorr. His comrades called to him but he didn't respond. The blade he'd been brandishing had fallen from his fist to the ground.

Charmed. The man had caught the eye of the Gorr as it came away from feeding off the fallen guard. The creature fell into a crouch, bright blood dripping from its fangs. It coiled, then sprang. As it launched its body on powerful hind legs to attack the paralyzed Tassagon, Tao let an arrow fly.

A satisfying *thwunk*—the arrow sank into its rib-cage with a spray of black-red blood. The leaping Gorr continued to fly at the man's throat, but it was already dead.

Tao's last glimpse of the near-fatal attack was the guard sitting up, blinking in astonishment as he shoved a limp Gorr off his chest.

Tao gripped the prancing mare with his thighs, waiting for a clean shot at the last Gorr. By the time he could safely take aim, the Gorr had taken a spear in the withers. Navi's whoop was unmistakable.

"Good shot, Navi!" Tao reloaded to fire on the wounded Gorr. His mare stumbled. The arrow went low, skidding over the dirt. The fleeing Gore turned on him, panting. The vaguely human face and ears, the flat snout and fangs, the thin tail swishing in warning—it was a scene burned in his memory, a nightmare he'd lived for much of his adult life. Usually there were hundreds of them, relentless, indescribably vicious attackers. Now just this one last monster.

Tao lifted the bow and took aim in the name of all the men he'd lost, all the lives over all the long years that had been ended too soon because *of them*. The Gorr.

"Uhr-Tao," it growled. "Uhr-Tao."

Tao jolted with shock. Everything about this one indicated it wasn't an alpha, thus it should not be able to speak the human language, let alone know his name. It wasn't supposed to be any more than a mute foot soldier, a brainless beast.

Was something happening amongst the vanquished Furs that he'd never anticipated? Had the alpha blood become so concentrated that the traits of speech were being passed on to all pups?

No time to worry about that. If it got away, it could reach the palace in too few leaps, and he couldn't have that. Tao let the arrow fly as the Gorr came at him in a suicidal leap. It met its end in midair and fell to the ground. A few twitches, and it lay still.

Tao turned sharply back through the gates into the ghetto. He was still a fugitive, to be arrested, and likely shot, on sight. Shock on the part of the guards had been the only thing saving him so far.

The pounding of hoofbeats met him inside the gates. Clearing dust revealed a makeshift, ragtag cavalry coming up the main street of K-Town. Kurel had mounted horses and even a mule. Others were driving a motley assortment of carts and wagons, speeding toward him. Behind them, a second wave of Kurel militia came on foot.

His reinforcements. When they saw him thrust a triumphant fist in the air, a gesture emulated by Navi and the many Kurel who had created the blockade, they cheered.

Tao soaked in the feeling of victory that was made even sweeter when he saw a woman running toward him, holding a spear with bandaged hands, flame-red hair streaming behind her.

He jumped down from the horse, his heart still kicking hard from battle. Seeing her agonized, tear-streaked face kicked his pulse up a few notches higher.

She crashed into him, the spear clattering to the ground as he crushed her to his chest. His hand was spread on the back of her head as he drew in her scent, her essence, using her to anchor him to the real world, and away from death and the pounding, blinding, bloodlust of battle.

Only belatedly did he realize she was speaking to him. No, yelling at him. "Don't ever do that," she was saying, her voice muffled against his neck as she pounded him with a bandaged fist. "Never again. I looked and you were gone." Her voice shook. "I ran… I didn't know if I'd find you alive or dead."

He gently caught her injured fist, feeling helpless in the wake of her tears, the first he'd seen. "I had to fight them. There was no time to say goodbye."

"They never said goodbye, either." Her body shook. "I ran. I ran to this very place, and I found them." Her voice was a ragged, anguished whisper. "I found them *here*. Dead."

She meant her parents, of course. She'd run the same route again, today, chasing after him. Reliving the trauma of the day her parents were slaughtered.

The intensity of her reaction proved how much she cared for him. The intensity of his feelings for her shook him to the core.

He took her face between his hands. "Beth, I'm alive, not dead. This is the present. *We're* the future." He pressed his forehead to hers as she nodded, absorbing his words. "Take this moment, this day, this memory, and replace the other."

"HAVE YOU HAD CONTACT with your brother, Aza? Tell me!" Xim pressed his fists to his throbbing temples, trying not to rant, but he was so angry he could self-combust. He'd sent out the assassins and they'd turned up dead. Only Uhr-Tao had the expertise to fend them off. Rumors flying all over the capital spoke of a new hero, a Kurel warrior. One who looked and sounded suspiciously like Uhr-Tao.

Tao shook his fist at Aza. "Have you? Tell me!" His shout echoed off the walls of the luxurious bed-chamber.

Only Aza's pale face and rapid breaths hinted at her upset. She otherwise stood silent, her hands folded over her distended belly, their unborn child.

"You, of all people, making me look a fool," he said.

"Tao and I have not spoken since the night of the banquet. I miss him so." Her eyes filled with tears. He hated when she cried. It made him feel even more a failure. "I have not spoken with him, Xim. It's the truth."

"I don't believe you!" He swept a row of priceless perfume bottles off her vanity.

She startled at the smashing glass. "Stop it!" She grimaced, clutching her belly. "You're scaring the children."

He became aware of the muffled wails of the children, locked in the nursery next door. Aza was so petite, her chest heaving, but with her fierce maternal protectiveness, she suddenly loomed bigger and stronger than he was.

Protecting her children from their own father.

"You and Tao are too close," Xim argued. "He wouldn't have gone away without leaving word as to his welfare."

She reacted to that, the tiniest of twitches of the corners of her lips.

"I knew it. You're lying. My own wife." He closed the few feet separating them, almost slipping on the spilled perfume, his hands raised like claws to squeeze the truth from her traitorous lips once and for all.

His own shadow stopped him. He saw it loom over her fragile frame. She hadn't flinched, but waited with her head turned to the side, as if she didn't want to watch him kill her.

He couldn't. He'd never. Didn't she know that?

Or, could he? The curve of her throat was vulnerability incarnate—slender and white, the pulse visible. *Beautiful.* He wanted to touch her there, caress her... Yet, sometimes the darkness inside him welled up so powerfully it blotted out all reason. He'd been angry for as long as he could remember. So much injustice, so much unfairness. His father's doubts. Now this, betrayed again by those he loved the most.

He pulled his hands away from her. His entire body shook. He'd let Gorr loose on the city, and all four had been killed—by Kurel, no less—two on each side of the ghetto gates. Hundreds of Tassagons had seen the body of the slaughtered guard, and those of the Gorr, too, before Beck's men had removed the stinking corpses and disposed of them. Everyone was terrified.

They were looking to their king for guidance.

For leadership. As they'd once looked to his father.

He grabbed anguished fistfuls of his hair to keep from screaming in frustration. No one must know he was behind the Gorr attacks. His actions, his weakness, sickened him. But he'd been afraid, and he'd trusted Beck. "What to do now?" he cried out. "What to do, Aza?"

He choked on a sob. He'd failed her as he'd failed his father, Orion. "How did it all go so wrong, Aza? I didn't mean for him to die. It just...happened." He was shaking so hard; he couldn't help it.

As if in pain, she was standing slightly hunched over. "What happened? Xim, tell me." The smell of the spilled perfume was thick in the air. Distantly, his children were crying, calling for their mother. For his Aza.

He sensed he'd reached the end of his rope with her. She was the last one in the world who loved him. No one else did. If he didn't have her, he'd have nobody. Filled with remorse, he knew there was no choice but to come clean. To have a second chance and redeem himself.

He crouched down at her feet, his shoes crunching on glass. "I want to start over, Aza." He glanced up, trembling. "Do you think we can?"

He was afraid—afraid to tell her.

Afraid not to.

"I don't know what you mean." She stood there, waiting. So patient. So beautiful. Her eyes so kind, even looking at him now, a wreck of a man. A man willing to start anew.

"I never told you what happened the morning Orion died. We argued, and he had an attack. He sent me to summon help. But I was so angry, Aza. You don't know. In that moment I hated him."

She grew even paler, her eyes almost sunken in her fragile face, her mouth tight with pain—from what he was telling her, or from the child growing in her womb? "I know you hated him, Xim. But Orion loved you—"

"Not like he should have! You know it as well as I do." He clenched his fists. "I didn't go for help, Aza. I didn't." A wrenching sob welled up. "I stood there and watched him die, and, Aza, it was the first time in my entire life I felt as if I had any power, any control over my destiny." He let his face fall into his hands and wept. "I'm so sorry. I'm so sorry."

After a while, he realized he heard nothing. Fearfully, he lifted his head. He took in the sight of her gemlike eyes, the piles of glossy brown hair, a face shaped like a heart. Slender limbs. Rounded with child, his child. *My wife.* He'd never really, truly appreciated that fact until that moment. He'd never realized just what Uhrth had granted him, all his blessings. His family.

He reached for her with a trembling hand. "You're so beautiful, Aza." But those ever-forgiving green eyes were in retreat, horrified. Worst of all, disappointed. *Like father was disappointed with me.*

Panic exploded inside him and he shot to his feet. "No. Don't, Aza. Don't stop loving me, Aza. Please." His voice cracked. "I don't know what I'd do. I couldn't bear it."

Tears falling slowly down her cheeks, she shook her head and opened her arms. He walked into them. Stroking his back, she comforted him like a child as he wept.

"Love me Aza. Love me. Everything will be better, you'll see. You'll see. I won't keep you and the children under lock and key for long. I promise. Just until I get everything sorted out. You understand why, yes?"

"Yes. I understand, Xim."

"You always did understand me. You're the only one."

Determined to prove his competence as king—to her and to his subjects—he fled the chamber, ordering the guard to lock the doors behind him.

CHAPTER TWENTY-FIVE

THE ELDERS VIEWED THE two Gorr corpses that had been killed in the ghetto. The musky odor had faded some, but it was still pungent enough to wrinkle the noses of the uninitiated.

Farouk was solemn. "So they are what severed our ties with our mother world. Stranding us here. Leaving us all on the edge of extinction forevermore."

"We came back from the edge," Tao argued. "We survived." By Uhrth, if anyone knew it, he did. He'd dedicated his heart and soul to preventing the destruction of their race.

"Alive but alone." The elder's voice was tremulous, from emotion or age Tao couldn't tell. "We told them not to come after us, you see," the elder continued. "Not to attempt a rescue. We lied, making it seem as if there were no survivors, sending a final message that this world was destroyed." Farouk's eyes were hooded, veiling a mysterious, meaningful glint. "So it is written."

"Always written," Tao complained. "I want to see where."

"The Log is not here, young Tassagon. It is protected in the Barrier Peaks. It recounts our origins, and tells of the days of the Old Colony, the decision to cut ourselves off from our home. We did not want these Gorr finding the human birth world, and doing to it what they had done here."

"I never heard this," Elsabeth almost whispered. "We were not lost? We were not abandoned?"

"It has been kept secret to all but the elders," Farouk said, nodding. "Perhaps we were mistaken in doing so." His lips thinned. "Now that we've seen a real Gorr, I know so. The consequences of inaction and of leaving Xim in power are clear. The Kurel are fully committed to working with your rebellion."

"Our rebellion," Elsabeth corrected her elder firmly but with respect. "All the human tribes are at great risk if this king continues on his path of destruction."

"Yes, yes. If humans turn on each other, darkness will consume us and we will be lost to Uhrth forever. So says the final verse of the Log of Uhrth," Farouk said crisply.

Elsabeth remembered what the elder had said about lying to Uhrth about the Old Colony's fate, and the significance of the darkness passage hit her for the first time. "'Lost to Uhrth forever.' That means no chance of our mother-world learning what happened to us. Because we'll all be gone. Extinct."

She felt Tao's intense, suddenly curious gaze on her. Farouk nodded. "That is correct."

"I always believed the purpose of the Log of Uhrth was for us to learn about our origins, but it's not really that, is it, Elder Farouk?"

The old man's gaze observed her with the patience born of being alive for more than a century. She forged ahead. "It's to teach us how to survive. No—more than that. It's to teach us how to be victorious, so we can ultimately reunite with our human family, our ancestors. And go home."

All the elders gaped at her. The silence stretched out, and began to cramp her stomach with worry. Had she insulted them, or the holy Log? Then, finally, Gwendolyn turned to Marina and said smugly, "Of my blood, that girl is. Do not ever dismiss her as a halfie again."

"So, I'm right."

Farouk's nearly invisible lips receded, baring his teeth. It was a rare smile. "Yes, Elsabeth. You are right."

Her heart leaped. She thought of her dream of sailing the stars in an ark. "If the Log teaches us that we must defeat the Gorr so we can safely reestablish contact with Uhrth, then why is it all such a secret?"

"Because of ignorance. Because of fear. And because this cursed war is not yet over." He turned to Tao. "Show us what we need to do to ensure peace between our human tribes." Then he tapped the floor with his cane as if impatient to begin.

"YOU'RE A GOOD, BRAVE warrior." Elsabeth brought Prometheus to her lips, pressing a light kiss to his feathered, warm body as she prepared to send the pigeon out with news of what had transpired that day.

"I'm jealous," Tao said.

"I'd do the same for you if you were headed out on a dangerous mission."

"In that case, I'd want more than a kiss."

The promise in his voice made her grow warm with anticipation. Despite the danger and the sometimes choking fright, she knew that at the end of the day his kisses, his caresses, his body, would be hers. She came up on her toes and whispered in Tao's ear, "Believe me, you'd get more than a kiss."

His husky chuckle told her he was pleased with that promise. She carried Prometheus to the hatch on the side of the aviary where he'd been trained to fly to the Barrier Peaks. There, she set him down and waited. It was important that the pigeon take off on its own accord.

It would seem logical that a bird would want to stay close to the safety and security of home, but with much cooing and strutting, Prometheus made it clear he was anxious to be off.

"Warn the Kurel who live in the mountains," she said. "Tell them what has happened."

The pigeon cocked its head to look at her with its black bead of an eye. Then it hopped onto the perch and, with a loud drumming of wings, took off on its long flight.

"GUARD! GUARD!" The warning cries stopped the departing Kurel militia cold. A horseman had galloped through the ghetto gates and was making his way through the warren of homes.

Dressed in blue and white, the helmeted guard demanded, "Uhr-Tao! Where is the general? Show him to me."

When not a single Kurel cooperated, the rider pulled to a halt and jumped to the ground, then tugged off his helmet, his demeanor infinitely less arrogant. "Tell him it's Markam. His friend."

MARKAM TROMPED INSIDE Elsabeth's house. The sight of the broken furniture, the shattered picture frame sitting on the floor propped against the wall, the bloodstains that would need to be scrubbed clean seemed to barely register with him. His sharp features were made even more so with his facial muscles hard with tension. His lanky frame was as tight as the string on Tao's bow. "Aza is in danger."

CHAPTER TWENTY-SIX

ELSABETH SERVED THE MEN tea as Markam briefed Tao.

"We're going to get her out." Tao's simple, firm statement set the tone of what was to come. Xim had imprisoned the queen and the children in her chambers. Given Xim's erratic behavior, there was every reason to believe Aza's life was in jeopardy.

"Xim never stopped believing the priest's reading of the bones. Even after we searched high and low for you, Tao, he wouldn't give it up. Beck got him alone, and talked him into sending a Gorr out to find you. There were four of them locked up in the old wing."

"You had Furs at the palace?" Tao bellowed.

"It was news to me, too." Markam was seething. "Beck's plan was to release only the alpha as an assassin, and he did. Then Xim had second thoughts about keeping any Gorr around, and wanted all of them gone."

"The alpha followed my scent here," Tao said tersely.

"Then the lessers followed his. It all makes sense now. They made a pact with our Tassagon king." His bitterness and disbelief was evident in every word.

"I had no way of getting here in time to warn you." His dark, troubled eyes scanned the mess in the living room. "Xim's grown wary of me. Perhaps he suspects my actions even now. He may know I've been protecting you, that I'm plotting Aza's rescue."

Elsabeth shivered with a sudden chill, picturing Tao captured and killed, the ghetto burned as punishment for the Kurel role in Tao's escape. There was a time she might have called all that a necessary risk in order to rid Tassagonia of its cruel ruler. Her vow of vengeance had been the only thing important to her. But ousting Xim wasn't her sole priority anymore. Preventing Tao's capture had become just as important to her heart.

Perhaps even more so.

Somehow she sensed her parents would have approved.

She moved next to Tao, and he stroked a reassuring hand down her back. Markam's sharp gaze didn't miss the interaction. *He can see how it is with us.* A flicker of warmth in those reserved eyes. *He approves.* He was gradually calming, becoming more the Markam she knew. "Xim has no intention of admitting he released the Gorr on his subjects."

"To do so would be suicidal," Tao said. "The Tassagons would turn on him in panic."

"Luckily, the Gorr deaths will take attention off finding you and put it on protecting the capital and the palace. We need the king to be focused on reassuring his terrified subjects—and not on what we're orchestrating."

Getting Aza and her two young children out from under Xim's paranoid nose. Butterflies took flight in Elsabeth's stomach. With his identities as a rebel and the king's confidante in danger of colliding, Markam's existence had become truly precarious.

They hunched around the table and their cooling cups of tea, hashing out the details of how Aza's rescue would be accomplished. The best way into the palace was the same as the best way out—through the spillways and the dungeon.

"Xim didn't order the loading dock grates sealed?" she asked.

"I took charge of seeing that the repairs were done," Markam said with faint, dry humor.

With the palace guards essentially neutralized under Markam's command, the one complication was Beck. "We'll need a diversion," Tao suggested.

"I'll make sure he's distracted," Markam said.

Tao downed his tea, looking to Elsabeth as if he longed for something stronger. She went to fetch the spirits that the Riders had given them, pouring a finger's width in each of the men's cups and a little less in hers. Markam sniffed at the liquid and broke into a tired smile. "Have the Kurel been trading with our friends from the Plains?"

"No. But Tao and I crossed paths with some. The night you searched the ghetto, we slept out in the countryside."

"Pax and two Riders from the Blue Hills band were sizing up our herds." Tao's hint of a smile hardened. "I warned him about Xim. And none too soon." He emptied his cup, tapping a finger against the rim. "Markam, before we part and commence our plans, I have to know something. I wasn't particularly fond of Elsabeth's people until I came to live amongst them, and know them. But how did you come to be such a great champion and protector of the Kurel?"

Elsabeth leaned forward in eagerness. "I often wondered the same thing myself."

Markam's jaw compressed. "I supposed it's time you knew. Both of you." With a glance around for listening ears, a habit engrained after years living where it often seemed even the walls could hear, he confided, "The crown prince became sick with fever as an infant. Maxim was only a few months old, and he weakened quickly. The palace healers tried but could do nothing for him. Aza could see her babe was dying. She was desperate. Xim said if it was Uhrth's will, his son would live. That wasn't good enough for the queen. Without Xim's knowledge, I accompanied her to see a Kurel healer. He treated Prince Max, and cured him."

Markam glanced over to Elsabeth, his eyes crinkling with warmth, and something more: gratitude. "That was your father."

"Mercy," she whispered.

"It changed everything. After that I was motivated to learn to read. The palace accountant, Navi's predecessor, taught me."

"Mikhail?" Elsabeth asked with a smile. The jovial accountant was retired now.

"Indeed. Because of that visit to your father, I discovered books, and the whole world opened up. And," his voice gentled, "Aza and I…" He cleared his throat then sat up straighter. "We fell in love. We've never acknowledged it, never spoken of it—not once. I respect her marriage, and so does she. I am a rebel, yes, but those aims can be—and will be—accomplished without murder. I could not live with myself with Xim's blood on my hands."

Markam stood then, picking up his helmet and preparing to depart. He locked hands with Tao in a farewell gesture. "Nor could I live with your blood on my hands. Xim believes the rumors that you were spotted slaying Gorr outside the ghetto. He's feeling more and more threatened. His imprisonment of Aza is proof. My friend, the king wants you dead. My influence is tenuous. As today's events have proven, do not expect you can rely on me for an early warning."

CHAPTER TWENTY-SEVEN

SUNLIGHT SWIFTLY RETREATED from the streets of Tassagonia, replaced by shadows and moonlight. On a balcony overlooking Palace Square, with his two highest-ranking officers in attendance, but not his queen, King Xim stepped forward to address the Tassagon populace.

The square hadn't been this crowded since General Uhr-Tao's homecoming. *With one difference,* Markam thought. This evening the citizens of Tassagonia had gathered under the threat of arrest if they did not attend the speech. Beck's men had gone door to door, ordering all those not too sick or too old out into the night.

Not everyone was so easily coerced. As Markam had planned, one wagonload of dissenters had been carried to the palace stockade, which kept attention diverted from the raid now being launched from the palace dungeons, nearly a hundred feet beneath the king's platform.

Xim's voice rang out. "K-Town is infested—with

Gorr and with Gorr sympathizers. The curfew has not kept us safe from such threats. Thus, the curfew will end, and Kurel Town will be sealed off around-the-clock until we have rid our city of the threats facing us. But fear not, my subjects. General Uhr-Beck's Domestic Defense Army will enforce the closure. Rest assured, these courageous guardians will keep you safe."

Domestic Defense Army? Pure, undiluted Beck. Xim would never have thought of it.

It took all Markam's self-discipline to hide his disdain as he glanced over at Beck. With stars freshly sewn on his epaulets, the bastard listened to the speech while making a show of flexing his arms over his chest, dishonoring their uniform once again by rolling up his sleeves.

The man could posture and preen all he wanted as long as he remained ignorant of what was transpiring many stories below. Markam willed Tao to hurry. *Get in and get out, with my Aza safe in your hands.* The queen couldn't escape soon enough. This charade had become an almost impossible balancing act, one he would not be able to sustain much longer.

"The foreigners who live amongst us have weakened us from the inside out," Xim continued. "No more. I will allow a few, specially screened Kurel to apply for extended-stay permits. All others will be exiled forevermore. Tassagonia will once again be for Tassagons!"

Subdued applause and some scattered cheers met the king's proclamation. The impression that Kurel practiced sorcery persisted, of course, but after witnessing the ghetto dwellers defend the city from the Gorr, after actually seeing the monsters that were the human race's mortal enemy, Tassagons were now more inclined to build a relationship with the Kurel than sever it. But General Uhr-Beck had assigned soldiers to "work the crowd." Nothing like the sight of a sharp blade to spur a man or woman into pretending enthusiasm.

Or a bottle of wine to dull a man's senses. "After this," Markam said out the corner of his mouth to Beck, "let us raise glasses in a toast to your promotion." Many glasses. Until Beck was falling-down drunk, Xim right along with him. So they'd miss what was happening under their noses—or rather, who was disappearing. By Uhrth, the queen and her children would be safe from this madness by morn.

"And so we shall." Beck's hand landed hard on Markam's shoulder. "A toast, my comrade. To new beginnings."

ELSABETH NEVER KNEW excitement and mortal terror could exist so compatibly side by side until she set foot in the foul and cold pipes with Tao and Navi. Was this how Tao felt each time he marched into battle? Mercy. And he'd repeated the act, an act of courage, over and over. He was a hero. More than that, he was her hero.

With disparate emotions coursing through her, she dove forward into the deep, stinking darkness.

Only the sounds of their breaths and boots splashing through muck accompanied their progress. There was no need for words. Everything had already been briefed and briefed again. Tao was meticulous about the details of the raid, from the disguises that would turn the men into guards and her into a kitchen wench, to the exit point they'd use to slip inside the palace via the dungeon, guarded tonight by Markam's handpicked men.

Still, before they had even lowered the grate at the loading docks to set foot inside the spillway, and before they had left Chun sitting on the driver's bench of the same wagon they'd used the first time they'd sneaked into the palace, Tao had asked her, "Have I missed anything? Is there anything you see that isn't as it should be?"

"No," she'd assured him, her hand resting briefly on his chest, over his pounding heart. His good and brave heart. "Now let's go get your family out."

With Chun, they exchanged nods of luck and hope and everything else good that a silent gesture could hold. Then they pulled the grate up behind them, leaving behind the physician, who looked convincing as a drowsy merchant waiting for his wagon to be loaded. No one would notice the bow and a quiver of arrows hidden under his coat, or the blade in his belt, but they'd certainly learn of the weapons if they tried to attack. This time around, the good doctor had more than a scalpel with which to defend against attackers.

So did they all.

She and Navi carried blades for self-defense. Tao was armed with the crossbow, a spear, two blades, one long and one short, and Uhrth knew how many other tools to maim and kill. For all her protestations against violence, she'd always had a distinct lack of remorse at the thought of using it against Xim. But tonight, she hoped no confrontations forced them to do so. Aza and her children's safe passage out of the palace was their goal. This was not the night to end Xim's reign.

Ahead was the confluence of pipes where Navi had slipped into the moat, causing Tao to dive in after him. Elsabeth shivered, smelling the dank stench of the water and knowing better than she ever had the deadly nature of the monsters swimming beneath its surface. "Take it slowly," she warned Navi in a loud whisper, seeing his bobbing lantern up ahead.

"Beth, if I were moving any slower, I'd be sitting," he reassured her.

"If you fall in, you're swimming to shore on your

own this time," Tao said, and Elsabeth could hear the humor in his voice.

The truth of it was they were a team. They'd come here together, and they'd leave together. No matter what.

"THEY LIKED TAO MUCH better," Xim complained to Beck over goblets of red wine. It was the most expensive vintage in the cellars, worthy of a celebration... like victory over the Gorr, or ridding the kingdom of its Kurel parasites. Unfortunately, Xim couldn't seem to work up enough levity to suit the occasion.

Markam's glass sat partially drained, his chair empty. The man was off again on his incessant rounds. He never seemed to rest. *I'll have to drink enough for the two of us.* It would mute the anger that continued to make his insides burn. "They were falling all over themselves for Tao. When they cheered that bastard, we could hardly hear ourselves think."

Beck leaned forward, his weight on his elbows, his elbows on the table. "You had to broach serious topics, My Liege. Something like that doesn't invoke a giddy response."

"True, true." Tao had been given the easier task. Of course. Still, it didn't make Xim feel much better. His entire life, no matter what he did, Tao had appeared out of nowhere to do it better. Xim was glad he'd confined

Aza, lest Tao find her and influence her against her own husband.

He drank more wine, splashing some on his brocade jacket. Irritably, he dashed the droplets away and gulped down another swallow. "I want him dead, Beck. I've done everything you have advised—promoted you to general, given you an army, for Uhrth's sake! And still, Tao runs free. Taunting me with his very existence. I'm sick of it." He shook a fist at Beck. "I had him in my hands, and he slipped away." He opened his fist, spreading his fingers, and then plunged them through his hair. "Out the dungeon of all places, Beck, the part of this fortress that should be unquestioningly secure. It's embarrassing."

"It was indeed embarrassing, My Liege, but not for you. The breach was the responsibility of your commander of the Palace Guard. As far as we know, the security of this palace may still be unsatisfactory."

Xim shifted his gaze from Beck to Markam's goblet of unfinished wine. Half done, just as the palace's security inspections had been. Xim didn't want to lose faith in Markam; he truly didn't. Markam was a good man— likable, efficient and, most of all, soothing, which was a quality Xim valued above most others. Markam had long been a salve for his constantly jumpy nerves— rather like Aza. But he'd also learned the consequences of too much trust. It was awful being let down.

"Markam did discover how Tao escaped the palace,"

Xim reasoned, and hoped his sudden dread wouldn't bloom into something bigger and more horrible.

Markam is friends with Tao. What if his loyalty is with him, not me? Doubt filled his chest with as much chill as winter fog. But, of course Markam knew Tao, but he hadn't known him any longer than he'd known Xim. All of them had grown up together, had known each other for years. More, Markam was the kind of man who had always placed palace affairs first.

Or had he? Xim's stomach did a nervous flip. His nerves jangled. "Won't he have seen to plugging the holes since the escape?" he asked Beck almost plaintively.

"Who was in charge of the repairs?"

"He was."

"There's your answer, My Liege. We don't know." Beck pushed to his feet. "It seems the good colonel's nightly rounds don't necessarily include a thorough security inspection. Luckily, you have me to back him up."

"Yes, yes. Go. Double-check his work. Tell me if you find anything lacking."

Beck arched the brow over his good eye. "As you wish, My Liege."

The dining hall was suddenly huge and cavernous without Beck there to help fill the void. *Again, I am alone.* Xim snapped his fingers for a servant to refill his goblet, but he had the feeling drinking was futile.

It would take more than wine to numb his growing anxiety. He did not feel safe in his own palace. No, not at all.

He shivered. *Aza, I need you.* Oh, did he ever! Why was he sitting here, alone, when he could be with his wife? The fur cape around his shoulders was a poor substitute for her warm arms. He'd go to her and spend the night in her bed. Yes, and she'd comfort him as she always did.

BACK TO THE DUNGEON—*but voluntarily this time*, Tao thought, supporting the grate as Navi unscrewed it and together they lowered the heavy iron slowly to minimize noise. Tao slid the lantern into the passage to the dungeon with his foot. After a look and listen convinced him it was clear, he pressed a finger to his lips and motioned Elsabeth forward, then Navi. Tao helped Navi lift the grate back into position as silently as possible, leaving it unscrewed.

Hunched over, they ran along the passage until the basket containing their disguises came into view in the circle of light thrown by the lantern. There were two guard uniforms, a servant's ware for Elsabeth and a bag that contained more servant ware, disguises for Aza and the children. *Good man, Markam.*

Now, dressed as a pair of guards and a kitchen wench, they grabbed their standard military bows and proceeded ahead. Once out of the passage they could run comfortably.

The stink was eye-watering as they passed the empty cells. Ahead, the tall stone staircase led to the palace's higher floors. "There are three doors. Each is guarded and locked. Usually. But not tonight." He hefted his crossbow and took the stairs to the first door. "Flat against the wall," he told her and Navi. Once their backs were pressed to the stones, he shouldered open the first door. A hard knot inside him eased a little. No locked door, no unhappily surprised guard.

The process repeated uneventfully and reassuringly for each of the next two doors. All of them unlocked. All of them unguarded. Markam had always been scrupulously well organized, sometimes to the point of obsession. But this was one of those times Tao was grateful for his friend's extreme attention to detail.

Tao turned to his unlikely raiders. "We go directly to the queen's chambers, gather her and the children and escort them out. Elsabeth, on the way in, you're simply a servant seeing to the queen's needs." She carried the satchel Markam had provided to hide the disguises for Aza and the children. The sack was richly embroidered and fit for royalty, making her ruse all the more convincing. "Navi and I are two guards on escort duty."

Navi's nod was both nervous and earnest. Tao remembered what it felt like as a boy being called upon to do brave deeds. He took hold of Navi's shoulder and gave him a firm, steadying squeeze. "You're going to do well, young man."

Navi smiled. "I won't disappoint you, General Tao."

Tao turned to Elsabeth. Her achingly lovely gaze looked up at him from under her bonnet. It had never felt this wrenching, poised on the threshold of a raid.

Because your heart was never involved.

He tucked in the few strands of her brilliantly colored hair that weren't hidden as deeply under the bonnet as he'd have liked. Normally this was the time he'd offer his men a few fortifying words of wisdom and hope. But the protectiveness surging inside him for Elsabeth left him at a loss for words.

Her lips eased into a hint of a smile, as if she'd guessed the reason for his silence. Then she shook her head, telling him nothing more needed to be said that hadn't been already.

He touched his palm to her cheek, let it linger there for a heartbeat, then turned away, lest his lover's eyes charmed him and caused him to be frozen in place.

He and Navi donned their helmets before Tao opened the last door and let them into the palace.

"Walk," he told Elsabeth in a curt, all-business tone. She was now under his escort, and several rungs below a guard on the social ladder.

Nary a glance came their way as they traveled toward the queen's apartments. They walked swiftly enough not to waste what little time they had, but not fast enough to attract notice. In the expansive central foyer, a tile mosaic depicting achievements of the kings and queens over the years covered the floor. It wasn't his imagination that Elsabeth's shoe landed dead-on the likeness of Xim wielding a warrior's broadsword, something Tao doubted the man could lift off the floor, let alone raise above his waist. Each portrayal of Xim was similarly desecrated as they walked over it, the one in the very center given an extra turn of her toe, as if to grind in her hatred of the king.

As long as she expressed her loathing symbolically while in the palace, he wasn't worried. *Just don't kill the man if we happen to cross paths.* He'd made a career of leading battle-hungry soldiers; he'd just never predicted his woman would be one of them.

As they turned toward the corridor leading to the private area of the palace, an ear-splitting horn jarred them all out of step. He thrust out an arm, stopping Elsabeth, turning to see what was happening.

"To your stations!" a sergeant of the guard bellowed. "To your stations!"

Guards were running to their posts. Had their presence been discovered? Had someone found the unlocked grate below? Remote, but still possible. He immediately calculated how much time they'd need to get Aza to their alternate exit points, the spillway entrance through the kitchens or, failing that, through the wine cellars.

Adrenaline poured into Tao's veins. Navi's throat bobbed, but he kept up his guard's stance, thank Uhrth, although he drilled Tao with a look that begged directions. Elsabeth had gone pale, but didn't stick out for doing so; any servant would have been alarmed in such a situation. But, within a moment, Tao and Navi were the only guards left.

They'd soon draw notice for not being where they were supposed to be. His mind calmly sorted through all options. There were many places to hide—alcoves, little-traveled passages.

Tao squared his shoulders. "Keep walking. With purpose. We're not turning back." Not yet.

They started toward Aza's chambers.

"You! *Halt.*"

Tao instantly recognized that familiar raspy yell— damn it to hell. *Uhr-Beck.*

CHAPTER TWENTY-EIGHT

BECK WORE GENERAL'S STARS on his shoulders and gripped a loaded crossbow. Two guards accompanied him, men unfamiliar to Tao. Elsabeth was standing very still off to the side, but her hands, wrapped together and pressed to the waist of her dress, were trembling. Tao would do anything in that moment to see her safe, including giving up his life.

"Why aren't you two fools at your posts?" Beck snarled as he approached.

Then he drew up short, shock breaking his stride as Tao marked the moment Beck recognized him. A look of utter hatred drained all hint of humanity out of that one, narrowed, brown eye.

Beck aimed his bow at Tao.

Everything crystallized in that moment, sounds fading away, the scene before Tao in perfect focus, tunneling to the bow and the man behind it. He'd faced near-certain death more than a few times in war, but never did he feel the utter futility, the senselessness, of what was about to happen: his own countryman sinking an arrow in his heart to settle an old score, with the tacit permission of their king.

The crashing of boots on stone broke the spell. "Why aren't these men at their posts?" Markam strode up to them with his own pair of guards. *Thank the arks.* Tao swung his boot up in Beck's blind spot and kicked the bow out of his hands. The weapon skittered across the stones.

Tao started to reach for his own bow when he heard the sounds of swords being unsheathed, and Markam's voice. "Touch that weapon, Uhr-Tao, and it'll be your last act on this world."

He straightened to see Markam's eyes dark and cold, his sword drawn and Beck marveling at the man before he turned back to Tao and smiled.

"Helmets off and weapons down," Markam ordered Tao and Navi. Tao let his crossbow fall to the floor, and then the rest of his arsenal. Navi followed suit, tossing down his blade. Their helmets were taken by one of Markam's guards.

Tao didn't dare make the error of trying to catch Markam's gaze. His friend's survival depended on not appearing to be aligned with Tao. And Elsabeth and Navi's lives were balanced on Tao not revealing how much he cared for them, especially Elsabeth. His true feelings for her were the one weapon he wouldn't be able to wrest back from Beck's control.

"General Uhr-Tao, the people's hero," Beck sneered. "The legend. The Butcher of the Hinterlands. I knew you'd fight to the end. I knew you'd make another run at the palace. That's why we have the Uhr in our name. We live to fight, and we fight to live. But this is the end. I assure you." He took a double take at Navi. "What is this? A Kurel! Uhr-Tao, have you fallen so low that you only lead Kurel now?"

Elsabeth stood quietly off to the side in her rough-hewn dress and bonnet, drawing little notice from the men. Tao wished she'd dropped the blade hidden in the waistband of her dress. True, she hadn't been ordered to, but she was flirting with extreme danger, defying Beck. Admiration collided with his white-hot fear for her. She was a warrior, through and through. But by Uhrth, she was also his woman and deserving of his protection.

Beck picked up Tao's bow, testing its weight, aiming it, and then glaring at him with revulsion. "This is a Rider bow. Arming Kurel, and trading with Riders? Your treachery knows no bounds, Uhr-Tao. No wonder you like to use the pipes and not the front door. You can rest assured you won't be going out the same way you got in."

His raspy laugh at the obvious threat of execution made Tao want to strangle the man. "I didn't come here to harm anyone, Uhr-Beck."

"Then why are you here, hmm?"

"To say goodbye to my sister. That is all." Tao had no intention of giving away more and endangering Aza. "She doesn't know. It was my idea alone. I ask you, Uhr to Uhr, allow me to leave, and you'll never have to see me again."

"Why should I, when you forced me to come back here—and *rot?* You thought you didn't need me. That I was useless—too damaged and weak to serve in your forces." Beck's voice was emotionally laden, hate-filled. "Now I get to repay you in kind. I'll put you at the mercy of the king, which I assure you won't be plentiful." He turned to Markam and the guards. "Lock the men in wrist cuffs. Bring the wench, too. March them to the king's private-audience room. He'll be interested to know that this traitor had planned on paying his wife an unplanned visit."

IN THE KING'S CHAMBERS, Elsabeth stood as still as possible to avoid notice. All through her childhood, going unnoticed was something she'd done unintentionally. Now she called upon that trait, seeing in it an unexpected value: survival. Victory. Revenge. Finally, after so long, the chance to fulfill her vow of vengeance against Xim may have arrived.

Yet, the feel of the blade tucked in her waistband horrified as much as it emboldened her. Her two ancestries collided, Tassagon and Kurel. She could kill the king and avenge her parents and all the Kurel who had died because of him. But by doing so she'd also kill the father of innocent children—Aza's children.

Xim killed my *mother. He killed* my *father.*

At what point did the violence end?

As they waited for Markam to arrive with Xim, Tao was watching her intently. Worriedly. He always seemed to know what she was thinking. *Planning.* When they caught each other's gazes for a brief second, he gave her an almost imperceptible shake of his head. *No,* he told her.

No—what? No rescuing him and Navi? Or no attacking Xim if she had the chance?

The door banged open and Xim lurched in with Markam. Beck waved a gloating hand at her, Navi and Tao. "Look what I netted you tonight, My Liege. The traitors. It seems your intuition about that passageway was right."

"My intuition is always right!"

Xim was drunk. Elsabeth could smell the alcohol on his breath. He'd been in the middle of washing up for bed, apparently. His hair was messy and slightly dampened, and he was clad in soft pants and a plain white shirt unbuttoned halfway down his torso. All adornment had been cast aside. Oddly, it embarrassed her to see the king of Tassagonia this way, as if he were naked without all the usual trappings of his position and power, the furs and jewels and golden crown. Standing in the shadow of Beck's maniacal charisma worsened the effect: Xim looked even younger, and somehow vulnerable. Like a lost boy.

But his angry pout and shifty eyes reminded her who he really was. An intolerant, insufferable, incompetent king. Murderer of innocents.

"I trusted you, Tao," Xim seethed. "You were my highest-ranking military officer. My brother-in-law. Yet, you thought nothing of criticizing my laws, speaking ill of me. Then sneaking away before you could be properly punished."

Tao's jaw hardened, but he gave the impression of calm, taking the full force of Xim's tantrum with his hands cuffed behind his back. Markam, standing close to Tao under the guise of guarding him, observed with perfect military bearing, but inside she knew he must be heartsick. No doubt his sharp, tactical mind was considering countless ways out of this debacle, as was Tao's.

"Now you bring Kurel inside this palace after I issued an expulsion order to rid our city of the damned spellmongers!"

Elsabeth's heart lurched. *My Uhrth, no.* The Kurel— exiled? To where? When? Was this what the evening's speech had been about?

"You've defied me on every level, Tao. Humiliated me." Xim jammed his hands through his hair and glared ferociously at Navi, who for all his inexperience didn't cower. Then he shifted his focus to Elsabeth and shoved her bonnet back with such force, she choked for a second on the strings around her neck. "You," he hissed. "Aza's sorceress."

Her heartbeat was banging in her ears, a metronome of terror. She tried to work moisture into her mouth, tried to calm her nerves. Would she be able to remove the blade in time? Would Tao try to defend her and get killed in the process?

"I forbade you from coming here ever again, Kurel." Xim shouted inches from her face, his alcohol-laden breath and spittle striking her with every word. "You disobeyed me. You—"

"I came to see Aza," Tao broke in. "That is all. Aza is my only blood, the only one of my family left. She and the children. If nothing else, give me the chance to say goodbye."

"My Liege," Beck said. The old warrior's eye was aglow, his lips frozen in a smirk as if he'd been hit with sudden inspiration. "I find it curious that the night they chose to say farewell to the queen is the same night you confined her to her quarters."

Elsabeth watched from only a hand's distance away as the king's countenance changed. Furor froze, then gave way to doubts and dismay. Beck stepped closer to murmur in the king's ear, whispers and insinuations that reached Elsabeth's ears, too. *What if Aza summoned them here? What if they're all plotting against you? To leave with the queen, and leave you with a curse to make you sicken and die? Don't forget, you caught her reading—more than once...*

With a cold surge of horror, Elsabeth realized what Beck was doing. *He thinks this is his big moment of triumph, and he's going to prove to Xim that both Tao and Aza are disloyal.*

Xim's lips fluttered as he shook his head, an expression of wrenching emotion too confused to decipher. "Aza," he whispered, shaking his head.

Beck crossed the room and yanked open the door connecting the royal couple's private apartments. "Your Highness," he called into the adjacent room. "The king requests the honor of your presence."

"What has happened, Xim?" Aza stepped into the room anxiously, looking like one of Uhrth's own angels, swaddled in a sparkling pearl-white robe, her hair soft and loose, her hand, as always, resting on her stomach. Taking in the scene before her, she turned so pale with shock that Elsabeth feared she'd go into early labor. She couldn't blame the woman, being greeted by a man she neither liked nor trusted; reuniting with the tutor who for three years had been a trusted friend; then discovering the proof that her brother was alive, only to plunge almost immediately into confusion seeing him handcuffed and gripped by Markam, the man she secretly loved. But of course her gaze went to Xim first, her husband, the king, who held all the power over her, and all the answers.

"The Kurel tutor has put you under a spell," Xim said.

"Of course not. She could not."

Elsabeth was jerked toward the table in the center of the room by the wrist by Beck, who then held her hand up for all to see. "There's only one way to tell," he announced, drawing all eyes to himself.

Cuffs and all, Tao lunged for her, but Markam caught him around the waist, almost throwing them both to the floor.

No, Tao. Elsabeth willed him to be still. He was thinking of the blade in her dress, fearing she'd use it.

She couldn't guarantee she wouldn't, but she'd be damned if she'd let him get killed over the prospect. *We're going to survive this. We're going to be together.* Elsabeth commanded him not to fight, sending the message with what she hoped was a chilling glare, trying to keep her pleading, her terror, from leaking through.

Beck yanked her hand down to the table, forcing her palm to slap the wood. His hold on her was crushing. Needles prickled her arm. "In the days of old, we'd cut off the hands of accused sorcerers." He unsheathed his sword and raised it high, focusing his eye with maniacal intensity on her face. "Save yourself, Kurel witch," he hissed.

Everyone froze in horror, until Tao ripped free from Markam's hold with a warrior cry and lunged for Beck—but his sister was closer. With a screamed *"no,"* Aza threw herself in the path of the sword just as Beck began his downward slice.

Everything slowed down. In that second, with the queen's arm stretching toward her, Elsabeth saw the flash of awareness on the king's face: where the sword would fall, whose flesh it would slash and destroy, which woman would crumple with a quick, soft scream, selflessly taking the blow...

Xim hurtled forward. The sword impacted his ribs. Blood sprayed. The sound of Beck pulling the weapon free was a sound Elsabeth knew she'd never forget, to be burned into her memory along with the sight of Xim, who, taking that sword, twisted it free of Beck's startled grip and plunged it deep into the old, one-eyed warrior's heart.

WHEN ELSABETH OPENED the eyes she hadn't realized she'd squeezed shut, she was being crushed in Tao's freed arms, trying to absorb the blood-soaked scene before her, like something from a battlefield.

It was a battlefield.

"You're safe," Tao told her in a harsh whisper, his hand spread on the back of her head, holding her tight to his chest and the thunder of his pounding heartbeat.

Xim sat down hard on the floor, his legs splayed as blood pooled under him. With trembling fingers, he touched the gaping wound in his upper torso. His expression was one of almost childlike surprise that such a thing had happened to him. Then peace such as she'd never witnessed suffused the perpetually troubled king's face. "You're all right, Aza," he told the queen.

Sobbing, Aza dropped to her knees beside him and squeezed his bloody hands in hers. "Oh, Xim, My Lord. My husband..."

He took great, hiccupping breaths. "I didn't know it would hurt this much to die."

Aza pressed his face between her hands. "Soon, dear, the pain will be gone."

Xim nodded, the strange hiccups wracking his body. "It is...easier." Then his head lolled forward. His body shuddered, and the king of Tassagonia was dead.

CHAPTER TWENTY-NINE

THE BELLS TOLLED FOR the passing of King Xim, who had become in death what he'd failed to be in life: a hero. He'd saved the queen from Beck the Madman, who now bore the blame for everything that had plagued the kingdom, from the massacre in Kurel Town to the unjust arrest of the adored General Tao and the release of the Gorr to the bloody assassination of the king.

Bells clanged in all four banner-topped spires of the palace, joined by the bell at the top of Kurel Town's tallest power-generating windmill. It became more than a sound of mourning; it was a harmony of two previously estranged peoples, celebrating an end and also a beginning. Before the last bell stopped tolling, the gates of the ghetto were thrown open, never to be closed again.

The peals carried from the walls of Tassagonia to the sweeping grasslands of the Plains, where another people long apart paused to listen and to consider the promise of humanity's reunion—Tassagon, Kurel and Rider—as it had been the day an ark named *Discovery* had set sail on a sea of stars with 3,032 colonists bound for this world.

Or so Elsabeth imagined, as she savored the bells' melody from the open window of a guest bedchamber in the palace. Maybe the Sea Scourge and their shameless scoundrel of a leader, Commander Yarr, heard the ringing, too, as their wooden ships plied faraway, heaving seas, these bells calling out to their human sides, which perhaps longed to be welcomed into the fold.

"Daydreaming?" Tao padded up behind her. His hands landed lightly on her bare shoulders, followed by the tingling delight of his lips pressing a kiss on the side of her neck. He'd bathed, and his hair was still dripping wet, smelling of soap and man, her man.

She turned in his arms, their kiss instant, feverish. *I can have you now. The danger is gone.*

They fell to the bed, a huge bed, the likes of which she'd never lain upon. He was naked, but a knee-length chemise still draped her body. "That blade," he said, kissing her in between his words. "You didn't give it up when Navi and I were disarmed."

"No one asked me to."

He rolled her beneath him, trapping her between his powerful thighs. "I know. I couldn't decide if I wanted to applaud your daring or shake some sense into you." Another kiss. "You were playing with fire."

"*You're* fire," she confessed against his teasing lips, and he buried his hands in her hair to kiss her fully.

Her chemise was discarded seconds later, as if they could no longer bear even the smallest bit of physical separation. They gripped each other, their mouths never parting even when he rolled her off the mattress, placing her atop him. The lovemaking was fierce. Breathless. She'd never imagined such a tempest of sensations, the intensity of the emotional bond she felt with Tao, coupled with an overpowering physical need that did not abate until they both lay sprawled and tangled together, utterly exhausted, like two shipwreck survivors washed up onshore after a storm.

Or, how she *imagined* it might feel being a shipwreck survivor. After reading a few fictional accounts. But Tao was better than any book—

She must have been gazing at him with the silliest of expressions, for his green-gold eyes turned as warm and sweet as honey-tea. He propped himself up on an elbow, his finger lazily drawing a circle around her belly button. "Do you love me, Elsabeth?"

"Yes. I love you." She lifted up to kiss him. "I am besotted."

He stretched both arms over his head with a hearty victory groan, then rolled back to her, grinning. "Well, wouldn't you know it? I love you, too."

ON A SUNNY AUTUMN morning, thousands crowded outside the palace to witness the official coronation of Crown-Prince Maxim and the continuation of the Tassagon dynasty.

Holding his mother's hand, the little boy was led to the priests, who had, for the occasion, and at the request of the elders of Kurel Town, carefully carried the Seeing Bowl outside.

The relic, made of the same kind of metal as Tao's amulet, had not seen the light of day for untold centuries. It was a piece of wreckage from an ark, something called a starship thruster cowling, Tao had learned from Farouk, and he wondered if it had been from the same vessel that had given him his amulet.

The water filling the Seeing Bowl reflected the cloudless sky. Within those waters it was believed the rightful king of Tassagonia could be viewed and the future revealed. Perhaps it shared the same magical powers as his talisman. Or maybe, magic had nothing to do with any of it at all. Just good timing, hope, determination and the unfathomable influence of something greater than them all.

Dressed in his ceremonial dress uniform one last time before his retirement became official at midnight, Tao slipped his fingers between Elsabeth's. The incessant breeze from the Plains ruffled her curls, tumbling them over her dress of brilliant green, the color of the grassy lawn at the vineyards, where they'd marry.

Together, they watched little Max crowned king. Until he came of age, his rule would be overseen by his mother and Markam, who together would provide the guidance and education Max would need if he was to become the ruler who would sustain the peace and unity required in the Log of Uhrth before humanity could contact the birthplace of its ancestors. There was still more work to be done on that account before such a day would come, but for two of the human tribes, the journey to bridge their differences had begun.

Tassagons and Kurel—the Kurel of Tassagonia, at least. While Farouk, Gwendolyn and the other Kurel elders at the coronation looked on approvingly, their brethren in the Barrier Peaks had sent no emissaries. Prometheus had returned with a response that had said only that their message had been received and "noted." Where those Kurel stood was still to be determined.

But going forward, Tao was confident there would be good men to lead the army in his place, forces that would be kept strong for defense of the realm, and all who were welcome to join them. It did Tao's heart good to see his officers, Nunez, Mandalay, Pirelli and Sandoval, standing with him on this peaceful, sun-splashed morning with no murderous, mutinous colonels or stinking Gorr in sight.

His nephew, Max, kneeled to accept the blessing of the priests. Then, after some whispered coaching on Aza's part, the child king joined her and Princess

Sofia on the platform overlooking Palace Square. Tao was glad to see Markam take his place with them.

The crowd went wild at the sight of the new royal family. Tao had heard cheers and applause on the day of his homecoming, but it hadn't come close to the thunderous approval greeting the new king. Today, the Kurel were clapping, too.

"MAX! *MAXIM*." AZA SHOOK her head in exasperation, exchanged a suffering glance with Elsabeth and went after her young son, who had run off with his sister to chase float flies, leaving the adults who'd gathered to eat a post-coronation brunch.

Laughing, Elsabeth followed. Markam and Tao strolled out after them, for the day was fine and everyone was in high spirits.

"Max," Aza scolded, her walk more of a waddle as her birthing time neared. "Just because you're king doesn't mean you can run off whenever you please."

"But I want to see inside it!" Max climbed up on a chair and took hold of the rim of the Seeing Bowl, its radius too large for the breadth of his skinny arms to encircle.

The adults grew quiet as the child rose up on his toes and peered into the water. For long moments, he was utterly still, unusual enough for a three-year-old boy, but when he looked up at the sky as if to confirm what he'd seen wasn't a reflection from above, Elsabeth knew they were witnessing something astonishing.

Max turned and waved to his sister. "Sofia, come see, too."

With the aid of her brother's hand, the beautiful little girl climbed up to share the chair. And squealed. "I see you, Max!"

Aza caught Markam's arm, and he drew her close. Tao wrapped Elsabeth in his arms as he watched over her shoulder.

"And ships!" Max exclaimed. "Look at them all."

Sofia was nodding. "So pretty..."

Then the pair jumped down.

"What did you see?" Aza asked the question that they all seemed to share.

"Stuff." Max swatted at a float fly drifting close, and scampered off with his sister to chase them.

Aza's brow went up, her lips pursing. "Stuff?"

Markam commented, "Clearly Max saw himself, so he's the rightful ruler, but ships..."

"'Pretty' ships," Aza put in with a mother's baffled shrug.

Tao stepped to the side of the bowl, keeping his hand on Elsabeth's back. "I've seen the ships of the Scourge. I wouldn't consider them pretty. Though, a few of the vessels were exceptionally well crafted."

"Ships could mean a number of things," Elsabeth

said, and the three full-blooded Tassagons turned to her. "Anything. From pirate craft to star craft. Arks."

"Or it was just a reflection of a flock of birds flying over," Aza suggested hopefully.

But unease had taken hold. Ships, what did it mean? Pretty ships.

Elsabeth wished she hadn't mentioned arks. She hadn't intended to trouble them on the one day that was supposed to be free of trouble. "You know my imagination," she said with a laugh.

"A vision of our future nonetheless," Tao affirmed, his thoughtful gaze lingering on the Seeing Bowl.

They left the relic behind to return to the reception. Tao stopped her with a hand on her shoulder, his breath caressing her ear. "By the way, your imagination is one of the best things about you."

CHAPTER THIRTY

THEY WAITED UNTIL springtime to marry, when Tao
knew the sky above the vineyards would be scattered
with fat white clouds resembling sheep, and the freshly
sheared grass under his boots would be deeply fragrant. The hills surrounding his family's estate were
the shade of green that could bring a tear to a man's
eyes, especially a warrior who'd spent a good deal of
his life never knowing if he'd see these lands again.

When he leaned close to kiss his bride and seal their
vows, and her loveliness stole his breath, he knew deep
in his soul that this was the day he'd held in his heart
all those wretched nights in the Hinterlands, when such
dreams were the only thing that had kept him sane.

Later, with family and friends putting a dent in the
massive amount of good wine and simple country food
set out for their enjoyment, and with the lusty wails
of Aza's baby, a new prince, carrying over the more
muted sounds of happiness, Tao took Elsabeth by the
hand and led her up a small hill overlooking the grass-

roofed stone house where they planned to raise their own family. In the adjacent meadow, his warhorse, Chiron, grazed.

"I don't think he minds his retirement any more than you do, Tao," Elsabeth said, her blue eyes shimmering as she gazed out over their lands.

Turning to her, he took her hands in both of his. "I told you once that my aim was to find a compatible female using the same logical, carefully considered methods with which I conducted my military campaigns. Emotion would play no part in it. Remember?"

Surprise flickered in her eyes at the topic. "You said marriage was based on deliberate effort, not true love."

"That's correct. To which you replied you hoped someday I'd find a woman who'd love me so powerfully, so completely, that she'd prove every silly belief I had about love completely wrong." Tenderly, he brushed his knuckles across his wife's cheek. "I did," he said, and dipped his head to kiss her smiling lips.

* * * * *

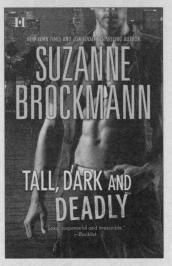

REQUEST YOUR FREE BOOKS!

2 FREE NOVELS
FROM THE SUSPENSE COLLECTION
PLUS 2 FREE GIFTS!

YES! Please send me 2 FREE novels from the Suspense Collection and my 2 FREE gifts (gifts are worth about $10). After receiving them, if I don't wish to receive any more books, I can return the shipping statement marked "cancel." If I don't cancel, I will receive 4 brand-new novels every month and be billed just $5.74 per book in the U.S. or $6.24 per book in Canada. That's a saving of at least 28% off the cover price. It's quite a bargain! Shipping and handling is just 50¢ per book in the U.S. and 75¢ per book in Canada.* I understand that accepting the 2 free books and gifts places me under no obligation to buy anything. I can always return a shipment and cancel at any time. Even if I never buy another book, the two free books and gifts are mine to keep forever.

191/391 MDN FDDH

Name	(PLEASE PRINT)

Address		Apt. #

City	State/Prov.	Zip/Postal Code

Signature (if under 18, a parent or guardian must sign)

Mail to the **Reader Service:**
IN U.S.A.: P.O. Box 1867, Buffalo, NY 14240-1867
IN CANADA: P.O. Box 609, Fort Erie, Ontario L2A 5X3

Not valid for current subscribers to the Suspense Collection
or the Romance/Suspense Collection.

Want to try two free books from another line?
Call 1-800-873-8635 or visit www.ReaderService.com.

* Terms and prices subject to change without notice. Prices do not include applicable taxes. Sales tax applicable in N.Y. Canadian residents will be charged applicable taxes. Offer not valid in Quebec. This offer is limited to one order per household. All orders subject to credit approval. Credit or debit balances in a customer's account(s) may be offset by any other outstanding balance owed by or to the customer. Please allow 4 to 6 weeks for delivery. Offer available while quantities last.

Your Privacy—The Reader Service is committed to protecting your privacy. Our Privacy Policy is available online at www.ReaderService.com or upon request from the Reader Service.

We make a portion of our mailing list available to reputable third parties that offer products we believe may interest you. If you prefer that we not exchange your name with third parties, or if you wish to clarify or modify your communication preferences, please visit us at www.ReaderService.com/consumerschoice or write to us at Reader Service Preference Service, P.O. Box 9062, Buffalo, NY 14269. Include your complete name and address.

MSUS11

SUSAN GRANT

77466	SUREBLOOD	___ $7.99 U.S.	___ $9.99 CAN.

(limited quantities available)

TOTAL AMOUNT	$ _____
POSTAGE & HANDLING	$ _____
($1.00 FOR 1 BOOK, 50¢ for each additional)	
APPLICABLE TAXES*	$ _____
TOTAL PAYABLE	$ _____

(check or money order—please do not send cash)

To order, complete this form and send it, along with a check or money order for the total above, payable to HQN Books, to: **In the U.S.:** 3010 Walden Avenue, P.O. Box 9077, Buffalo, NY 14269-9077; **In Canada:** P.O. Box 636, Fort Erie, Ontario, L2A 5X3.

Name: _____

Address: _____ City: _____

State/Prov.: _____ Zip/Postal Code: _____

Account Number (if applicable): _____

075 CSAS

*New York residents remit applicable sales taxes.
*Canadian residents remit applicable GST and provincial taxes.